"I had one bad moment. Let's just let it go."

Gracie looked out the window, blinking hard to hold back the tears that stung behind her eyes.

"Look," Adam finally said, "I'll let it go for today. But you and I need to have a talk about the rules we're going to follow. Whether we like it or not, we're a team for a few weeks."

Earlier today, it had been hard to picture him as a dad. Now Gracie could see it perfectly. How he'd be measured and fair and also a little strict with his kids. But he'd be kind, too. Like he was being kind now.

"Fine," she said. "We'll talk. But for now, let's just get back to the office and get to work."

"Agreed," Adam said. He kept them steady on the road back to Shelter Creek, but Gracie noticed he was still driving a lot faster than he had been before. Maybe Deputy Sears wasn't quite such a stick-in-the-mud after all.

Dear Reader,

Maybe it's the darker side of my writer's psyche, but occasionally I enjoy shattering my characters' worlds. Sheriff's deputy Adam Sears was a happily married man in the first book of my Heroes of Shelter Creek series, but I kept wondering if his perfect life might be an illusion. And sure enough, here he is in *Falling for the Lawman*, an overwhelmed single father trying to balance a full-time job and caring for his kids. Adam isn't fond of taking risks, so to shake up his life just a little more, I sent Gracie Long to Shelter Creek. She's his opposite—an impulsive loner who can't settle down.

Gracie and Adam have a lot to learn from each other as they team up to stop poachers from hunting bears around Shelter Creek. When they fall in love, their path to a future is as prickly and tangled as one of the blackberry thickets growing out in the forest. Good thing they are both skilled at finding their way through the woods!

I had a lot of fun accompanying Gracie and Adam on their bumpy journey toward love. I hope you enjoy *Falling for the Lawman*!

Claire McEwen

HEARTWARMING

Falling for the Lawman

—

Claire McEwen

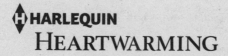

HARLEQUIN®
HEARTWARMING™

ISBN-13: 978-1-335-42639-0

Recycling programs for this product may not exist in your area.

Falling for the Lawman

This edition published by arrangement with Harlequin Books S.A.

For questions and comments about the quality of this book, please contact us at CustomerService@Harlequin.com.

Harlequin Enterprises ULC
22 Adelaide St. West, 40th Floor
Toronto, Ontario M5H 4E3, Canada
www.Harlequin.com

Printed in U.S.A.

Claire McEwen writes stories about strong heroes and heroines who take big emotional journeys to find their happily-ever-afters. She lives by the ocean in Northern California with her family and a scruffy, mischievous terrier. When she's not writing, Claire enjoys gardening, reading and discovering flea market treasures. She loves to hear from readers! You can find her on most social media and at clairemcewen.com.

Books by Claire McEwen

Harlequin Heartwarming

Heroes of Shelter Creek

Reunited with the Cowboy
After the Rodeo
Her Surprise Cowboy
Rescuing the Rancher
Second Chance Cowboy

Visit the Author Profile page
at Harlequin.com for more titles.

This book about bears is dedicated to the most wonderful bear I know. Mr. Bear, Wee Bear, Bear-ski-doo, B'ear, Bean Bear-ito, BEAR... whatever we call you, I am so grateful that you are my bear. When you showed up on that airport baggage claim carousel and put your little paw in mine, my heart grew a million sizes, and the best adventures of my life began.

Acknowledgments

Falling for the Lawman would not exist without the encouragement, support and author-rescue skills of my editor, Johanna Raisanen. My gratitude is profound! And thank you to my husband, Arik, for his infinite patience with me and my writing efforts this past year.

Before researching this book, I didn't understand the extent of the wildlife poaching problems we have in the United States. I had no idea how much effort wildlife officers expend, or how many risks they take, to try to stop poaching. They are true heroes, and many articles about their investigative skills, bravery and persistence informed and inspired this book.

CHAPTER ONE

ADAM SEARS SHOVED his chair away from his desk, wincing as one of the ancient wheels screeched in protest. He stood up, relishing the faint breeze from the fan turning slowly back and forth on the battered metal file cabinet. The Shelter Creek sheriff's office was a small satellite to the main office in Santa Rosa. Adam had worked here for over ten years, but the old clapboard building still felt like a temporary setup. There was barely any heating in winter, and definitely no AC in summer.

Plucking at his shirt, Adam tried to pull the thick fabric of his uniform away from his damp back. Tomorrow was supposed to be even hotter. Where was the fog that usually rolled in from the ocean and cooled things off during summer nights?

He reached for the diet cola on his desk and took a sip as he glared down at the email on his computer screen. The message thanked him for his application, and informed him that his kids were on the waiting list for the final session of summer day camp at the community center. *A waiting list?* Shelter Creek was a small town. How could there be a waiting list for a summer program?

If he'd known the last session would fill up so quickly, he'd have registered the kids weeks ago. But it was just one thing on a long list of things he still didn't know about managing his kids on his own.

He set his drink down and tried to think. What would he do with Jack and Penny for the next two weeks if they couldn't go to day camp? He could ask his sister, Sara, to watch them, but she was pretty busy these days. She'd been running the family cattle ranch ever since their parents retired to their little cabin on the Oregon coast. He could ask his younger brother, Wyatt. No, bad idea. Wyatt was so irresponsible, he'd probably have the kids driving the tractor or swinging from the barn rafters if he were in charge. And Adam's older brother, Ryan, was still on the road, living out of his truck chasing glory in the rodeo arena.

A tap at the door had Adam slamming his laptop shut like he'd been viewing something illicit. He had a pile of paperwork he should have been working on. "Come in," he called, trying to sound casual.

Josie pushed the door open and stepped inside. "The captain wants you in his office."

"Sure, Josie, thanks." Adam waited for Josie to leave so he could follow her out the door.

But the receptionist stayed where she was, twisting her hands together in front of her, her shoulder-length brown hair waving slightly in the fan's breeze. "How are you doing, Adam? Everything okay?"

He had come to hate that question. *Was everything okay? No. Was there anything he could do to change that? No, again.* "We're hanging in there. The kids are enjoying the first session of day camp."

"Oh good. Let me know if you'd like me to take them at any time on a weekend. Brendan loves playing with Jack and I'm happy to have Penny, too. It would be fun to have a little girl around to spoil."

As always, when someone tried to help, Adam's mouth developed a paralysis that made speech almost impossible. People assumed he was grief-stricken that his wife had walked out on them, but he was too overwhelmed to be sad. Too angry to be heartbroken. Tanya leaving had hurt like heck, but he was a grown man, he could handle it. What grieved him, what almost broke him, was that she'd practically abandoned their kids. She'd crushed their hearts, and she seemed to have no understanding of the hurt she'd caused.

Adam forced his jaw to move and fortunately, the rest of his voice followed. "That's kind of you, Josie. I may take you up on that offer."

"Are you sure there isn't anything you need?"

Adam thought about the email he'd just received. "You don't happen to know anyone who works at the community center camp, do you? I forgot to register the kids for the final session."

"Ah." Josie's smile was full of sympathy. "A common mistake. You've got to get in there the moment they open registration or you're out of luck. The last session always fills faster than the others, because a lot of families are back from vacation and getting ready for school to start."

"I didn't realize."

"That's a shame. Brendan's going. He'd be so happy to have Jack there." Josie looked thoughtful. "I have a hair appointment this afternoon. I'll ask my stylist what you should do."

Had he heard her right? "Your hairstylist?"

"Monique. Over at Monique's Miracles. She has the scoop on everything that goes on in Shelter Creek. She'll know if there are any strings we can pull to get your kids in."

The load of worries Adam carried felt just a little lighter. He was acquainted with Monique. If she wanted something done, she found a way. "I'd really appreciate that. If I can't get them in, I'll have to figure out some last-minute childcare."

"If it comes to that, I know a few ladies around town who would be happy to babysit."

"Sears!" The frustration in Captain Dean Carson's voice carried easily from his office down the hall. "You gonna make me wait all day?"

Josie grinned. "Guess you'd better get going, before he blows a fuse."

"Thanks for helping me out." Adam followed her out of his office.

"Of course." Josie stopped next to her desk and turned to face him. "You and the kids have been through a rough year."

"Yup." It had been eleven months and four days, but it sure felt like a year or two since he'd found Tanya's goodbye note on the dining room table.

Josie's bright smile was probably meant to be reassuring. "Hey, it can only get better from here, right?"

Adam wasn't used to talking about his personal life, let alone having it be brought up at work, or when he was out doing errands, or at kids' birthday parties. Everyone in town wanted to offer their advice and support. It was kindly meant, but sometimes he thought he might suffocate under all that concern. "That's what I'm hoping."

"Sergeant Sears!" There was a definite edge to Dean's voice now.

Adam glanced down the pale green, chipped linoleum hallway. "I'd better get in there."

"I'll call you tomorrow if I can find a way to get the kids into camp."

"I'd really appreciate that." Pulling in a deep breath, Adam forced himself to let his childcare worries go for now. His shift wasn't over for another half hour. He was at work and he'd better start acting like it. He walked down the hall and tapped on his boss's half-closed door.

"Sears. Finally." Dean yanked the door open. "Come on in."

Dean Carson was in his midthirties, just a couple years older than Adam. They'd worked together for over a decade, but only Dean had moved up the ranks to Captain. Adam preferred to work with people, not paper.

He followed his boss into the office. A woman was seated on one of the blue plastic chairs that Dean kept for visitors. Her straight black hair was long in front, flopping over her forehead like a horse's forelock. It was cut really short in the back, giving her an edgy look. She stood up and fixed Adam with a cool, assessing gaze.

He nodded in response. "Hello."

She didn't return his greeting. Instead, she looked at Dean as if he'd offered her a moldy sandwich. "Is this him?"

Dean seemed oblivious to her dismay. "Sergeant Adam Sears, meet Officer Gracie Long. She's with the State Department of Wildlife. Pull up a seat, Adam. I've got to talk to you about her work."

Gracie wasn't dressed in the usual khaki uniform of a wildlife officer. She wore faded jeans and a T-shirt that matched her striking, light blue eyes. She plunked back down in her chair and crossed one long leg over the other, the toe of her scuffed brown cowboy boot tapping the air.

"Okay." Adam took a seat in the other plastic chair and turned slightly toward her. "Good to meet you." She nodded in response and Adam looked at his boss for guidance.

Dean had remained standing. He leaned against the front of his desk and crossed his arms over his chest. "Gracie is pursuing a possible poaching case in the area."

"I'm required to notify you all that I'm working around here," Gracie added.

"There's a little more to it than that." Dean tilted his head toward Gracie. "Why don't you give him the background?"

The blue of Gracie's eyes just visible under the long thick bangs that had fallen over her forehead. She reminded Adam of a wild animal peeking through a thicket. "You probably know that black bears have been showing up in the northern part of the California Coast Range. They're moving south from Oregon, looking for new habitat as their numbers grow." She paused, as if waiting for confirmation.

Adam nodded. "We've had a few bear sightings around here in the last couple years."

"And when you get bears in the neighborhood, you also get bear poachers." She fixed him with a stern look. "Do you know anything about bear poaching, Sergeant Sears?"

Her condescending tone was a little annoying, but years of working in law enforcement had taught Adam not to show his feelings. "I know it happens."

"It's a brutal crime. Poachers kill bears, chop off their paws, cut out their gallbladder and leave the carcass to rot. Those few parts they take can be sold on the black market for a whole lot of money."

Adam could do without the images she'd just put in his head. "That's pretty disturbing."

"Gracie thinks we have poachers around here," Dean said. "A mutilated bear was found by the side of the highway, about five miles north of here."

"Was it a roadkill?" Adam glanced at Gracie. "Maybe someone just took advantage of an opportunity."

"Maybe. Though that's illegal, too," Gracie said. "I suspect it might be the same people I've been trying to catch farther north in Mendocino County. I haven't had any leads on them for a couple weeks, so I figured I'd better check this out." She shrugged. "Whoever they are, I'll track them down."

"Okay, good to know." Adam glanced hopefully at Dean. Now that this introduction had been made, maybe he could get back to his office and finish a little more paperwork before the end of his shift.

Dean gave a slight shake of his head, indicating that Adam should stay. "Gracie needs a partner while she's here."

"I usually work alone." Gracie sat up straighter. "I don't need a partner, just someone I can call on for backup, if it comes to that."

"How are you going to call for backup if you're out in the middle of nowhere chasing a poacher?" Dean looked more irritated than Adam had seen him in a long time. Maybe they'd already been arguing about this before he showed up.

"I've worked out in the backcountry on my own for years."

"And your supervisor told me that you were working alone when you ended up in the hospital." Dean's voice sounded a little gruff. "From what he told me, you're lucky to be alive."

Adam studied Gracie, trying to process Dean's words. What had happened that had landed her in the hospital?

Gracie's sharp cheekbones flushed a deep rosy pink and she stood up so fast her chair slid a few feet back. "That was one incident out of many successful arrests."

Dean held up his hands in a don't-shoot-me posture. "That may be true, but you've got your supervisor pretty spooked. He asked me to assign someone to work with you in our district, and that's what we're going to do."

Adam knew that resolute tone well, and it seemed like Gracie recognized it, too, because she didn't answer. But from the way she'd pressed her lips closed, it was clear she was holding back some choice words. What a prickly attitude. Pity the poor fool who had to work with her.

Then Dean's words sank in and landed hard. "You're assigning...me?"

"I figured you could use a change of pace." Dean gave Adam an apologetic shrug that didn't help one bit. "Plus, you're my most experienced investigator. I need you on this job."

"Full-time?" He glanced over at Gracie, unable to hide his dismay.

"Full time whenever Gracie is working in the area."

Great. Adam had too much on his plate right now as it was. He didn't need any more stress, and this woman was a whole lot of stress poured into jeans and a T-shirt. "I don't get it," he said. "How can it take all day, every day, to deal with a couple of hunters taking bears without a license?"

"Apparently they're not easy to catch," Dean said, glancing at Gracie, who had sat back down and was jiggling her foot again. "You'll probably spend some time looking for them out in the backcountry. Gracie has her horse with her and you're the mounted patrol sergeant most familiar with the area."

Adam was starting to feel a little desperate. "What about my shifts? My paperwork?"

"Deputy Turner can take a few of your shifts. So can Deputy Leary. I'll help them with the paperwork."

Worry crept in. This smacked of a demotion. But it couldn't be. No matter what Adam had dealt with in the past year, he'd shown up here and done his job as carefully as ever. He studied Dean's face, trying to read the expression there.

"He obviously doesn't want to do it," Gracie interjected. "How about this? I'll check in with him by phone once a day. If I'm headed anywhere remote, he can come along." She pulled her car keys out of her pocket and they jangled in her restless fingers.

"You and Adam will be on this case together. End of story." Dean reached for the phone on his desk and held it out to her. "You want to call your supervisor and complain to him? Go for it. I'm just doing what he's asked me to do."

Gracie's pale skin went a little whiter. "Fine." She shot Adam a glance armed with resentment, then shrugged. "Guess we're working together."

"Adam, when you're not on horseback, you two will use Gracie's unmarked SUV for this investigation. You'll dress in civilian clothes and carry concealed weapons."

Now he was being stripped of his uniform? To follow a wildlife officer around? To baby-sit bears? What had he done to get on Dean's bad side?

"Wear hiking boots, if we're going on foot," Gracie said. "I hope you're in decent shape. We'll be covering a lot of ground."

Adam was in the worst shape he'd ever been in. Without Tanya there to help watch the kids, he'd had to give up his daily run. He couldn't exactly leave a seven-year-old and an eleven-year-old at home alone. Some days he talked them into a bike ride so he could jog beside them, but the pace was uneven since Penny wasn't too sure of herself on a bike yet. "I'll be fine," he muttered.

"I hope so. Poachers tend to move fast. They're savvy. We need to be faster than them and anticipate what they'll do next."

Her lecturing tone scraped his bruised pride. "Of course."

"I guess we're done here, then." Gracie stood, so Adam did, too. She looked a little surprised at the courtesy. "It's okay, I can see myself out."

"You two will check in here at 8:00 a.m. every day, starting Monday," Dean said. "I'll need to know your plan for the day, including your expected itinerary. You'll check back in here at the end of each shift. Got it?"

"Yes, sir."

Adam heard the bitterness in Gracie's tone loud and clear. What was her problem? He was the one who should be bitter, getting reassigned out of the blue to go chase poachers.

"See you Monday," he told her, but she didn't answer, just raised a hand in a curt wave and strode out the door.

His boss reached over and shut it behind her.

"What did I do wrong?" Adam watched as Dean made his way around the back of his desk to slump in his chair. "Whatever I did, however I messed up, just tell me and I'll fix it."

"I'm not giving you this assignment as punishment," Dean said. "You're the most levelheaded guy I've got."

"You mean I'm the only one who won't shove her out of the SUV and leave her by the side of the road to commune with those bears she's so crazy about?"

Dean flashed him a weary smile. "Yeah, that, too." Then his expression sobered. "I know you've been through a lot lately. Think of this as an easy gig. No paperwork, no major issues. Just driving around the countryside watching for poachers that you'll most likely never find. And you'll probably get to ride out on Bodie a few times. You haven't had a chance to bring your horse to work in a while."

Adam fixed Dean with a skeptical look. "You think you're doing me a *favor* with this assignment? Nothing about that meeting gave me the impression that this will be an easy gig."

Dean leaned forward, resting his clasped hands on his desk. "Okay, let's be honest. I'm doing *me* a favor because I know you'll be able to handle her. She'd run circles around Turner, and Leary is way too green. He'd do something stupid right along with her."

"So my job is to keep her from doing stupid stuff?" Adam shook his head. "Look, I love my kids, but I spend most of my free time keeping *them* from doing stupid stuff."

"Then you'll be really good at this. And if you can catch some poachers while you're at it, that would be great, too." Dean's mouth twisted into a grimace. "Scum of the earth."

"That's for sure." Adam wouldn't mind rounding up anyone who killed and mutilated animals for a few bucks. He just wasn't looking forward to doing it with Gracie. But his boss had decided, so there wasn't much more to say. "I'll do my best, but I can't promise you anything. Gracie seems like a real wild card."

Dean nodded. "She sure does. But she's caught a lot of poachers, so I guess her methods must work."

"Except you said she ended up in the hospital." Adam leaned forward, resting his elbows on his knees. "What do you know about that?"

"Not that much. Just that she was arresting a poacher up in the Sierras. He turned on her. Beat her up pretty badly, I guess."

Adam winced at the image. "Did they catch the guy who did it?"

"Yeah, he's waiting on his day in court."

"Hope they lock him up for a good long time." Adam pictured Gracie, so tense and testy in the office just now. "How long has she been back at work?"

"Just a few weeks I think."

Adam rarely got mad at his boss, but he certainly didn't want to be sold a bunch of manure either. "You know I'll do whatever you ask me to. But stop trying to sell this as a nice, easy gig."

The expression in Dean's eyes got a little desperate. "You're my most experienced sergeant and the only one who's going to be able to keep up with her on foot and horseback."

"I hope I can." Adam glanced at the clock behind Dean's desk. "If that's all, I have to go pick up the kids."

"We're done. Except… I hope you know I appreciate you."

"Aw, that's sweet. Just add a little something extra to my Christmas bonus." Adam smacked his hand to his forehead like he'd forgotten. "Oh wait, we don't get bonuses."

Dean laughed. "I owe you a beer or two, at least. Have a good weekend. Say hello to Penny and Jack for me."

"Will do." The kids adored Dean, looking up to him with a little awe, now that he was "Daddy's boss." "They're going to be with

Tanya all weekend, so let me know if you have time to buy me that beer."

"Tanya's back?" Dean clamped his mouth shut like he regretted the surprise in his tone. "Sounds good. I'll give you a call."

Adam shut the door to Dean's office behind him and thanked God for Friday. Despite the unpleasant prospect of working with Gracie, Adam was looking forward to the weekend. Tanya was coming into town and she'd rented a vacation cottage out near the coast. The kids would finally have some quality time with their mom and Adam would have a little peace and quiet. Maybe he'd even call up a couple friends and put some burgers on the grill.

When he stopped by his office to close up, there was a note from Josie promising again to try to fix his summer camp fiasco. He sure hoped she could.

Adam pushed through the creaky glass door and stepped outside into the late-afternoon sun. A faint breeze shifted the heat around and he welcomed it. If Gracie wasn't so upset about working with him, Adam might agree with Dean about his upcoming assignment. It would be nice to be out in the fresh air, and to ride Bodie on the job again. Seemed like lately he'd been spending so much time indoors—cooking, cleaning, playing with the kids and their toys—trying to give Penny and Jack the quality parenting time they needed so badly, now that their mom had walked away.

But she'd be here this weekend. The kids had packed their bags this morning, excited for time with their mom. The next two days stretched out in front of him, suddenly full of possibility. Maybe he'd get out for a hike, or even a run. The memory of Gracie's words, that she hoped he was in shape, stung a little. Yeah, he'd go for a run, for sure. Both days.

Adam's phone buzzed in his back pocket as he unlocked his truck. He pulled it out and saw Tanya's name on the screen. "Hey," he answered, sliding behind the wheel. "I'm just leaving work. I have to pick up the kids and get them home. Then they'll be ready for you."

"There's been a change of plans," Tanya said. "I feel terrible but I'm not going to be able to make it this weekend."

"What?" Luckily Adam hadn't started driving because if he had, he might have crashed into something. The hurt that slammed his heart wasn't his own. It was the pain their kids would feel when he had to tell them. "Why not? What happened?"

"I feel horrible about it. I really do. But Neil has a lot of work and his parents are in town. I need to play tour guide for them. They flew in all the way from Delaware."

"Neil." The name still tasted rotten in Adam's mouth, no matter how many times he said it. Neil was the old friend Tanya had connected with on social media. The guy she'd eventually left him for. "Tanya, you barely know these people. You don't even know if this thing with Neil will last. Don't you want to see your kids? Aren't they more important than Neil's parents?"

"Neil and I are going to last," Tanya said. "I've met his parents before and I really like them." She paused and took an audible breath, as if she was trying to maintain her patience. "I know it's hard for you to understand, but my relationship with Neil is very important to me."

"Clearly." Adam looked around at the empty parking lot and said goodbye to his weekend plans. Though maybe he could still have his buddies over for a barbecue. It would be a distraction for the kids, and they were going to need one.

"I'm sorry to change plans at the last minute."

Something cracked inside him, down in his chest. Maybe it was his heart. He couldn't be diplomatic anymore. "It's not me you should be apologizing to. It's your children. They miss you, Tanya. A lot. Penny cries sometimes. Jack is more stoic, but his temper is a lot shorter than it used to be."

"Don't guilt trip me, Adam." Her voice rose. "You can't just blame this on me. It takes two people to ruin a marriage."

He took the bait. "Does it? Because as far as I can tell, our marriage was just fine until you went online and reconnected with your summer-camp crush."

"And do you think I would have done that if you'd been there for me? *Really* there? You were always so serious about your job, so stuck in your routine. Our marriage was boring. Stale. There was no room for us to grow anymore."

Years of law enforcement had taught him to keep his temper in check. But it was rising now. She wanted to blame *him* for her affair? Adam pulled in a deep breath and watched his knuckles go white on the steering wheel. This conversation was going nowhere. It was just a distraction from the real issue. He forced the turbulence out of his voice. "I'm sorry you were so unhappy in our marriage. But what matters now are the kids. Can't you keep your promise to come see them this weekend? I'm sure you could explain the situation to Neil's parents. They're adults. They can do their own sightseeing."

"They live on the east coast, Adam. They can't just come here anytime. This is my chance to get to know them better. Just tell the kids that I'll come up soon."

"Why don't you call back in about half an hour and tell them yourself? I think it would mean a lot more coming from you."

She sighed, as if he'd just asked for a huge favor. "I'll try. But I have to go pick up Jackie and Dave from the airport."

He could hold back his temper, but not his sarcasm. "Jackie and Dave. That would be Neil's parents, whose happiness is more important than your children's?"

"Oh, come on. The kids will be okay. I even read an article that said children of divorce are more resilient than—"

"Stop." He said it quietly, because how could he yell when his throat was closing up with the hurt his kids would soon be feeling? "Just stop making excuses. You don't want to see them. That's the real truth."

"Don't paint me as the bad guy here. I'm just postponing until next weekend."

Adam closed his eyes, wanting the conversation to be over. "If you show up next weekend, great. You can wait while they pack and get ready. But I'm not going to let them count on you until you're here, in Shelter Creek, ready to pick them up."

"Don't you undermine my relationship with them, Adam Sears."

He was too tired to care about her scolding tone. "I don't want to do that and honestly, I don't have to. You're doing it all by yourself."

She hung up and Adam sat for a moment, listening to the silence on the other end of the phone. Then he plugged it into the charger and started his truck toward the community center to pick up the kids. He wasn't looking forward to telling them that their mom had changed her plans, again.

CHAPTER TWO

GRACIE TIED HER sweatshirt around her waist as she walked down the gravel lane that led from her friend Maya's house to the barn. It was only nine in the morning, but yesterday's heat had never really broken. The sun was up and blasting the landscape it had already bleached to straw.

She'd stayed behind to finish up the dishes from their decadent Saturday morning breakfast while Maya went to the barn. Gracie was determined to be a good guest. It was so kind of Maya to offer her a room, and a stall for Rio, Gracie's Appaloosa mare.

The sunny morning tempted her to stop and look around. Maya had married a man named Caleb, who owned this big ranch just north of Shelter Creek. The property rolled out over the golden hilltops in every direction. All that land and sky filled this weekend with a sense of promise Gracie hadn't felt in a long time. Maybe she and Maya could go for a ride later on. Or take a drive. Gracie wanted to get familiar with any roads that led to the more remote regions of this part of the Coast Range.

The pasture and shed reserved for Rio was on the way to the barn. The blue roan trotted to the fence when Gracie called. The mare's tail was up, her ears forward, she seemed to have adapted to her temporary quarters just fine. Rio was an experienced traveler, going with Gracie from one assignment to another, living in a new situation each time.

"Let me get you some breakfast." Gracie had stored some alfalfa hay in a bin behind Rio's shed last night. The mare followed her along the fence line in eager strides. "You're hungry, aren't you?" When they reached the shed, Gracie pulled a couple flakes of hay out of the bin and tossed them into a wooden feeder near the water trough. "Munch up, girl. I think we'll be going for a ride later on. I have to help with the chores first." Gracie walked down the hill toward the barn, glancing back to check on Rio one more time. The mare was too busy eating to notice.

Gracie found Maya outside the barn, hold-

ing up the hoof of a big black horse she'd tied
to the post of a wooden fence. Stopping a
few yards away to give Maya and the horse
space, Gracie kept her voice quiet. "What's
going on?"

Maya glanced up. "Hey. This is Caleb's
horse, Amos. When he crossed the pasture
to get his breakfast just now, I thought I noticed a limp." She had a hoof pick in her hand
and she used it to gesture at the horse's hoof.
"There's a rock stuck in here and I can't get
it out." She set the hoof down carefully and
stepped away, rubbing her lower back. "He's
heavy."

Gracie approached, holding out her hand
to let the big black horse sniff her knuckles.
"Hey, Amos, nice to meet you."

Amos blew out a long breath on her hand
and Gracie carefully moved her fingers up
to stroke the velvet skin between his nostrils.
"What a cutie," she told Maya.

"A cutie who is always getting into something. That rock is lodged in his hoof at a really strange angle."

"Poor guy. Is Caleb coming back today?"

"Not until tomorrow. He's speaking at a
veterans' event out in Reno. Whoever thought

my closemouthed, tough-guy husband would become a public speaker?"

"What does he speak about?"

"Sobriety. Healing." Maya went to Amos's shoulder again. "Let's try this one more time."

"Let me do it," Gracie admonished. "You're starting your second trimester. Maybe it's time to slow down a little."

"Says the woman who's chasing poachers all over Northern California."

Gracie returned Maya's smile, but she wasn't going to back down. "That's different. I don't have to worry about growing a baby at the moment." She held out her hand. "Come on, hand over the hoof pick."

Maya glanced from her to Amos, as if she wasn't sure. "Maybe. But he's a rescue horse. He had a lot of problems at first and he still doesn't warm up to people easily."

"I grew up with horses, you know. And I spend most of my life with Rio." Gracie placed a gentle hand to the horse's forehead. "Plus, he likes me. Right, Amos?"

Amos moved his head up and down, probably trying to scratch an itch against Gracie's hand, but it was perfect timing.

"See? He agrees."

Maya shook her head, but she was smiling. "You two are a couple of clowns." She held out the hoof pick. "Just be careful. Let's untie him and I'll hold his lead rope. Sometimes he does better that way."

Gracie moved alongside Amos, stroking his neck and feeling the tough muscle beneath his soft coat. "Hey, buddy, I'm going to help you out, okay?"

Maya untied the big horse and backed him a few steps away from the fence. "Be good, Amos. Gracie is our guest. Mind your manners."

Gracie ran a hand down Amos's leg. She leaned gently into his shoulder and he picked his hoof up immediately. It was easy to see the problem. The rock was triangular in shape, with the narrow end jammed between the edge of the hoof and the frog, the soft wedge of flesh that went from the back toward the middle of the hoof. "Ouch," she murmured. "No wonder this is bugging you, buddy." Carefully she hooked the pick under the wide end of the rock and tried to pry it up, but that only pushed the stone farther against the side of the frog. "Hang on there, big guy." She scooted closer into the big gelding's side and switched hands, so she was holding the hoof pick in her left hand, his hoof with her right. Angling the pick carefully along the side of the frog, she tried to find some leverage with the stone. Amos shifted his weight.

"Easy there," she heard Maya murmur.

Gracie could feel the horse's impatience as if it was radiating off his coat. He wasn't going to let Gracie mess around with his hoof much longer. She quickly hooked the pick behind the stone and pushed toward the front of the hoof. The rock slid. It wasn't much, but enough that she could get under it now, lever the pick and wiggle the stone loose. She used her fingers to pull it out. "Got it." She set Amos's hoof down and patted his shoulder. "Good job, friend. You should feel better now."

"You did it!" Maya put a hand to her shoulder as if to hug her. Gracie flinched and took a step backward. *Not again.* It happened all the time now. Sudden motions. Loud noises. People wanting to touch her. It all sent her anxiety rocketing and her senses recoiling. She put her focus back on Amos to cover her confusion and slow her speeding heart. "Let's take another look at his foot now, and see if he has a bruise. If he does, we might need to treat it. Will he be willing to spend the night in a stall to give it a rest?"

If Maya noticed her overreaction she was kind enough not to say anything. "He'd rather be out with his buddies but he doesn't seem to mind being in a stall." She glanced at Gracie. "You could be a vet, you know. You're great with animals."

"I'd become a vet if I could just work with the animals," Gracie said. "It's the people I can't deal with."

Maya laughed softly. "I know what you mean. I felt the same way when I first moved back to Shelter Creek. But the more I got to know everyone, the more I realized that most people are pretty good." Her glance was full of compassion. "It's easy to forget that when you're trying to catch poachers."

And when one of them smashed the end of your own gun into your head. "True." Gracie leaned into Amos again, picked up the hoof and examined it. "There is a bruise. It's not too bad, thank goodness. See?" She glanced over to Maya who came close to peer over Gracie's shoulder. "That faint shadow where the rock was?"

"Maybe I should call the vet," Maya said.

"I hate to bother her on a Saturday morning, though, if it's not urgent."

"I don't think it's an abscess or anything," Gracie said. "Let's soak it in Epsom salts and water, then apply some iodine just in case. And we'll put lots of bedding in Amos's stall so it's very soft on his feet."

"You're hired," Maya said, grinning. "You can live here with us, take care of the animals, and I'll get to have an old college friend around as well."

"I might like to have my own ranch someday," Gracie admitted. "Out here on the coast, not in Texas where I grew up. Now that I've lived in California for a few years, I'm not sure I could handle working in that Texas heat."

"You'd be fine." Maya laughed. "You're the toughest person I know. Remember that research trip we took in college? Where we went to survey mountain goats up in the Rockies? You out-hiked everyone. I remember getting to the top of the highest peaks and you'd be sitting there, sipping your water, looking like you'd been napping while you waited for us."

"Growing up with five older brothers might have made me just a little competitive," Gracie confessed. "Plus there's what my mama called 'an excess of energy.'" She smiled at the bittersweet memory. "She made me sound a lot nicer than I truly was. Loud. Hyper. Always competing with my brothers."

"You must miss her," Maya said softly.

Gracie tangled her fingers in the comfort of Amos's thick mane. "I just wish I'd spent more time with her, you know? I always assumed she'd be there whenever I wanted to go home and visit. But then she was gone." Her mom had succumbed to a heart attack a year ago and it was still hard to talk about. Gracie should have visited more. She shouldn't have gotten so mad whenever her mom questioned her choice of career. She'd give a lot to hear those questions now.

The tears prickling Gracie's eyes were a weakness she didn't need. "Let's get those Epsom salts ready for this guy." Just then an orange cat wandered up and wound its way around Amos's feet, rubbing against his legs. "Kitty, get out of there," Gracie exclaimed. She glanced at Maya. "It's going to get hurt."

Maya laughed. "Nah. This is Hobo. He and Amos are old friends and they adore each other. In his younger days, Hobo would leap right up onto Amos's back. Now I usually give him a lift." She scooped up the rangy cat and deposited him on Amos's rump. The big horse looked around curiously, then placidly stood while Hobo circled a few times, then flopped down to rest as if the horse was a big black couch.

"We're going into the barn like this?" Gracie asked Maya.

Maya grinned. "We sure are." She and Amos started toward the barn, the cat still lying down as comfy as you please. In the pleasant shady interior, they were greeted by Maya's dog, Einstein, who'd been snoozing in the cool aisle. The big dog, with his floppy ears and missing leg, had jumped up on Gracie in greeting when they met yesterday, and landed straight in her heart. He was a survivor, this one, and he seemed to realize how good a life he'd found with Maya. He wasn't a young dog—Maya thought he might be getting close to ten years old—but he had the joy of a puppy. He stood now, and wagged his tail excitedly at all of them, as if he were in charge of welcoming their odd procession into the barn.

They tied Amos in the wide barn aisle and Maya filled a tub with warm water and

Epsom salts. She hung a bucket of grain on the post in front of Amos. "Bribery will make him stand still," she told Gracie.

Sure enough, Amos was so busy gobbling the treat that he barely seemed to notice them putting his hoof into the water to soak. Hobo didn't much like the ruckus, though. He leaped onto Maya's shoulder, then down to the ground, and walked off into the shadows, his tail twitching back and forth to signal his displeasure.

Gracie found a wheelbarrow and loaded it with a bale of wood shavings. Maya pointed her to one of the empty stalls and she spread shavings wall to wall, creating a soft, thick bed for Amos. Then she sat down on a bale of hay and played with Einstein's floppy ears. The big dog grinned up at her then rolled onto his back for a tummy rub.

Maya was still standing by Amos, making sure the horse kept his foot in the bucket. It seemed like a good time to ask the question Gracie had wanted to ask since she'd arrived on Maya's ranch the evening before. "So what do you know about a sheriff's sergeant named Adam Sears?"

Maya looked at her sharply. "Did you get pulled over *already*?"

"No!" Gracie laughed at the assumption. "I don't drive *that* badly. Though maybe a ticket would be preferable." She tickled Einstein's big paw. "He's been assigned to babysit me."

"Babysit you? What does that mean?"

"It means that my supervisor thinks I can't handle my job on my own anymore. They assigned Sergeant Sears to help me."

"Oh." Maya was quiet for a moment, stroking Amos along his neck. The big horse seemed to like it. His ears dropped and he let out a horsey sigh. "Because you were attacked?" She fixed Gracie with a compassionate gaze in her wide dark eyes. "I haven't asked you how you've been doing with that. I don't want to bring it up every time we see each other, but I always want to know."

"I appreciate you not always bringing it up, honestly. It feels sometimes like it's come to define who I am. How everyone sees me." Gracie tried to focus on Einstein, but tears blurred her vision. "I hate that. Someone assaulted me and it's like they left a tattoo on me that says *victim*. I don't want to be a victim. But it follows me everywhere. And now, thanks to my boss, it followed me here to Shelter Creek."

"You're not a victim. You're a warrior. A fighter. You came back from those injuries and you're still working. You're still doing what you love. I saw you in the hospital. I know how bad it was. But look at you now. You're stronger than ever."

Gracie was quiet, not wanting to contradict her friend, but not wanting to lie either. She wasn't strong. She was as cracked as an old mosaic underneath her skin. One wrong move or unexpected event could crumble her to fragments. "Thank you," she finally said. "For your faith in me. For being there for me in the hospital. For inviting me and Rio to stay here with you while I'm in the area."

"I'd be upset if you stayed anywhere else," Maya assured her. "We have plenty of room for your horse and I want the chance to spend time with you. I'm happy you can get to know Caleb better." She smiled. "And it's paid off already. You've only been here one night and you already helped Amos."

"I want to be helpful. Maybe I can cook and do some chores and you can take it easy while I'm here." She owed Maya so much. Her friend had spent a few days with her in the hospital after the attack. Maya had held her hand, listened and talked her through the fear and shock—and strangely shame—that were almost harder to handle than the pain of her injuries.

"That is a sweet offer." Maya pressed her lips together and Gracie could tell she wasn't going to be diverted from their original topic. "I guess I don't quite understand why you're so upset about having a partner to work with. Haven't you been working with some other officers since getting out of the hospital?"

"Yes. They both have families, so they stayed up north. I volunteered to come here so they wouldn't have to." Truth was, she'd been hoping for some time alone. Hoping no one would be there to witness it if she fell apart again. Heat prickled along her spine as that horrible day last week came rushing back. The flood of nameless fear disorienting her senses. The ground spinning, then rushing toward her as she toppled over. Her coworkers' anxious faces as they pulled her up from the ground. What was wrong with her? She'd never panicked on a case before. If she could just get some time alone, she was sure she could connect with her courage again.

Gracie stood and reached for a broom

and swept some loose straw into a neat pile, wishing she could sweep up the mess she'd made of her career. "Adam seems like such a straitlaced guy. I don't have time for someone who's going to preach at me about rules and regulations. I don't work that way."

"I'm sure he won't be *that* bad," Maya said. But her friend didn't contradict her, which meant Gracie's intuition had been right. From his perfectly combed hair to his square-shouldered stance, Adam worked 100 percent by the book.

"Catching poachers isn't like everyday law enforcement. You have to be able to make quick decisions. Sometimes rules need to be bent. I don't think Adam seems up for that."

"I'm sure there's a good reason Dean assigned him to work with you," Maya said. "It will be fine. Adam is a good man."

"Maybe." Gracie swept up a few more specks of dust. "But he seems like kind of a stick-in-the-mud. And I don't think he's happy to be working with me."

"What did you do?"

Maya knew her too well. "I may have taken some of my frustration out on him and Captain Carson."

"Right." Maya smiled. "I've met your temper before. I thought you'd learned to keep it in check."

"I thought I had, too." She'd thought she had everything together, until the attack had stripped it all away.

Maya regarded her with a thoughtful expression. "Show Adam that you know what you're doing, and that you're just fine on the job. Then he'll tell Dean, who will tell your boss, and you probably won't have to work with anyone else ever again."

Gracie nodded. "I'll try."

"And go a little easy on him. He's a single dad. Newly divorced."

"Just what I need," Gracie muttered. "A sad stick-in-the-mud."

Maya looked shocked, and then burst out laughing. "You're not being very nice to him, but it's good to see some of your old attitude coming back. I think you're getting better, my friend, but try to be patient with the poor guy."

It was Gracie's turn to laugh. "Patient? I'm pretty sure no one has ever used that word to describe me."

Amos must have finished his grain because he nudged the feed bucket out of the way and shifted restlessly. Maya lifted up his dripping hoof and got the bucket out from under it. "Speaking of patience, I think we've used up Amos's supply as well. Let's put him in a stall for now. We may have to give him some attention later, though, so he doesn't get too bored."

"You big baby," Gracie told the horse. She went to him, let him snuffle her knuckles, and ran a hand down his neck. "You and me are a lot alike. We don't like to sit around doing nothing." Amos nuzzled his grain-flecked lips along her sleeve. "Oh, so now that we're friends, I'm just a napkin for you, huh?"

Maya laughed. "You really do have a great way with horses. Want to put him in the stall?"

"Sure." Gracie took the lead rope and walked Amos into the large, cool stall. "Not a bad place to spend a hot day," she told him. She glanced at the empty feed box by the door. "Maya, can we get some oat hay for him to nibble on?"

"Sure," Maya called, and Gracie heard the heels of her boots clunking away across the barn.

Gracie leaned against Amos, wrapped her arms around the big horse and gave him a hug. "You and me, we've got to make a recovery this week, okay? We've got to turn things around."

Just then Hobo the cat leaped onto the stall door and gave Gracie an indignant *meow* that made her smile. "I know, kitty…he's your best friend. I'm just borrowing him for a moment."

Amos moved toward Hobo and nuzzled him, nickering softly. Hobo rubbed his head against the horse's soft nose. They looked so cute that Gracie pulled her phone out of her pocket and snapped a photo.

Maya appeared on the other side of the half door and tossed the hay into the manger, startling Hobo. The cat took a wild leap, landing unsteadily on the horse's back.

"At least we know Amos won't be lonely," Gracie said. She unbuckled the halter, slipped it over Amos's head and let herself out the stall door. "Let's get the rest of the chores done."

"You can stay here forever, you know." Maya grinned as she took the halter from Gracie and hung it on a hook outside the stall door.

"Good to know." Gracie smiled back. "I don't think Caleb would appreciate that, but I'm definitely spoiling you while I'm here."

"Awesome. You can spoil me by helping feed the cattle."

They walked outside the barn to an older white pickup truck already stacked with hay. Gracie took a deep breath of the dry air, filled with the herbal scents of grass and shrubs and the earthy smells of manure and feed. She'd been right to accept Maya's invitation to stay on the ranch. Already the constant ache in her shoulders was easing. The part of her mind that had been so vigilant and afraid for months now, was a tiny bit more at ease.

A rabbit darted out of the bushes near her feet and Gracie jumped back, her heart hammering against her throat, every nerve on red alert. Okay, so maybe she wasn't really at ease. Not yet. But she was in a beautiful place, with a good friend, and that had to be a step in the right direction.

CHAPTER THREE

ADAM FOLLOWED GRACIE out of the sheriff's office and toward her black SUV. It felt weird to be in civilian clothes on a workday. But the jeans, T-shirt, sweatshirt and hiking boots he was wearing for their undercover work were a lot more comfortable than his uniform. He was very conscious of the gun and Taser hidden under his sweatshirt, in a holster at his hip. He'd always carried them openly on his belt. Somehow they felt more lethal like this.

This whole mission was ridiculous. What were they going to do all day? Though apparently Gracie had big plans. All during their Monday morning meeting with Dean she'd been tapping her foot, twisting the hem of her T-shirt between two fingers and glancing longingly at the door. Maybe she had a problem with authority. Or sitting still.

She walked quickly ahead of him, as if she were hoping to lose him before she got to the car. She wasn't exceptionally tall, shorter than his own five eleven by a few inches at least. But her strides covered ground like she was used to walking miles in a day. She had an athletic build, and he could see the defined muscles in her upper arms. She might be annoying, but it was kind of impressive how she radiated energy.

As if she somehow knew his thoughts, she glanced back at him as she aimed her key fob at the SUV. A series of beeps announced that the doors were unlocked. Adam climbed into the passenger side, taking in the unfamiliar dashboard and glove compartment. He'd always driven during his marriage. He drove for work. Now he drove his kids everywhere. "Want me to drive?"

"No." Gracie shut her door, jerked her seat belt over and fastened it in what seemed to be one motion.

"Okay, then." Adam put his own seat belt on and as soon as he was settled Gracie zipped backward, spun the wheel and drove out of the parking lot so fast that Adam grabbed the handle above the door. "Hey, slow down." Annoyance sharpened his tone. "This is a small town. There are kids everywhere. You need to drive carefully."

"Yes, Sergeant Sears." She glowered at him, but slowed the car.

"Also, we're supposed to be undercover. You drive like that around here and people are going to notice." Adam pulled the brim of his baseball cap a little lower on his face. He was pretty sure he'd met and talked with every resident of Shelter Creek multiple times in his life. He wasn't going to be able to pull off this undercover thing while they were within the town limits.

Gracie pointed toward her speedometer. "Twenty miles per hour. You happy?"

"Now I am," Adam muttered and gazed out the window. The community center was just two blocks away. The kids were in day camp there again this week, thanks to the miracle Josie had managed to pull off at her hair appointment on Friday. Apparently, Monique was good friends with Priscilla Axel, who'd taught school in Shelter Creek for generations. One of Priscilla's former students ran the community center summer program, so Mrs. Axel had used her influence to plead Adam's case. For once he didn't mind the sympathy, or even the pity, of his fellow residents. Poor-Adam-who-got-dumped-by-his-wife was able to get his kids two last-minute slots in summer day camp. He'd take the pity if it gave his kids a fun place to go while he was at work.

"How was your weekend?" Gracie asked.

That was unexpected. She'd barely spoken a civil word to him since they'd met.

"It was fine. Uneventful." Friday night had started out rough when he'd told Penny and Jack that their mom couldn't visit after all. Seven-year-old Penny had cried. Jack had stomped off to his room like the tween he was becoming. Adam had consoled them with ice cream sundaes and a movie, and by Saturday morning they'd seemed happy again. He'd taken them riding up in the hills that day, just them and the horses and a picnic lunch. On Sunday they'd gone on a bike ride around town, with a stop at the park to play in the creek that gave the town its name.

Adam was glad he'd been able to salvage their weekend, but he couldn't shake his anger at his ex-wife. Or his worry about what her choices might mean for the kids. Maybe he should start putting some money aside for their future counseling sessions. No movies or ice cream sundaes could truly fix the pain of their mom leaving them.

He'd become lost in his thoughts, when he should be meeting Gracie's attempt to make conversation. "How about you? How was your weekend?"

"It was good. I'm staying with an old friend. It's been nice to catch up."

He'd pictured her staying alone in some motel somewhere. Or camping out. She seemed so intense and stressed out, it was hard to picture her hanging out comfortably with friends. "That's nice. Who is your friend?"

"Maya Burton."

He turned to face her in surprise. "You're friends with Maya?"

She glanced at him for a brief moment, humor in her light blue eyes. "She says she's known you for ages, that you're practically an institution in Shelter Creek, you've been working for the sheriff's department for so long. You don't seem old enough to be an institution, though."

"An institution?" The word didn't sit well. An institution was unchanging, always there, and…boring. Did Maya think he was boring? She and her husband, Caleb, were his good friends.

Wait, how did this woman get him questioning his own longstanding friendships with just a few words? That was her thing. Putting people on edge. Making them uncomfortable. Why? To keep them at a safe distance? To hide her own insecurities?

Or maybe Tanya's words on the phone were getting under his skin. *You were always so serious about your job. So stuck in your routine. Our marriage was boring. Stale.*

"I don't think I'm an institution. I was just lucky enough to find work I like at a very young age." He glanced out the window. They were heading east toward the highway. "Where are we going?"

"We're investigating the site where the bear carcass was found. Highway patrol had it hauled off already, but I want to look for footprints, tire marks, anything else we can find."

"Okay." Adam stifled a sudden yawn. Penny had woken in the middle of the night from a bad dream and it had taken him ages to get her back to sleep. By the time he'd succeeded, insomnia had its grip on him, and he'd spent another hour or two staring at the ceiling and revisiting every doubt he had about the way his life had turned out.

"Sorry if this assignment is boring to you," Gracie said.

"No, I'm just a little worn out today, that's all."

"Right." The set of her jaw said that she didn't believe him. Well, he didn't exactly want to be here with her, so her instincts weren't wrong.

On the highway, a few miles north of Shelter Creek, Gracie asked Adam to look for mile marker seventy-seven. He watched the little numbered signs go by on the side of the road, grateful for a reason to avoid the awkward silence that had been growing between them. Apparently neither of them was very good at small talk.

Just past marker seventy-six, Adam saw a dirt area on the right-hand side. "Pull over there," he told her, and Gracie hit the brakes hard enough that his hand went to the dashboard on instinct. They skidded in the dirt and came to a stop a few feet before a big pile of boulders.

Adam gaped at Gracie as she calmly shut

off the engine and put the keys in her coat pocket. "Do you always drive so badly?"

Her grin was totally unrepentant. "Probably." She hopped out of the truck and Adam followed, feeling slightly nauseous. He was going to insist on driving from now on. He might have to work with her, but he wasn't obligated to risk his life just so she could feel in charge.

They crossed the empty two-lane highway that wound through this forested area. Big firs rose to touch the sky around them. As they scrambled up the bank from the highway Adam inhaled the deep refreshing scent.

"The bear was left right here." Gracie pointed to a flattened area in the fallen fir fronds and dust. "You can see where it was dragged away from the road."

Sure enough, Adam could see marks in the dirt, as if something heavy had been dragged up the bank. There were darker stains here and there. Blood. Broken ferns and flattened grass. "Wait." He walked closer to the marks and knelt down. "Gracie, look at these ferns here. The way they snapped. And this grass. The bear was dragged *toward* the road, not away from it."

"I knew this wasn't really a roadkill." Gracie pulled out her phone and took a few photos. Then she glanced up at him and Adam noted the tiny flicker of respect in her gaze. "Nice work, Sergeant." She turned away and prowled like a cat, silent and fluid, studying the soil between them and the highway. Suddenly she knelt to look at the ground. "Boot print," she said.

"It could be anyone's." Adam crouched next to her. "Look, there's another one."

Gracie snapped a couple photos. "Yes, it could be anyone's. Or it could be the poacher's. If we come across other prints later on, maybe they'll match."

"Why do I get the feeling you go down a lot of dead ends in your job?" Adam stood up and glanced around them. There was a tuft of dark fur on the ground and for a moment he couldn't look away from it. The whole situation was heartbreaking and futile. The bear was dead. The poachers had moved on. "What else are you looking for?"

"You never know. When someone leaves an area in a hurry, they might drop all kinds of things. A knife. A wallet. A wrapper from their favorite snack. It's all potential evidence."

Adam's phone vibrated in his pocket and

he pulled it out. It was work. "Josie, is that you? What's going on?"

"Hey, Adam, I had a call from a guy named James Freely. He owns a large property out in the hills around County Road 39. He just spotted an unfamiliar truck turning onto a fire road that goes through a few hundred acres of his managed timber. He's on his way to a medical appointment and couldn't pursue it, but he's concerned. I guess he's heard some gunshots in that area recently."

Adam's adrenaline kicked up. Maybe this day with Gracie wasn't going to be boring after all. "We're pretty close by. Did he give specific directions?"

"He sure did. Go west on County Road 39. There's a turnoff on the right, just after mile marker four. That will put you on the fire road."

Adam glanced at Gracie, who was watching him intently. "What else do we know about the terrain out there?"

"Not much. The fire road makes a loop and eventually goes through some Forest Service land. You'll end up back on the county road, several miles west of where you started."

"Did he get a description of the truck?"

"He said it looked pretty new. Black. Shiny. Double cab. Gun rack behind the cab."

"Thanks, Josie. We'll check it out." Adam hung up and turned to Gracie. "We have to go. Someone reported trespassers, just a few miles from here. It might be nothing, but it might be your poachers."

She was down the bank and across the road before he'd finished his sentence. He followed and put a hand on her arm as she reached for the driver's-side door.

He might as well have hit her with his Taser, she jumped away so fast. Her lips parted in a high-pitched gasp, her eyes widened with visible fear. "Don't touch me," she ordered.

Adam held his hands up. "I'm sorry, Gracie. I was trying to tell you that I'd like to drive."

She shook her head. "I'll get us there faster."

"I'll get us there in one piece."

Her hands went to her hips while her eyes rolled to the heavens. "Please just get in the car. We don't have time for this."

"I have two little kids, Gracie. They rely on me completely. I'd prefer not to die today, and your driving makes me think that could actually happen."

She stared at him for a moment and then

shoved the keys into his hands. "Okay, fine. You drive. But hurry."

He got behind the wheel, adjusted the seat to fit his height and buckled up. Glancing at Gracie to make sure she was set, he turned on the engine and backed up the SUV. Checking the highway carefully for traffic, he accelerated onto the road.

It didn't take more than a minute for Gracie to start tapping the dashboard. It took another minute before she complained. "You're like a turtle, Adam. Can't you speed up a little?"

"Nope. Our exit is right here." He signaled and steered the SUV down a small off-ramp, then took a left on the county road that cut under the highway. It was just barely a lane wide in either direction.

"Okay, hurry now, please."

"We won't be any help to your precious bears if we crash on the way."

That seemed to sink in because she was silent as he drove them out to mile marker four. There was the lane, just as Josie had described it—a dirt road leading across a field and into the woods. Adam glanced at Gracie. "Are you ready?"

She nodded. "Let's do it."

"What's your plan if we find these guys?"

"Arrest them."

"What if they're out here but they haven't shot anything?"

"Then we'll take photos of them. And their truck. We can pretend we're out for a nice, quiet drive in the country." She flashed him a mischievous smile. "We can do some four-wheeling, if you want."

"Ha. No. We'll stick with the nice, quiet part of the plan."

It would have been a pleasant ride if they hadn't been pursuing possible poachers. Once in the forest, the road ran along the top of a ridge. If the firs had ever been logged up here, it had been a long time ago. Their thick trunks and canopy of branches cooled the warming day and gave the sunlight filtering through them a hazy golden hue.

Adam braked carefully as the road dipped sharply downhill along one side of the ridge. There was a steep drop-off up ahead and he eased the truck around the corner. This area got a little more sun. There were gaps in the trees where shrubs and grass had taken root.

"Those are huckleberries." Gracie pointed to a large stand of dark green bushes. "They'll attract bears and other wildlife at this time of year."

Just then a shot rang out from somewhere up ahead of them. Instinctively, Adam slammed on the brakes.

"I knew it," Gracie said. "Poachers. Let's go."

"Do you carry a gun?" Adam glanced over as she opened the glove compartment and pulled out a revolver. "Okay, so yes, you do."

"I'm getting it out just in case."

Adam started forward again, going slowly now, uncertain of what was ahead of them. Around the next corner, the trees opened up to reveal an exposed hillside of shrubs and rock, and there, a few turns ahead of them on the far side of the hill, was a truck. Black, with a gun rack, just like Mr. Freely had described. Adam stopped the SUV. "Quick. Let's get a picture of that truck."

Gracie used her phone to snap a few photos, and then reached under her seat for a higher quality camera with a long zoom lens. "I'll get a couple really good ones with this." She opened her window and leaned out. The click of the camera's shutter seemed too loud in the quiet woods. She nodded to Adam as she settled back into her seat. "Let's go see what they're up to."

But whoever was in that truck must have heard them coming. Two figures emerged from the hillside above the vehicle and jumped into the cab. The truck accelerated and disappeared around a corner in a cloud of dust.

"Go!" Gracie was pressing buttons on the camera and Adam realized she was pulling up the photos she'd just taken, zooming in, trying to see the vehicle's details. "Those jerks. No license plate."

They were approaching where the truck had been. Adam glanced at Gracie. "Should we stop and see if they hit anything with those guns?"

Her eyes were fixed on the road ahead. "I'd rather catch them, arrest them for trespassing and find out who they are."

"I think they've got too much of a head start on us. Once they get back to the county road, we've lost them. They could turn either way."

Gracie closed her eyes briefly, as if it was physically difficult for her to end the chase. "You're right. Let's stop. I hope they didn't actually shoot anything."

As soon as Adam put the SUV in Park,

Gracie was out the door, aiming her camera at the dusty road. "Look," she called as Adam walked over to join her. "We've definitely got tire tracks."

Adam's mood ticked up at the sight. "They're deep in that dust. The tread looks new."

"Their truck looked new. That might help us figure out who they are." Gracie snapped several photos.

"There have to be some footprints in this dust." Adam crouched down, scanning the ground around them. "There." He pointed. "Sneakers."

Gracie took a photo. "Let's check the passenger side."

They stepped carefully over the tire tracks and walked to the middle of the road.

"Bingo." Gracie pointed just as Adam saw them. "They're a little blurred. Probably because the guy was running."

"But still." Adam knelt by the prints. "They look a lot like the one we saw back by the highway."

Gracie gave him a wan smile. "Our sleuthing may be paying off." Her gaze drifted to a spot over his head. "Stand up," she whispered. "Walk slowly to the car. Be ready to get in if we need to."

He heard what she did now. A rustling and cracking of sticks in the bushes. The sound was coming from the hillside above the road, a little behind where they'd stopped the car.

They walked quietly to the rear of the SUV. Adam's blood was pumping hard through his temples, his chest, his wrists. He'd forgotten what it felt like to be this awake, this alert, with all his attention focused on just one thing.

A few more heartbeats and it emerged. A black bear cub. Not tiny, but definitely not grown. Cute as could be, with a black sleek coat, a pale brown muzzle and round ears that reminded Adam of the teddy bear that slept with Penny at night.

The cub scrambled down the bank and padded out into the middle of the road on paws that looked a few sizes too big. Stopping several yards in front of them, the little bear raised its nose in the air and let out a plaintive, raspy squeal.

"It's only a few months old." Gracie spoke in a whisper, but Adam could hear the worry in her voice. "If they killed the mother…if they orphaned it…" She didn't finish, just watched the cub as it sniffed at the dust in the road.

"Does it need to be rescued?" Adam's heart

ached as the cub let out another pitiful yowl. "It looks too young to survive on its own."

"Way too young," Gracie agreed. "But we can't jump to conclusions. We have to wait and see what happens."

They watched while the cub wandered away from them, back the way they'd come, sniffing at some bushes growing alongside the fire road. It was so small, and looked so confused, it reminded Adam of a child, lost in the woods.

"How long do they stay with their mother?" he asked in a low voice.

"Up to about two years," Gracie answered. "They learn everything from her. How to hunt. How to forage. How to find or build a den. How to climb trees and get back down again. It won't survive out here on its own. If its mom doesn't come soon, we'll have to figure out how to take it with us."

The bear cub gave another whimpering yowl and turned off the road, heading back uphill. "Let's follow. Come on." Gracie started walking and Adam stole a moment to swipe at his eyes. Maybe being a dad made him sentimental, but that cub, on its own like this, was getting to him. He didn't want to follow it into the woods. Didn't want to see what he was afraid they'd find there. Its mother... killed by a bullet.

He followed Gracie as she clambered up the hill and disappeared into the trees behind the baby bear. They stayed a good distance away from the cub as it ambled along the side of the hill, parallel to the road below. Occasionally it paused to sniff at something, or tried to reach its mama with a squeaky call.

Just when Adam was giving up hope and starting to wonder how in the world they'd catch an orphaned bear cub, Gracie held a palm out behind her to signal him to stop.

The land in front of them sloped down toward a seasonal creek, dry in late summer. Looking over Gracie's shoulder, Adam saw a full-grown black bear standing at the base of a big fir near the creek bed. Her front paws were on the trunk, and she was looking up into the tree.

There was another cub, clinging to a branch several yards up the trunk. It was peeking down at its mama, obviously hesitant to climb down. The little lost cub they'd been following broke into a shambling trot and reached its mother, greeting her with a series of small squeaks and growls. The mother bear dropped to all fours to nuzzle her baby.

Gracie took a few silent steps backward to stand next to Adam. A huge smile revealed creased dimples in her cheeks and crinkled lines around her eyes. Her hands were clasped in front of her as if in prayer and she glanced at him with eyes that were bright with unshed tears.

She gave him a thumbs-up and motioned for him to follow her back the way they'd come. Adam did his best to walk as silently as possible, glancing over his shoulder in case an irate mother bear was on their heels. But there was no sign of her. She was probably busy coaching her other cub down that tree.

They got into the SUV and sat for a moment. Adam tried to swallow the bear-sized lump in his throat. Finally, Gracie spoke. "That was the best outcome we could hope for."

"It sure was." Adam closed his eyes, trying to wipe the image of the bear cub, so alone and scared after the gunshot, from his mind. "Lucky for us, whoever was in that truck only got off one shot, and didn't have the best aim."

"I don't recognize that vehicle," Gracie

said. "These might be different guys than I've been trying to catch up north. Or they may have bought a new truck. We can check DMV records to see if anyone has registered a new pickup around here."

"Let's do it." Adam had thought this assignment was a waste of his time. He'd thought he'd been demoted. But now he was angry.

He started the engine and fastened his seat belt. Gracie pulled her gun out of her belt, checked the safety and put it back in the glove compartment. Once she was buckled in, Adam hit the gas. Maybe they could spot tire tracks at the intersection with the county road and figure out which way those men had gone.

Gracie gripped the handle above the door as they bounced and rattled over the ruts. "Now you're starting to drive like me," she said. "What's going on?"

Adam tried to smile but only managed a tight grimace. But despite his anger, or maybe because of it, he was more alive and ready to work than he had been in months. "We're going after those poachers," he said. "Hang on tight."

CHAPTER FOUR

THE TRUCK RATTLED and bumped as the fire road wound up and over rolling hills, the forest giving way to fields rippling with long grass parched by the summer sun. There was no sign of the black truck. Gracie tried to look casual while she gripped the handle above her door with sharp knuckles. Adam's jaw was set in a tight line. The guy was going to crack a tooth, he was wound so tight. "Hey," she said quietly. "Let's stop a minute and make a plan."

"We can talk and drive."

"Adam!" She smacked him lightly on the shoulder to jolt him out of his mood. "I'm supposed to be the one who needs a babysitter on this job. Stop the truck."

He glared at her and hit the brakes a little hard, so the SUV slid to a stop surrounded by its own cloud of dust.

Gracie put her palm to her forehead. What

had her boss been thinking? She sure didn't need this kind of help. Adam was wound as tight as the top on a bottle of soda.

He wasn't who she'd thought he was. The uptight, disinterested man she'd met up with this morning had vanished. His forearms were etched with corded tendons as he gripped the wheel. His eyes had lost their detached expression and darkened with anger and determination. He sat up straight, squaring shoulders so sturdy that a different girl than her might want to lean on them. He'd yanked off his baseball cap somewhere in the last few miles, tossed it into the back seat and run frustrated fingers through his thick, dark hair. Now it stood on end, erasing the carefully combed impression she'd had.

He was handsome. Tough. And the intensity of his pursuit was a little breathtaking. Not that *her* breath was taken.

He looked over at her, his breathing shallow, his fingertips tapping the wheel. "I stopped. What's up?"

"What's up is that you need to slow down. We're not catching any poachers if we end up rolling my car into a ditch."

"*You're* telling *me* to slow down?" The

sheepish quirk at the corner of his mouth softened the defensive words. He knew he was out of line.

"What's going on with you? One moment you're completely unenthusiastic about working with me, the next you're so angry you're about to go nuclear."

Adam rolled down his window, leaned an elbow on it and upended his hair with his fingers again. "I saw that cub wandering around, so alone and scared, and a switch in me kind of flipped."

They might be very different people, but Gracie could understand what he was going through. "This is nature. Cubs get orphaned. They even die. If you're going to work with animals, you have to try to toughen up."

He nodded, looking away from her out the window, silent for a long moment. Gracie studied him, or the part of him she could see—the neat hair at the nape of his neck, the curved edge of his ear, the cut line of his jaw. She watched him swallow once, hard, before he spoke. "It was a rough weekend. I've got two little kids. Their mom left last year. She was supposed to come see them this past weekend, but she changed plans at the last minute."

It took a moment for Gracie to absorb the impact of his words. Motherless cub. Motherless kids. An ache kindled deep in her chest. "I'm sorry. That's rough."

"I guess I sort of connected that cub's situation to my kids. I don't know why. I'm not someone who usually gets riled up on the job."

She hadn't gotten riled up either. Until recently.

He turned to face her and a shadow of humor softened the bleak lines around his mouth. "How about we just forget this happened?"

"What happened?" Gracie threw in a nonchalant shrug of her shoulder. This was what she wished her colleagues had done last week, instead of notifying her boss that she wasn't fit to serve. One moment didn't mean that. Adam's moment, just now, didn't mean that. "How about we get on the road and see if we can figure out where that black truck went?"

"Sounds good." Adam released the brake and started to put her car in gear, but Gracie put a gentle hand to his shoulder. She tried to ignore the sensation of rock-solid muscle beneath her fingertips.

"Hang on. I think it's my turn to drive."

He gave a short, sharp laugh and shifted back to Park. "Guess I earned that." He set the brake and got out of the SUV. She hopped out her side. As they passed each other in front of the vehicle Adam held up his palm for a high five. Gracie smacked it hard as she went by.

By some miracle, or because everything was so dry and dusty at the tail end of summer, they spotted tracks as soon as they arrived at the county road.

"Stop," Adam said, but Gracie had already seen them. She pulled along the verge of the road and left the car running as they both got out to look.

"There's no guarantee it's the guys we saw." Adam pointed to the dusty tracks on the pavement. "But someone peeled out of here recently and turned right."

"Well, at least it's a start." Gracie shaded her eyes and looked west. "What's down this way?"

"The road winds on for miles, all the way to the coast. There are a couple small towns along the way."

The information extinguished her momentary flicker of hope. "They could be anywhere."

"Yup." Adam glanced at his watch. "But we've got some time, and no other leads."

He was right. "Let's do it." Gracie turned back to the SUV and Adam followed. "We might spot the truck, but also keep an eye out for any house that seems like hunters live there. Antlers over the door. Or a skinning rack in their yard."

"A skinning rack?"

Gracie studied Adam from across the roof of the SUV. "Are you sure you live in a small, rural town?"

"I live on a cattle ranch, to be exact."

She shook her head in disbelief. "A skinning rack is what hunters use to hang a deer carcass."

"Oh." Adam shrugged. "I never knew what they were called. Like I said, I live on a cattle ranch. We prefer beef."

Gracie got behind the steering wheel and she and Adam buckled up. A rancher? Again, not what she'd pictured when she'd met him in the office last Friday, wearing his starchy uniform and an uptight expression. But suddenly she could see it—the physical confidence of someone who spent a lot of time outside, in motion, working hard. Gracie waited for a car to pass, then pulled back onto the county road, heading west. "How do you have time for ranching when you work for the sheriff's office?"

He smiled slightly. "I don't. My brother and sister run the ranch. I have a house on the property, and I try to help out when they need me. Mostly weekends." But not very often, since he'd become a full-time dad. Maybe it was time to get his kids more involved. By their age he'd had a full schedule of ranch chores. It would be a good way to build their confidence. A good distraction from the situation with their mom, too.

"And you have a horse."

"Bodie. I got him from Dean."

"Captain Dean Carson?" This town was getting interesting. Was everyone a cowboy on the side?

"He trains horses. He seems real tough but he has a soft heart in there. He read an article about those wild mustangs they're rounding up. They sell them off for almost nothing. Sometimes they get bought for meat and

Dean didn't like that idea. He has quite a bit of land, so now he buys them, trains them up and sells them to anyone who will take good care of them."

"Your horse used to be a wild mustang?" All of her first impressions of Adam were shifting, changing, falling away.

"Yeah. He was caught out near the eastern Sierras. Thus the name. Bodie is an old ghost town out that way."

Gracie had been scanning the houses they passed as she drove, but nothing looked suspicious. There were lush kitchen gardens ready for harvest. Horses grazing in pastures. One lucky family had a pool, and the day was so hot Gracie wished they could sneak in for a quick dunk. She shoved her damp hair out of her face and turned on the AC. "You mind a little cool air?"

"Not at all. I sure hope this heat wave will break soon."

"What does Bodie look like?" Gracie hadn't met too many mustangs. Growing up in Texas, she and pretty much everyone she knew rode quarter horses, so perfect for working with cattle.

"He must have a little Appaloosa in him,"

Adam said. "And something else, too. He's pretty tall for a mustang. His coloring is all over the place. I guess if I had to give it a name, I'd say he was a black roan. Black face, black legs, and a whole bunch of mottled black, gray and white all over him."

Gracie hadn't thought she'd have anything in common with Adam. But apparently, they had this. "I love Appaloosas," she told him. "My horse Rio is a blue roan. But she also has a blanket of spots on her rump. She's pretty unusual looking."

"We'll be a motley, spotted crew if we hit the trails together." It was the first time she'd seen Adam really smile and Gracie almost swerved into oncoming traffic. His whole face creased when he grinned. He had dimples. Real dimples on both of his cheeks. Gracie swallowed hard and focused on the road. Good thing she did, because otherwise she might have missed the barn.

It was high up on the ridge to their right, but she could see it at the top of the grassy hill. Sagging roof, chipped paint and the look of a place that no one visited very often. But there were two posts along the side of it, with a beam set across—a skinning rack. She braked hard and pulled over, just before the narrow lane that led up to the barn.

Adam grasped the handle above his window. "What the—give me some warning next time!"

"Sorry," Gracie muttered, studying the three mailboxes at the base of the lane. People lived up here. The road must go on past the barn.

"I think I made a mistake when I let you drive," Adam said. "Why are we stopped?"

"Check out that barn."

He looked up the hill. "What am I looking for?"

"They've got a skinning rack and I've got a feeling." She started forward and turned up the lane. The pavement became gravel after a few yards, and she shifted to low gear to navigate the steep hill.

"This is how you work? You get a *feeling*?"

"Pretty much." There was no point in explaining it to a practical person like Adam, but her hunches had served her well in the past. "Doesn't that barn seem like a good place to deal with an animal you weren't supposed to have in the first place?"

"I guess…but there are a whole lot of old

barns like this around here. They can't all be poachers' hideouts."

Gracie pulled off the lane and parked in a patch of dirt by a gate that led to the field below the barn. "Let's walk from here."

"Do you have a plan?" Adam's disbelief was written in raised brows and a skeptical tone. "Or is walking right onto private property just part of how you work, too?"

"Yup." Gracie grabbed her camera and got out of the SUV. She started up the lane, then realized Adam hadn't followed her. She stopped. He was still in the car. She blew out a long breath, hoping it would instill some patience. Then she went to get him. "Are you coming?"

"Not without a plan. You really think those wannabe poachers from the woods are up here?"

"I don't know. It just seemed like somewhere they'd be."

"Let's say we check out the barn and we find someone in there. What's your plan then?"

"We arrest them."

He raised his hands in obvious exasperation. "They haven't committed a crime. We didn't actually see them fire that gun, Gracie. Even if their truck is here, even if it matches our photos, even if they have a shotgun and the barrel is still warm, it's not enough to stand up in court."

He was right. She couldn't seem to think straight anymore. She'd told him to keep his emotions in check back on the fire road, but hers were all over the place. "Let's just take a peek at the barn since we're here. See if we notice anything suspicious."

"It's private property and we have no warrant."

"It's abandoned property as far as I can tell. Come on." She waved her arm to summon him and started back up the road again. This time she heard his door shut and his boots on the gravel and she slowed her pace so he could catch up. When he did, he spoke softly, but it was loud enough that she could clearly hear.

"Did anyone ever tell you you're stubborn as a mule at feeding time?"

She grinned. "Yeah. Maybe not in those exact words."

"What words did they use?"

"Let's see." Gracie kept her voice quiet, too.

They were getting closer to the barn. "Tough as a pine knot. That was my daddy's favorite. My mama just said things like, *Gracie, you'd argue with a fence post, if it could talk.*"

Adam made a snorting sound and covered his mouth and nose with his hand. The smile lines around his eyes were deep, but he managed to contain his laugh. Good. They'd reached the dirt drive that led to the old barn. There was no black truck, or any vehicle, parked nearby.

"I think your *feeling* might have led us wrong," Adam whispered.

He was probably right. But from the main road, this barn had seemed like the perfect spot to hide. Then Gracie saw the tire tracks. She pointed to the dusty ground in front of the wide barn doors. "Those are similar to what we've been following."

Adam knelt down to study them. Then he stood and shook his head. "These are from older tires with a lot less tread."

"Maybe these are from the poacher's old truck. Then he bought the new one we saw today." She was being ridiculous. She knew it. But she could feel that this place was important. A glint of metal caught her eye. "There are new hinges on these doors. And a new padlock."

"That means nothing."

"Not by itself. But it *could* matter. Let's just see if there's a window." Gracie started along the side of the building.

"Wait." Adam was following her, but he didn't look happy about it.

This was why she hadn't wanted to work with anyone. She whirled to face him.

"What if someone's here? What if they're hostile?" Adam's voice was barely loud enough for her to hear, but his stern tone came through loud and clear. "You're walking straight into an unknown situation. It could be nothing, but it could be something ugly."

"No one is here, Adam. I'm positive." It was impossible to hide the irritation in her voice. He was just what she didn't need right now. Uptight. Upstanding. Upset.

"Well, that still doesn't excuse this. You don't have a warrant. You don't even have probable cause." His jaw was back in that stubborn line, his eyes focused intently on hers. They were brown. Dark brown with thick lashes. How come he had lashes like that? A total waste on a guy.

Focus, Gracie. She crossed her arms over her chest. "I don't work that way."

"Well, you need to start working that way or you won't be able to prosecute these poachers when you find them."

"I'm not collecting evidence right now. I'm following a hunch. Come on…just one peek?"

He was wavering, she could tell. "I'm feeling like that fence post your mama used to talk about."

"Ha. I guess some things never change." Gracie had only taken a few steps when she heard the hum of an engine on the lane, and the crunch of wheels on gravel. She pressed her back to the barn wall and Adam did the same. They waited for a few long seconds. A big black truck with a gunrack came into view, driving away from them on its way down to the county road. Gracie's racing heart seemed to crash right into her lungs. She gasped and grabbed Adam's arm. "I told you!"

He was staring at the truck as it disappeared out of sight, his lips parted slightly. "I don't even know what to say right now."

"How about, 'Gracie, you have amazing intuition.'"

He looked at her with humor and a touch of awe. "You were right. I'll just leave it at that."

"Do you think they'll recognize my car from the woods?" Gracie put a palm to her forehead. "Oh gosh, I can't believe I parked right in plain sight."

"We were pretty far away from them, and they took off right away," Adam said. "Plus I think they might have only seen your SUV from the front…"

"But we can't be sure," Gracie finished for him. She pushed herself away from the wall. "Come on. Let's see if we can find a window." She led the way around the back of the barn and pointed. "Jackpot."

"Except we can't see in." Adam was right. Someone had taped newspapers over the inside of the window.

Gracie stepped closer and shaded her eyes with her hands. "This newspaper isn't very faded. Someone did this pretty recently."

"And put new hinges and a lock on this door, too."

The sunlight was reflecting off the glass, making it hard to read the newspapers on the other side. Gracie tilted her head and shaded her eyes again.

"What are you doing?" Adam came up beside her.

"I'm trying to see where these papers are from." Gracie squinted. "I'm pretty sure this article is about a shop in Eureka. Maybe this guy in the truck really is the same poacher we've been looking for up north."

"Hello? Anyone here?" The shout from the road jolted Gracie from her bones to her skin. She threw herself back against the barn wall, her breath shallow and useless in her throat. Where had all the air gone? Her pulse pounded in her temples, faster and faster. She pushed her palms to her chest as if she could slow her heart that way. *No, this couldn't be happening again.* But her lungs were shrinking, and the ground was getting further away.

"Gracie, we need to get out of here," Adam whispered. He turned to look at her and his eyes widened. "What is going on?"

"Nothing," Gracie gasped. "I'm fine. Let's go."

"Are you okay?"

Why wouldn't her heart slow down? She needed to breathe. Needed to come back down to earth, but how could she, when she could barely feel her legs? Three words repeated in her mind like a mantra. *Get a grip, get a grip, get a grip.*

Adam wrapped an arm around her back before she could protest. "Lean on me," he whispered. "Put a hand on my shoulder. Act like you hurt your ankle."

His arm anchored her, strong and steady, pulling her back from the whirlpool of panic. Gracie put her hand on his shoulder and leaned into his side.

"That's it," he whispered. "Let's go."

They retraced their steps toward the lane. Gracie clung to Adam's side, his warmth grounding her, the rise and fall of his breath guiding her own until finally her heart slowed its frantic pace. But it couldn't seem to completely settle. Not with Adam's arm around her back, and his breath so close to her ear.

As they rounded the corner he called out, "We're here."

An older man with a thick gray beard stomped toward them. He wore a blue baseball cap and a faded red flannel shirt that barely closed over his belly. His baggy olive pants ended in a pair of scuffed, brown work boots. "This is private property," he said.

"Sorry, sir." Adam's voice conveyed a

practiced, calm deference that must come in handy when he was working. "My girlfriend and I heard there was a hiking trail up here. We were looking for it when she twisted her ankle."

Gracie glanced at Adam in surprise. Girlfriend? Hiking trail? The straitlaced lawman knew how to fib? Adam's hand tightened on her waist, reminding her to act her part. The man was eyeing them suspiciously. He'd stopped, hands on hips, right in the middle of the driveway.

"I'm sorry if we're in the wrong place," she said. "I read about the trail on a website, and I thought I had the directions right."

The man shook his head so vigorously that his beard waggled back and forth. "No trails in this area. There's one at Johnson's Wood, about four miles farther west."

"That's the one I read about." Gracie feigned regret. "Though now that I've messed up my ankle, we may have to take that hike another day."

"That's okay, honey," Adam said. "We can visit some of those wineries you were wondering about on the drive over."

Honey? A quick glance at Adam revealed

a slight twitch at the corner of his mouth. He was messing with her now, which was just what she needed to make the last of her anxiety fizzle away. "Okay, sweetie. But you have to promise not to drink too much this time. It's called tasting. Not guzzling."

The bearded man grinned, revealing teeth that were begging for a trip to the dentist. "I never did understand that tasting idea. You put some free wine in front of me, I'll just drink the stuff down."

"See? This guy understands." Adam reflected the older man's hearty tone and faked a laugh, pulling Gracie a little closer to his side. "You can be my designated driver, honey."

"Now you're talking," their new buddy chimed in. "Trust me, young lady. This guy will have a lot more fun than if you'd gone hiking."

He and Adam shared a manly guffaw of laughter. Then Adam sobered, and put that earnest tone back in his voice. "We really didn't mean to intrude on your property."

"No problem." The man gestured vaguely to the structure. "It's just an old barn. My nephew stores some gear in there sometimes.

Though why he'd want to, when the thing is going to fall down in the next strong wind, I'll never know." He shrugged and moved off the driveway so they could get past. "Have fun with the wine tasting."

"Thanks," Adam said. "We will." He started forward, and Gracie hopped alongside him.

"Other ankle," Adam muttered.

Oops. Gracie quickly shifted position and flashed the man what she hoped was an innocent smile. "Goodbye. Thanks for your understanding."

They hobbled to the end of the driveway. When they reached the lane and turned downhill toward Gracie's SUV, Adam stopped, crouched, and put his free arm behind Gracie's legs. He scooped her up to carry her.

"What are you doing?" Her face was going up in flames. He was holding her close to his body, the rhythm of his stride jogging her up and down. "You can't carry me."

"I'm your boyfriend, remember, *honey*?" He smiled down at her. Though it might have been more of a grimace. She wasn't exactly light as a feather. "It was going to take you forever to hop down this hill. I don't want to give that guy time to change his mind and call the cops on us for trespassing."

"That would look bad," Gracie agreed.

"Bad? Gracie, we were basically searching a property without a warrant."

"But did you hear him?" Gracie couldn't keep the triumph out of her voice. "His nephew uses the barn? This man doesn't understand why? I bet his nephew is one of the guys in that black truck."

They'd reached her car and Adam set her down, perhaps a little roughly. "Give me the keys. I'm driving." His voice didn't allow for argument, and Gracie didn't have any fight left in her anyway. Even though they were safe, echoes of her panic by the barn were still there, making her knees shake and her bones feel mushy. She handed Adam the keys and went to the passenger side.

Once they were settled in the car, Adam drove them down the lane and took a right at the county road, heading east toward the highway. "I think we may as well return to the station. Maybe we can figure out who registered that truck we were chasing."

"*If* it's registered." Exhaustion had set in now that her panic was gone. She was ready for some time in the office, a sentiment she'd never thought she'd feel.

They drove in silence for a few miles, and Gracie was grateful for the quiet. She looked out the window, felt the sun on her face and wondered what was happening to her mind. How had she gotten so weak? Was this lasting damage from her head injury? The doctors had told her it was completely healed.

"Want to tell me what happened back there?"

When Gracie glanced his way, Adam was watching the road ahead. "It was nothing," she told his profile.

"That wasn't nothing, Gracie." Adam glanced at her briefly and she hated the concern she saw in the angle of his brows. She might have been battered, but he was looking at her like she was broken.

"I just got startled, I guess. I wasn't expecting anyone to be on that property."

"You were more than startled. You were practically hyperventilating. You could barely walk."

"I was faking a sprained ankle." She couldn't explain what had happened when she barely knew the words to describe it. And if she did describe it, he'd report her, and she'd be assigned to a desk job. Or put on leave.

"You weren't faking that you needed to hold on to me."

"*Hold on?* You were the one who put your arm around me." Gracie instantly regretted the words. He'd saved her back there. "Can we just forget about it? I promise it won't happen again."

"I can't forget it. Not when it put us in danger. Not when I thought you were going to pass out on me. Are you sick? Is there some medication you should be taking?"

"No!" He'd called her stubborn, but he was the one acting like a dog with a bone right now. "I'm fine. I had one bad moment. Let's just let it go."

Gracie looked out the window, blinking hard to hold back tears of frustration. No way was she going to start bawling on the job.

"I'll let it go for today." Adam's tone was patient, but firm. "But you and I need to talk about how we're going to work together. Whether we like it or not, we're a team for a few weeks. We need to figure out how to act like one."

Earlier today, it had been hard to picture

him as a dad. Now Gracie could see it perfectly. How he'd be measured, and fair and also a little strict with his kids. But he'd be kind, too. Like he was being kind to her, now.

"Okay," she agreed. "But not now. The guys who shot at those bears might have better aim next time. We have to find out who they are and stop them before they get another chance."

"Agreed." Adam kept them steady on the road back to Shelter Creek, but Gracie noticed he was still driving a lot faster than he had before they'd met those bears. The memory of him calling her honey and making wine tasting jokes had her smiling as she watched the scenery race by the window. Sergeant Sears definitely believed in playing by the rules, but maybe he wasn't such a stick-in-the-mud after all.

CHAPTER FIVE

ADAM STEPPED OUT of his front door with his kids, grateful that the hot day had turned into such a peaceful, warm summer evening. As they started up the lane toward the barn, he felt his shoulders relax. This was the golden time of day, with the light getting low and Penny and Jack on either side of him. Just what he needed after such an intense first day working with Gracie. "So how was the new session of camp?"

"It was fun." Penny grabbed Adam's hand, jumping up and down next to him, her wavy light brown hair bouncing in an unruly mess around her face. He hadn't reminded her to tie it back, again. "There were a lot of kids there. We played tag. And there were Popsicles for afternoon snack."

"That sounds just about perfect." Adam ruffled Penny's hair. "Jack, how about you?"

"It was okay." Jack shoved his hands nonchalantly into the front pockets of his jeans, a new gesture that looked so grown up it made Adam's head spin. "It was fun hanging with Brendan. Sam and Diego were there, too. We played some basketball."

"That sounds good." Adam put a hand on his son's shoulder, resisting the urge to tug on Jack's straw cowboy hat, a smaller version of his own. "You and I should go down to the school this weekend and shoot some hoops."

"Can the other kids come?"

"Um…sure. Why don't you ask them about it at camp tomorrow and see what they say?" Was it wrong to feel a twinge of regret? Father-son time was getting replaced with son-friends time. Of course that was how it should be. Jack was eleven now. But still…

Penny's tug at his hand pulled him back to the moment. "Daddy, can I ride Comet?"

"Tonight?"

"C'mon, Dad, can we ride? Please?" Jack bounced up and down just like Penny, slipping right back into familiar boyhood. "We already had dinner and did the dishes. And it won't get dark for almost another three hours."

The longest days of the year. He used to ride out with Wyatt and Sara on evenings like this when he was just a little bit older than these two. "We should probably just get the chores done and get to bed. You two have camp again in the morning."

"Puh-lease?" Penny skipped ahead a few paces, then stopped and pressed her palms together. "Just a short ride?"

Adam looked from Penny to Jack, whose dark brown eyes held a plea like Penny's.

They were approaching the barn. Could they make it work? Adam started on a mental list of chores waiting for them. They had to clean the corral tonight. He'd hoped to replace a couple boards on the side of the shed that had come loose. Tanya's words cut into Adam's train of thought. *Stuck in your routine...boring...stale.*

"Sure. Let's do it."

"Awesome!" Jack started running. "C'mon, Penny. Let's get the wheelbarrow and clean up real quick."

And just like that the kids were running up the lane ahead of him, eager to get started. Adam jogged after them. Might as well get some cardio in wherever he could. He'd learned a few things about Gracie today, and one of them was that he was going to have to be on his toes to keep up with her.

The thought should annoy him. Except that there'd been exhilarating moments today. For almost a year now he'd been slogging along, learning to be alone, trying to be everything for his kids. For years before that he'd been focused on Tanya, and trying to live up to her most recent set of expectations.

Today he'd felt like someone more than that. Seeing those bears had made him realize that there were things that mattered outside of his ever-shrinking world. It had even felt kind of good, until Gracie started shaking behind that barn. Something had happened there, something that almost caused her to pass out. He'd kept quiet about it all afternoon, back in the office while they'd searched online for any record of the truck they'd seen. But he'd caught her studying him a few times, and wondered if she was going to let him know what had made her fall apart. She never did, though. Just said goodbye promptly at five o'clock and slipped out the office door.

It was her business. Her health. Except that if she was going to fall apart on the job like

that, it affected him, too. They couldn't rescue any bears if he was busy rescuing her.

When he reached the corral, the kids were
already hauling the wheelbarrow and shovels
out of the barn. His brother Wyatt followed
them out. He'd taken off his cowboy hat and
as Adam approached, he could see the shadows under Wyatt's eyes.

"You look like hell, bro." Worry made
Adam's tone sound a little more accusing than
he meant it to.

"Nice to see you, too." Wyatt ran a hand
through his shaggy, light brown hair and
yawned. "Long day."

"And a late night, I'm guessing."

Wyatt shrugged. "Just went out for a few
hours and played some pool."

Adam was pretty sure that "played some
pool" was code for "drank too many beers."
Ever since Wyatt's fiancée had broken things
off last year, to travel the world and experience life, Wyatt had been kind of a mess.

"What has the kids so enthusiastic about
scooping manure?" Wyatt looked over at
Penny and Jack, in the corral with the horses
now, arguing over who was going to push the
wheelbarrow next.

"I promised them a short ride tonight, if they got it done."

Wyatt's tired eyes narrowed. "Wait a minute. You're letting them stay up late on a weeknight?"

Adam shrugged. "It's a nice summer evening."

"You know what I mean." Wyatt watched the kids as he spoke. "You've been pretty rigid since Tanya left."

Adam winced. Rigid? The word made him seem like some overly-strict father from a different era. He wasn't *that* bad at this single-dad thing, was he?

"Have you talked to Tanya since she bailed out this weekend?"

"Nope."

"Women." Wyatt scrubbed his palm over the few-days stubble covering his jaw. "They don't make much sense. I remember back when Tanya was bugging you night and day to start a family. Now she's checked herself out of it entirely."

Adam had spent many nights wondering about the same thing. And whether he'd done something to make his former wife so miserable that she'd abandon her kids, her hometown, everything. He wasn't always great at communicating, he knew. He'd come home from work tired and just wanting some quiet. That certainly must have played a part in how unhappy she'd become.

Which made him think of Gracie today, refusing to tell him what was wrong. Was that because she was too stubborn to admit there was a problem? Or because Adam wasn't someone who inspired her confidence? "I've got a question for you. About a woman."

Wyatt put his hands up in protest. "No way. You know I've got no good answers in that department. Hang on." He turned and fled toward the barn. Adam was staring after him, wondering whether he should be worried, when Wyatt came back with their sister, Sara, in tow.

Sara scowled at both of them as she approached. Her long hair, a lighter brown like Wyatt's, was twisted into two braids that hung down her chest. There was a smear of mud on the rim of her straw cowboy hat and another one on her cheek. "What do you two clowns want? I'm almost done patching the water trough that you promised to fix last week, Wyatt Sears. Anything that gets between me and the shower I desperately need better be important."

"I'll go finish the trough," Wyatt said. "Adam has a question about women."

Sara, just a year older than Adam but always the big sister, folded her arms across her chest. "Ah. Women. Not sure I understand most of them myself. But I'll do my best."

This was getting awkward. Adam hadn't meant to get both his siblings involved in his problems. But heck. Sara was a tomboy and Gracie seemed like one, too. Maybe his sister would have some insight.

"I started working with this woman today. Gracie. I'm supposed to be helping her catch some poachers."

Sara grimaced. "Poachers. Scum of the earth. I hope you get them."

"Me, too. But I think this woman has some kind of problem. She ended up in the hospital a while ago, after some guy she was trying to arrest turned on her. Then she froze up on the job today."

"That's not good. Did you ask her what's wrong?"

Adam nodded. "She told me she was fine. To just forget about it."

Sara grinned, suddenly. "Are you intimidated by this woman? You're law enforcement! You've had to reason with practically every person in and around this town."

"Let's just say my track record for communicating with women hasn't been that good lately."

"Are you thinking of Tanya?" Sara rolled her eyes. "You can't judge yourself by that. Leaving was her choice."

"Yeah, but it was partially my fault. I didn't exactly make her happy."

Sara shook her head in disgust. "When someone wants to leave town as badly as Tanya did, no one can make them happy. I think the two of you married way too young. She probably never had a chance to figure out who she really was."

Sara's words rang true. Today's events had Adam wondering who *he* was, exactly. He'd been so upset over that lost bear cub. So furious at the idiots who fired that shot. He'd lost control afterward and driven so badly that even daredevil Gracie was upset. Looking back on his career, he could safely say he'd never lost control on the job before. But he sure had, today.

And then there was the discovery that even though Gracie made his head spin with her contradictions and chaos, she'd felt so good when he'd held her in his arms.

"Daddy, we cleaned the corral!" Jack jogged toward them with a shovel in his hand. "Hi, Aunt Sara."

"Hi, Jack. I don't think I've ever seen you guys clean that corral so quickly."

"Dad's taking us for a ride now."

Sara's brows arched as she looked at Adam. "At bedtime?"

"It's not bedtime yet," Adam said.

Penny rumbled up with the empty wheelbarrow. "We're finished, Daddy. Can I go catch Comet?"

"I'll help you," Sara offered. "I love that little pony of yours."

"She's not that little. She's a Pony of the Americas." Penny was a little obsessed by that fact. Adam figured she wanted everyone to know that her pony wasn't a tiny one, like a Shetland.

"It's quite a mouthful to say." Sara flashed a smile at Adam. "Can we stick with POA?" Penny reached for her aunt's hand, to tug her over to where Comet was waiting by the fence.

Hay was sticking out of the side of the little mare's mouth. She was just about twelve hands high, white with all kinds of brown spots scattered over her body. Like comets, Penny had decided when they'd brought her home. So June the pony had become Comet, and never seemed bothered by the name change.

"Hang on, Penny," Sara said. She extricated her hand and walked back to Adam, took him by the arm and pulled him a few yards away from the kids. "If you want my advice? Don't let whatever happened with Tanya get in the way of doing your job now. Talk to this woman. Let her know that she can trust you. That you'll have her back. That's all anyone wants. I know that much."

Then she returned to the kids. "Grab the halters, small ones. I'll help you catch your horses so you can go on this ride. Past your bedtime and everything. Who is this man, and what did he do with your dad?"

Adam listened to them laughing as they wandered off, wondering why his sister sounded like she spoke from experience. Who had broken Sara's trust? Who hadn't had her back? He'd probably never know; his sister was so closemouthed about anything personal. But she'd given him good advice and he'd try to use it tomorrow. For now he was going on a ride with his kids. Past their bedtime. His siblings were right—this was pretty out of character for him. But hey, he'd already broken a few rules today with Gracie. No harm in breaking another one now.

CHAPTER SIX

Rio was saddled and ready, but there was no sign of Adam. Gracie glanced down at her phone. Where was he? She'd called him almost an hour ago. Maybe he'd gotten lost. This dead-end dirt road northwest of town wasn't easy to find.

Gracie buckled on her saddlebags, double-checking that she had enough food and water to last the day. She also had her water purifier, in case she needed to refill.

The sound of wheels on gravel had her turning to see a silver pickup hauling a darker gray horse trailer, driving slowly, oh-so-slowly, along the dirt road through the field. Gracie smiled and shook her head. The snail-paced vehicle *must* be Adam. When he finally arrived, he gave her a wave, pulled off into the grass alongside her and cut the engine. "Morning," he called, his arm resting casually on the frame of the open window.

The memory of that arm around her back, supporting her at the barn yesterday, sent a kaleidoscope of butterflies fluttering to her stomach. Gracie froze. She *never* got butterflies. Not since the eighth grade when she'd had a huge crush on her older brother Tyson's best friend, Jim. Tyson discovered Gracie's crush and told Jim, and they'd had a good laugh at her. Then she'd punched Tyson in the jaw, and he'd shoved her in a water trough. Jim thought it was hilarious, and any butterflies Gracie might have possessed flew away while she scrambled out of that trough, red-faced and furious and soaked to the skin.

They'd never returned, until now. She hid her shock with a sharp glance in Adam's direction. "It's Tuesday morning. A work day. Did you sleep in?"

He rolled his eyes as he got out of the truck and clapped a brown felt cowboy hat on his head. "I've got kids, remember? I was dropping them off at day camp when I got your message. Then I had to drive all the way home and collect Bodie and my gear." He walked closer and surveyed Rio. "That's a nice horse."

"Rio, this is Adam." Rio glanced at Adam from under her thick gray lashes and nickered.

"Does she always talk back?"

"Sometimes." Gracie ran her hand gently down Rio's nose. "We've spent so much time together, we understand each other, don't we, girl?" Rio took a step forward and rubbed her forehead on Gracie's shoulder, hard. "Or maybe I'm just your scratching post."

Adam smiled. "I'm pretty sure that's how all our horses see us." He motioned toward his trailer. "Let me get Bodie. It's a little uncanny how similar they look." He went to the trailer, calling to his horse as he reached for the latch. "Hey, Bo, time to get to work."

He opened the doors, lowered the ramp and entered the trailer. Gracie heard him say, "Let's go now," and a beautiful horse backed out. Bodie's coat was a darker version of Rio's. He was taller than Rio and a little leaner.

"They look like they could be cousins or something." Gracie waited while Adam took a better hold of Bodie's lead rope. "Can I say hi?"

"Sure. He's a good guy. He's put his wild ways behind him."

Gracie walked slowly to Bodie's head and held out her hand, fingers closed, knuckles up. The big horse snuffled her hand and then the sleeve of her sweatshirt, leaving behind a trail of green slime. "Ugh. Alfalfa for breakfast?"

Adam grinned. "Forgot to give him a napkin. Sorry."

Gracie laughed and wiped her sleeve on the leg of her jeans. "I'm sure it means that he likes me."

"Oh yeah. Any time a horse wipes his mouth on you, it's definitely a sign that you're something special."

"You mock me."

"Just a little." He was still smiling down at her, and Gracie suddenly realized how close they were standing. She took a quick step back. "Time to saddle up, Sergeant."

Adam walked his horse to the side of the trailer and dropped the lead rope to the ground. Bodie didn't budge, standing as securely as if he were tied.

"What a good boy," Gracie said. "He's well trained."

"Dean gets most of the credit. He doesn't miss a detail, on the job or when he's working with horses." Adam went to the back of his truck and returned with a brush. He ran it in quick strokes over Bodie's back. "What were you so worked up about on the phone? Why are we out here?"

"Someone called the tip line early this morning, saying they'd heard shots on their ranch. This is their property. It's big…one of those early land grants around here. The owners use the old ranch buildings as a vacation home. The rest of the acres are just their own private paradise."

Adam glanced at her over Bodie's back. "In other words, it's perfect for someone who wants to hunt without a license."

"Yup. I guess the owners haven't visited for a while. They arrived two days ago and they heard gunshots before dawn this morning."

"Do you have a map?"

"Of course." Gracie pulled it out of her pocket and motioned Adam a few yards away from the horses before she unfolded it. She pointed to the pencil mark she'd added earlier. "We're here. And all of this—" she drew a broad circle with her fingertip "—is their land."

Adam's eyes widened. "That is a lot of land."

"That's why I figured we'd need the horses." Gracie pointed out the star she'd drawn on the map. "The ranch house is way over here. And these lines represent these hills in front of us." She pointed to where tree-covered ridges rose sharply in the distance. "From what the man told me over the phone, my guess is that the shots came from up there."

Adam nodded once. "Give me a couple minutes to get ready."

"You brought water? Food? Extra clothes?"

He grinned, flashing a smile full of white teeth and disbelief. "I work with the mounted patrol. Search and rescue. Criminal pursuit. Trust me. I've got what I need."

"I didn't mean to offend your delicate sergeant feelings. Just wanted to make sure you were prepared for a day of hard riding."

"I'm definitely prepared. Are you?"

Now it was her turn to be offended. "This is what I do, most of the time."

"Well, I guess we're both gonna be just fine, then."

Gracie shook her head as Adam went to his truck to get his saddle. This thing between them was confusing. Competition. Humor.

Opposite ways of doing pretty much everything. But he'd already made her smile today.

Adam came back with a pad and his saddle and lifted them easily onto Bodie's back. He reached under the horse's belly for the cinch. After he buckled it, he looked up at her suddenly. "Hang on. Can I see that map again?"

"Sure." Gracie held it out and he came to take it, his brows drawing together as he studied. She bit her lip to keep from asking what he was thinking. They needed to get going. The longer they waited, the colder the poachers' trail. She tapped her fingers against her thigh, jiggled her boot heel against the ground.

"You just can't be still, can you?" Adam glanced at her with a bemused expression.

"Not my strong point," Gracie admitted. "Are you done with the map?"

"Let me show you something." He moved to her side and pointed to the dot. "We're here, right? And there is the ridge we're going to try to explore? And after that there's this valley, then another ridge. And look what's on the other side."

Gracie squinted at the map. "A road?"

"Not just any road. The county road we were on yesterday."

Suddenly all the topographical lines seemed to swim and re-form. Gracie jabbed her finger at a familiar-looking curve. "Oh, my gosh, then this must be where we took that fire road and first saw the black truck. And the bears."

"And I'd guess that the barn we visited was right about there." Adam pointed to a spot on the map almost directly on the other side of the hills from them. "Owned by our bearded buddy, who we now know is named Will Bateman. Except he hasn't taken out a hunting license in over a decade."

"But that doesn't mean Mr. Bateman doesn't poach," Gracie reminded him.

They'd figured out Will Bateman's identity in the office yesterday afternoon. But they hadn't been able to trace the black truck without a plate number.

"No offence to Will Bateman," Adam said, "but he didn't exactly look like he was in good enough shape to go climbing over ridges, hunting for bears."

"But his nephew might be," Gracie said. "The one who borrows Mr. Bateman's barn. I'm sure he's the owner of the black truck we saw. He could have climbed the hills behind his uncle's property and hunted from there. And the folks on this side of the ridge would hear the shots."

Adam glanced down at her with a quirk to his smile. "Please don't tell anyone that we're chasing poachers based on your hunch. I have a reputation to keep up in this area."

She laughed. "My hunch is already supported by evidence. But until we prove it, your secret is safe with me."

Adam attached his saddlebags. Soon they were ready to go, but when Gracie put a foot in the stirrup to swing up onto Rio's back, Adam's voice stopped her. "Hang on."

"What now?" It was starting to seem like she'd been parked by this lane, trying to get this ride started, for hours—even though it had only been about forty minutes.

"I'm not going into those woods with you until we talk about what happened by the barn yesterday."

"Are you kidding me?" Gracie gaped at him. "There are people out there possibly hunting bears or other animals and you want to have some big heart-to-heart right now?"

"I want to know why you froze up yesterday at the barn."

His words twisted in her stomach. "I told you it was nothing."

"I had to haul you out of there. So I know it wasn't nothing."

Gracie took a deep breath and exhaled slowly. Maybe she should just hop on Rio and leave Adam and Bodie behind. Take care of these poachers on her own. But no, that wouldn't be a great career move. "Okay, we can talk. But can we at least ride while we're talking?"

Adam glanced at the lane that narrowed into a trail and crossed a field before it disappeared into the forested hills. "As long as you talk fast." He put a foot in his stirrup and swung up onto Bodie. He tipped the brim of his hat down a bit and smiled at her. "You coming?"

Gracie let out an exasperated groan. "You are impossible." She got her foot back in the stirrup and was up on Rio in an instant. As always, the moment she was up on her beautiful mare's back, all the pieces of the world seemed to fall into place. If she had to open up to Adam, maybe this was the best way to do it.

"Let's see how the horses do together."
Adam walked Bodie up to Rio and the two
horses put their heads together and snuffled
a cordial greeting. "They seem fine." He
reined Bodie out to the dirt track and waved
an arm for Gracie to come up beside him.
When she and Rio were riding by his side,
he jumped right in. "So, what's really going
on with you?"

It was like trying to solve an impossible
math problem in her head. If she told him too
much—about the nightmares and the way she
jumped about ten feet in the air whenever she
got startled—Adam would push her to take a
leave from her job. Not because he was mean,
but because he clearly played by the rules. An
officer that couldn't be trusted to keep it together on the job was a danger to everyone.
Gracie knew that. But she also knew that she
was tough and that she could get through this
if she just kept pushing forward.

But if she downplayed her symptoms too
much, Adam wouldn't believe she was being
honest. After all, he'd seen her completely
lose her cool yesterday.

Gracie studied Rio's black-rimmed ears,
and the chaotic plumes of the mare's mane

that stuck up no matter how many hours Gracie spent brushing them down. When she started to speak her lips seemed almost numb, like her whole body wanted her to keep her secrets. "Did Dean tell you what happened to me?"

"He mentioned you were attacked on the job and spent time in a hospital."

"I was there for almost a month." She motioned to the back of her head. "The man I was trying to arrest grabbed my gun. He used the butt of it against me." She reached back and tugged on the short hair at the back of her head. "My hair used to be long, but it was shaved in the back when they put in all the staples."

There was a beat of silence before Adam spoke. "Sounds like the guy who hit you meant business." His words were clipped so short, Gracie glanced over at him. He was looking straight ahead but his knuckles on the reins were clamped tight and she could see the muscle of his jaw bulging. There was something about knowing he was upset for her that kept her talking.

"I don't know why he didn't just shoot me and get it over with. I was sure he would." Her words came out smaller and shakier than she meant. She took a deep breath and reminded herself to buck up. "It could have been much worse. Everyone said I was lucky. No brain damage."

He made a goofy face at her. "Are you sure?"

She couldn't help but laugh. "Hey! Not nice." How did he do it? Get her smiling when there should be tears? Making her relax when she was so tense her body felt like a sparked fuse.

"Seriously, I'm really sorry that happened to you. It's evil. Recovery must have been rough."

No…not kindness. Kindness was the worst. Kindness made tears flow. Gracie blinked hard. "It wasn't a picnic, but those are the risks we take, right?" She eased Rio into a jog. "The path is really smooth right here. Want to get these two warmed up?"

"You first," Adam said.

Gracie nudged Rio into a faster trot, and after a minute, into a comfortable, controlled lope. Relief and riding had her smiling. Their talk had been a lot easier than she'd anticipated.

It was a beautiful day. The weather had cooled a bit, and there was a breeze. Rio's lope was steady and strong, but they were approaching the trees now… Time to rein her in.

Gracie slowed her mare to a trot, then a walk, and heard Adam and Bodie behind them, doing the same. She turned in her saddle to look at Adam. "The trail looks really narrow up here."

He jogged Bodie up alongside her. "Then we'd better finish our conversation."

The relief faded. "I thought we talked already."

"Come on, Gracie, enough putting me off. I need to know why you got so shaky yesterday. I can't help if I don't understand it."

She admitted the truth. "I honestly don't know. That's the second time it's happened."

"Can you tell me what it feels like?"

Rio shuffled her hooves restlessly, uncertain where all of Gracie's tension came from. "It's okay, girl." She tried to relax a little before she spoke. "When I get startled, or too stressed, I get dizzy. My heart beats really fast. Not fast like it does when I run or something, but out-of-control fast. It's hard to breathe."

"Were you on the job when it happened before?"

"Yes," she admitted. "It was over a week ago. Up near Mendocino."

"Is that why I got assigned to work with you?"

Her face heated. She'd been so rude when she met him, and a few times since then. As if it were his fault that she needed him with her. "Yes."

"Why were you upset about us partnering together? If you need support, you should have it."

"Because I *shouldn't* need it!" It came out louder than Gracie had planned and she drew in a shaky breath to try to still the anger simmering in every vein. "I've done backcountry patrol on my own for years. I have never once needed a partner."

"You make *need* sound like a bad word," Adam said quietly, as if by staying calm he could get her calmed down, too. "There's nothing wrong with working together. It just means you're pooling your strengths to get more accomplished."

His words hit like only truth could. What strengths could she bring, when her mind and her emotions couldn't be trusted? She looked away, into the woods, wishing she were alone—just her and Rio riding beneath those tall, cool trees. "I guess I'm not used to relying on anyone."

"You're going to have to get used to it, then." Adam brought Bodie a little closer. "Look at me, Gracie."

She looked, wishing her eyes didn't feel so watery.

"I'll do whatever I can to help you track down these poachers. But you have to communicate with me. Tell me how you're doing. Even if it's not good news."

She nodded. He was right.

"We should have a signal, in case you start feeling bad and we're in a situation like yesterday, where we can't really talk."

"A signal?" That wasn't what she'd expected. "Like what?"

He shrugged. "I don't know…something pretty obvious. How about, if you start to get dizzy or anything, you put your hand on top of your head?"

The idea had her cracking a reluctant smile. "That's going to look ridiculous."

"Exactly. It's something you wouldn't normally do, so I'll know what's going on."

Would she even remember the signal? It

had been hard to think yesterday. Hard to do anything except try to breathe. But he could be reporting her to his boss and hers. Instead, he was offering to help. "I'll try it. Thanks."

"You're welcome. And one more thing. Let's both keep our cool and think before we act. I kind of lost it after seeing that baby bear all on its own. You got pretty impulsive up at that barn. If we're going to figure out this case, we have to be smart. Deal?"

"Yes." Relief lowered her shoulders a couple inches. The talk was over. She'd told him her problem, and he'd been nice about it, and they had a plan.

"And one last thing."

"You're torturing me!" Gracie glared at him.

He grinned. "You really don't like talking about stuff, do you?"

Gracie shook her head. "I can never get used to you Californians, and the way you want to share all your feelings. I was taught to put up and shut up. I guess that's ingrained in me now."

"Maybe that's part of your problem. You can't just ignore every negative feeling, and hope it magically goes away."

She didn't want him to be right. "It's so much simpler just to ignore things."

He fixed her with a sardonic smile. "And how's that been working for you, lately?"

There wasn't much she could say to that.

"There's something I learned once in a training I had to take for work," Adam said. "It might help you calm yourself down. I couldn't quite remember it yesterday, so I looked it up on the internet last night."

"You Googled for me?" Gracie rolled her eyes. "How sweet." It *was* sweet, and that was a problem. He'd been thinking of her in his free time. Wanting to help her. And now those butterflies were flying around again.

Adam grinned, calm and confident and definitely butterfly-free. He pulled a piece of paper out of his back pocket. "I even wrote it down." He unfolded the paper and glanced down at it. "If you start to feel anxious, remember the number three."

Three? It was so unexpected that she laughed. "Is it a magic number?"

He glowered at her. "This is serious. Three is a reminder. If you get anxious, take three deep breaths. Then look around you and name three things you see. Then touch three different things around you. Listen for three different sounds. Move three different parts of your body. It's supposed to connect you to your surroundings, so you don't get stuck in your head with whatever is misfiring there."

"Misfiring?" Gracie's indignation was quickly replaced by reality. "Actually, that's not a bad way to describe it."

"You'll try it?" Adam handed her the paper. He'd written it in neat block letters, using purple ink.

"Yes. Though I really hope I don't need it." She waved the paper at him. "I didn't take you for a purple pen kind of guy."

"It's my daughter's. She left it out on the table." He motioned toward the trees ahead of them. "Should we get going?"

"I thought you'd never ask." Gracie pressed her legs into Rio's sides and the mare started up right away, as if she, too, were impatient to get this journey started. As Rio followed the path into the trees, Gracie was conscious of Adam riding behind her. He was the first person she'd shared her situation with. Now it felt like he could see right into her. Hopefully he wouldn't notice the butterflies. They had no business hanging around and she planned to send them on their way as soon as possible.

Adam was a nice guy, and handsome, of course. But he wasn't *her* guy. He couldn't be. She wasn't looking for love, or even someone to date. Even if she was, she wouldn't get involved with a coworker, or someone so completely different from her.

The trail into the forest flattened out ahead, the path soft with pine needles. "Come on, Rio." Gracie clicked her tongue and pressed her legs into her mare's sides. Rio moved into a slow jog and then a trot. Adam and Bodie would catch up to them soon. But at least for a few seconds, Gracie needed to put a little space between herself and Sergeant Sears.

CHAPTER SEVEN

ADAM COLLAPSED INTO the chair closest to Dean's desk.

His boss looked up from the file he'd been studying. "Rough day?"

"Can we talk about that beer you promised me?" Adam ran scraped palms on the denim covering his aching thighs.

"I don't think you've earned your bonus yet. Isn't this just day two of your assignment?"

"Day two? Year two? I'm not really sure. You should have seen the terrain we were in today. We were hoping to cut cross-country to check out where those shots were coming from."

Dean set down his pen and folded his hands on his desk. "The ones reported on the tip line?"

"Yeah. Turns out that area is impassable on horseback. There's poison oak everywhere, and the hills are really steep." Adam held up his palms. "I climbed a hill on foot, to see if the ground was stable. It wasn't."

Dean laughed. "Took a fall, huh?"

"Went rolling right back down again. Gracie thought it was pretty funny, but she wasn't the one picking leaves out of her hair."

"Gracie has a sense of humor?" Dean shook his head. "I never would have suspected."

"Me neither." And Adam definitely hadn't anticipated how much her laughter would transform her. But when he'd picked himself up out of the dirt and limped back to the creek where she'd waited with Rio and Bodie, their eyes had met and they'd both started laughing, and there it was. Her whole demeanor had changed, lightened and sparkled, transforming her completely.

"So did you get any leads? See any evidence?"

"It turned out that the trail we were on was a dead end. It stops at a shallow creek, surrounded by steep, crumbling hillsides. That's where I fell."

"Thanks for taking one for the cause." Dean's gaze sharpened. "Did you get hurt?

You need to fill out a workman's comp form or anything?"

"Nah. I just came by here to look up a few things. I'm thinking we might need to approach the area where folks have heard shots from a different side of the hills."

Dean glanced at his watch. "It's late. Shouldn't you be home with your kids right now?"

"Josie wanted them to come to her house for dinner with her son, Brendan. They're having pizza. It gave me a chance to get Bodie settled, clean myself up a little and stop by here."

"To look at maps." Dean leaned back in his chair and folded his arms across his chest.

"Yes."

Dean's smile was laced with a shot of smugness. "Seems like you're getting kind of excited about this assignment. Maybe you're the right man for the job after all."

"Maybe." Maybe not. He hadn't felt professional today when he noticed how pretty Gracie was, laughing at him in the woods. That was wrong. She was a colleague. Someone he'd been assigned to protect. He had to stay neutral to do his job well. "What are you doing here so late?"

"Catching up. I stopped by home and fed the horses, but I still have a lot to do."

Adam wondered how many late nights Dean pulled here at the station. "You're making me happy, once again, that I didn't follow in your footsteps and go after a promotion."

Dean shrugged. "It's not so bad. Besides, what else would I be doing?"

"Oh, I don't know...going on a date, maybe."

Dean grinned. "With who? This town is pretty small. I'm pretty sure if some great love was out there, I'd have found it by now."

"Weren't you dating Summer Dornan not too long ago?"

"Nah." Dean ran a hand through his short, dark brown hair. It was starting to gray at the temples. "We got to know each other a little better last year, when her son did a few ride-alongs with me for a school project. We're just friends. Honestly, sometimes I get the impression Summer's still sweet on Wyatt."

"My *brother*, Wyatt?" Adam shook his head. "Nah, I'm pretty sure that flame burnt out back when Summer got pregnant in high school."

"Well, what do I know?" Dean said. "Women are a mystery that I can't unravel."

"Aw, come on. You have a sister. Can't you ask her for advice?"

"Jade? She's not exactly a girly girl." Dean grinned. "I kind of hope this baby girl of hers is born loving unicorns, sparkles and all things pink. I'm not sure Jade could cope, but I'd like to see her try."

Adam grinned. Jade was a firefighter, and tougher than most of the men she worked with. "So basically, you're just giving up? You're a confirmed bachelor?" Even though Adam was technically a bachelor now, too, the idea that it might be a permanent state didn't sit well in his mind. He hadn't given much thought to dating. But to just throw in the towel on ever finding someone else? It was a depressing thought.

"If it happens, it happens," Dean said. "For now, I've got a whole lot to keep me busy. Do you need any help finding those records?"

"I think I've got it." Adam pushed himself out of his chair, trying to ignore the twinge in his back where he'd rolled over a tree root on that hillside. He wanted to offer something to Dean. Encouragement. Hope. It was bleak to imagine his boss still sitting behind this battered desk thirty years from now, with no family and no life outside of the endless stream of crises that came through the squeaky glass doors of this old building. "Don't give up on finding someone," Adam said. "You never know what's coming down the road."

Dean looked a little surprised. "Thanks for the tip," he said. "Same to you."

Adam's boots echoed in the empty hall as he made his way to his office. He plunked down in his chair, turned on his laptop and put his boots up on his desk while he waited for the computer to warm up. His office seemed smaller than he remembered, the walls a little too close. Luckily, he'd probably be outside tomorrow, scrambling through the woods with Gracie. It might be dangerous, or chaotic, or both, but there'd be fresh air and sunshine, and it definitely wouldn't be boring.

CHAPTER EIGHT

"I'M SO HAPPY you made it back for the barbecue," Maya said.

Gracie looked around at all the people clustered around Maya and Caleb's barn and wasn't sure she shared the sentiment. She'd never been great at small talk, but that would be her fate here, today. She barely knew anyone at this party. At least she could hide behind this table with Maya for a while, getting the cold drinks organized.

"Of course I made it. You said it's a big annual event." Maya had told her that they threw this party every year to celebrate the way the community had come together to rebuild the Bar D ranch a couple summers ago. Caleb had even hired a band. There were tables loaded with food, and from the plume of smoke rising from out by the lane, Caleb was barbecuing enough meat to feed Sonoma County.

"How did it go up north?"

Gracie sighed in frustration and smacked the bag of ice she was trying to break up just a little harder. "I tried to follow up on that tip we got."

"The dead bear?"

Gracie nodded. "Two different people said they saw it by the side of a hiking trail, in the hills behind Fort Bragg. Rio and I spent a couple of days riding around out there, but I couldn't find a trace of it."

"It's possible that a mountain lion got ahold of it," Maya said. "They'd drag it away and bury it so no other animal could have it."

"That's a definite possibility. I just wish I could find out whether it was killed by poachers. While I was gone, there was no poaching activity down here. No shots fired. No trespassing calls. It makes me think that I might be chasing the same poachers in both counties."

"That would be convenient, right?" Maya smiled. "Two problems solved with one arrest."

"As long as I can figure out where they are for long enough to catch them, it would be great." Gracie glanced up and noticed

Adam talking to a couple of women about her age, who were sitting at a table near the stage. One of the women said something that made Adam laugh. Gracie quickly returned to pouring drinks. It wasn't her business who he spoke to at a party.

In fact, the more distance between them, the better. Gracie had been grateful to get the tip from up north on Wednesday morning. It was the perfect excuse to get out of Shelter Creek for a few days. She needed to be away from Adam's smile and the way she'd felt so close to him after their talk on Tuesday. She wanted to forget her terror when he'd first fallen down that hill. He was her temporary partner. So why did he already feel like a lot more than that?

A blonde woman arrived at their table with a big smile and a jug of lemonade. "Hey, ladies, I brought this from home. I think it's still cold."

"Trisha!" Maya put an arm around the woman's shoulders. "Just set it on the table. This is my friend Gracie, who's staying with me."

"Nice to meet you." Trisha set down the lemonade and gave Gracie a shy wave.

"I'm enjoying having Gracie here," Maya said. "She spoils me with really good food."

Trisha laughed. "That's exactly what you need when you're growing a baby." She smiled at Gracie. "I've had two of them, so I consider myself the resident expert."

"Trisha works at the wildlife center with me," Maya explained. "She's our technician, in charge of the animals' care. But more importantly, her husband, Liam, is from Texas. You two should have a lot to talk about."

"You're from Texas, too?" Trisha clapped her hands together. "You have to meet Liam. He'll be so happy to have another Texan in our midst."

"I'll make sure to find you two later on."

"That would be great. I'd better go look for him now. He's got both kids in his care. I'll see you in a bit, Gracie." Trisha waved and walked away.

Maya handed Gracie a stack of plastic cups. "Would you mind filling these with Trisha's lemonade?"

"Yes. I'm happy to help out." Gracie started setting the cups out in neat rows. "Please put me to work. All day."

"You can't work all day. You need to meet everyone."

Gracie gave her friend a baleful glance. "You know that chatting with strangers is not exactly one of my strengths."

"Oh, come on." Maya patted Gracie on the shoulder. "Don't sell yourself short. You're one of my favorite people on this planet. I want you to meet my other favorite people, and most of them are here today. Let me take you around and introduce you to everyone."

"How about we do that later," Gracie suggested. "Let me finish getting the drinks ready while you go greet your guests." Socializing with a bunch of people she didn't know made her itchy and fidgety and acutely aware of her lack of social graces.

"That's a really nice offer. Thank you." Maya pointed to a group of women sitting in folding chairs beneath the big oak that grew to one side of the barn. "But once you're done pouring drinks, you should go say hello to my grandmother and meet her friends. She'll be so excited to introduce you to them."

Gracie had met Maya's grandmother, Lillian, last weekend and really liked her. "I'll do that."

Maya hurried off to greet everyone and Gracie finished pouring the lemonade, smiling at a few kids who came by to take a glass. When she was finished, she looked over at Lillian and her friends, talking and laughing so animatedly together. In fact, everyone, all around the barn, was talking and laughing with friends. They all looked so comfortable with one another. Suddenly Gracie felt even more out of place. This happened to her at parties. One moment she was okay, the next she was standing around as awkward and useless as a bean pole after harvest.

That was something her mom used to say and the memory of it had Gracie missing her more acutely than usual. She hated that she couldn't hear her mom's funny expressions anymore. Or see her smile. Or get annoyed when her mom told her to quit running around like a ten-ton tornado, whatever that was.

Ma was always telling her to slow down, but Gracie had never had a low gear. Sometimes it stung to know that if she had just downshifted a little, she might have more memories of her mom. Maybe they would have cooked together, baked cookies or taken walks. But Gracie had always been charging after her brothers, trying to outrun them, out-ride them and outsmart them. Well, that last one hadn't been too hard.

Gracie drifted aimlessly away from the barbecue and wandered around the side of the round pen to the back of the barn. Here, the sounds of the party were blissfully muf-fled by the big building.

There were open fields behind the barn and Gracie spotted an old, wooden cattle chute out in the grass. She walked toward it. The wood had turned silvery and the whole chute sagged a little as it rotted away in the ele-ments.

Suddenly a little girl wearing a pink check-ered Western shirt, her miniature jeans tucked into miniature cowboy boots, came running around the side of the chute. She trotted up the ramp until she was standing on the platform at the top. It didn't look very safe. Gracie broke into a jog, but she was still too far away to stop the girl from climbing onto the railing. There was a splintering sound, and the girl and the railing disappeared into the tall grass.

Frantically Gracie ran faster, glancing around for help. Where were the kid's parents? But no one was back here so she sprinted for the chute, careening around the side of it to find the little girl on the ground, staring in dismay at a rip in the knee of her jeans, tears sliding down her face. Gracie knelt beside her. "Are you okay?"

The little girl nodded, her wavy brown hair bobbing in a cloud around her face.

Thank goodness no major first aid was required. But now what? Gracie studied the girl, who seemed to be barely keeping herself together. What did one say to a child this small?

"I'm Gracie. I'm a friend of Maya's. And Caleb's, too, I guess."

The girl nodded, still looking down at her knee.

"Does your knee hurt?"

She nodded again. "A little. And I ruined my new jeans."

Ah. Gracie tried to think of a way to console her. "I spend a lot of time outdoors, so my jeans get ripped a lot. I figure it's a sign that I've been having a lot of fun."

That seemed to get the girl's attention. She looked at Gracie and though there were still tears in her eyes, they weren't rolling down her face anymore. That was progress. Gracie tried again. "It's also a sign that you've been having adventures. You climbed up on that big old cattle chute just now. That was an adventure, right?"

The girl's lips pressed together in a hint of a smirk. "I guess so."

Gracie sat down in the grass next to her. "Have you ever taken a trip before, and your family let you bring back a special toy or magnet or something from the place you visited?"

She looked thoughtful. "One time my mom and dad took us to Lake Tahoe, and I got a wooden bear key chain."

"Okay, so things like your bear are called souvenirs." Gracie pointed to the rip. "That is your souvenir from the time you visited the Bar D ranch and climbed the old cattle chute." She didn't know much about kids, but Gracie was pretty sure that the little girl was looking at her ripped jeans with a new level of respect.

But then she glanced up at the chute apprehensively. "But I *broke* it."

"I don't think anyone will mind. It's old and rotting and falling apart anyway." It seemed like the right thing to add a lesson in here. "If you see something where the wood looks all gray and broken up like that, it might not be safe to climb on. When wood gets really old, it can break apart just like that railing did."

Gracie received a solemn nod as an answer. Then the girl's curly head dipped as she turned her hands over to look at her palms. There was a lot of blood. "Uh-oh."

Gracie wanted to kick herself. She should have asked to see her hands right away. The poor thing was probably so worried about her jeans that she didn't notice the pain at first. "Um, okay, we're going to have to get those hands cleaned up." She stood, trying to stay brisk and unemotional so the girl didn't start crying. Because if she melted down, Gracie had no idea how to handle it. "What is your name?"

"Penny." She was still studying her hands, a stunned expression on her face.

Did she have a puncture wound? Maybe a rusty nail went into her hand. "Penny, we really should get your hands clean right away. It's never good to let any dirt get into your cut and I don't know about you, but I see a whole lot of dirt around here."

Her words seemed to break through Penny's shock because the little girl got to her feet and Gracie noticed that again, while tears streamed down her face, she didn't cry out loud. It was as if she were trying to keep everything inside and private.

She'd been the same way. Not ever wanting to show her brothers that she was hurt or tired or scared. "Come on, then, let's go get you cleaned up."

They started back toward the barbecue, walking slowly, Penny holding her hands in front of her as if she didn't want to get any blood on her nice pink shirt. As they got closer to the crowd, Adam broke away and ran toward them.

"What happened, Penny?" Adam skidded to a stop in front of the girl and saw her palms. "Oh no, did you fall?"

Penny nodded. "And Gracie found me. And she helped me."

Adam put a gentle hand on Gracie's, and wrapped strong fingers around hers. "Thank you so much."

"Of course." His hand was warm and comforting. Thinking about her mom and then seeing Penny fall had shaken her up a little more than she'd realized.

"It's nice to see you. It was kind of strange, finishing out the week without my partner."

"It's nice to see you, too," she managed. It

was way too nice. All of her hopes that a few days away would banish the attraction she felt for him were gone in an instant. She took a step back and extricated her hand from his. "Glad to see you survived without me."

"It was tough." His smile was hard to read when the expression in his eyes was so serious. Was he teasing her? "Sorry you didn't have any luck up by Fort Bragg."

She shrugged. "It's how it goes, sometimes. Did you like being back on your normal beat for a few days?"

He nodded. "It was fine. Not quite as exciting, but it did give me a few days for my bruises to heal." He grinned. "And here's where you make a comment about my grace and dignity as I rolled down that hill on Tuesday."

"I would never tease you about an injury incurred in the line of duty." Gracie tried to hold back the smile building up, but ultimately failed. "I know I gave you a hard time about it, but I'm truly glad you're okay."

His wide smile reached his eyes and held her gaze to his. "Good to know that you care."

"Gracie is going to help me wash my hands and get the blood off," Penny announced.

Gracie laughed, grateful that Penny broke

whatever spell had her gazing way too long into her partner's eyes.

Adam shot Gracie an alarmed look. "I can do that, honey. Gracie probably wants to get back to the party."

For once, Gracie agreed with him. Now that the initial emergency was over, she was out of her element here. She had no idea what to say to such a small human. She had no idea what to say to Adam. She barely knew him. Why did she want to put her arms around his neck and tell him she'd missed him?

"I want Gracie."

There was no mistaking the stubborn note in Penny's voice.

"Penny, let me clean you up." Adam put a hand on her shoulder and attempted to steer her gently toward the party.

Penny dug in her heels. She fixed Gracie with a look that was one part mule and one part cherub. "Please, Gracie? Will you help my daddy clean me up? It will be like an adventure."

Using her own words against her. *Good move, savvy Penny.* "Well, if it's an adventure, then I'm in. Let's walk up to the main house and get your hands all better."

"An adventure?" Adam looked mystified for a moment, then shrugged. "Whatever you two want to call it is fine with me, as long as we can get this taken care of."

They cut around the side of the party so as not to draw attention to their little drama, and walked up the lane to Maya and Caleb's house. "Is this where you live?" Penny followed Gracie down the hall to the bathroom. "It's nice."

"This is Maya and Caleb's house," Adam said. "You know that."

"But I'm staying here with them," Gracie said. "For a little while at least."

"And then where will you go?"

"Um... I'm not sure. I travel a lot for my job." Gracie glanced at Adam, noting the serious expression in his eyes. Was she saying the wrong thing to Penny?

They'd reached the bathroom and Gracie led the way inside, turning on the faucet at the sink to let the water warm up. When she turned around, she realized just how small the bathroom was. With three of them inside, there wasn't much room to move. "Maybe I should go out, so you and your daddy can wash your hands."

"Okay."

Gracie could hear the reluctance in Penny's voice. Maybe she missed her mother and felt comforted having a woman around when she was hurt. "I'll just wait outside." She got past Penny easily enough, but Adam was a different story. The only way to get around him was to squeeze herself between him and the wall, which would be way too close for comfort.

He must have realized her dilemma because his eyes widened, and his smile was a tad self-conscious. "Here, let me get out of your way." He backed out of the bathroom and waited in the hall until she slipped by him. "Why don't you go on back to the party. I can take care of Penny from here."

Gracie hesitated, torn. She didn't want to let Penny down after she'd told her she'd accompany her on this "adventure." On the other hand, Adam was her father. If he wanted her gone, she should go. She nodded. "Bye, Penny, I'll see you later," she called.

"Bye, Gracie."

"And, Gracie?" Adam's voice was oddly rough. "Thank you again for taking care of Penny. I lost track of her at the party and

I shouldn't have. I'm grateful that you were there to help her when she fell."

"Anyone would have done it."

His smile curved in a gentle way Gracie hadn't seen before. "I don't know that anyone would have done it with the same kindness and creativity as you."

His compliment threw her off balance. "I'm just glad she's okay." She gave an awkward wave and hurried back out of the house.

Halfway back to the barbecue, Gracie realized that she was done. Worn out. Big social gatherings with a whole bunch of strangers just weren't for her. Instead of going back to the party, she hopped in her SUV and headed down the driveway. It was a perfect afternoon for a coffee in town and a quiet drive through the countryside. She just hoped that Penny was going to be okay. And that when Adam saw that hole in his daughter's new jeans, he'd have enough imagination to recognize a souvenir when he saw one.

CHAPTER NINE

"EXPLAIN TO ME how you got your brother to lend you his Jeep for this?" Gracie hung on to the handle above the door as Adam navigated a trench and the off-road vehicle rocked back and forth.

"You don't want to know." Adam downshifted as they lumbered forward and started climbing the ridge. The fire road was steep and had deteriorated into more of a rain-washed gully. "It involved me spending time with a whole lot of manure early this morning."

His words made her smile but from his grim expression she could see that he wasn't joking. "Well, I appreciate you making a sacrifice for the cause."

"It wasn't an ideal way to start my Wednesday. Plus, I'm beginning to wonder if this is a cause or just a wild-goose chase."

Gracie nodded. "Welcome to the joys of

wildlife protection. You never really know, until you know."

"That sentence doesn't even make sense."

"Sure it does." Gracie smiled. He was just so…so linear. "It's true that our progress has been a little slower than we wanted." It had taken them two days to track down the owner of this land and convince him to let them drive through to try to access the ridge top where they suspected the poachers had been active. "But at least we're not hiking through all that poison oak or trying to climb crumbling hillsides. You, of all people, should be glad of that."

"You're never going to let that one go, are you?" Adam glanced at her with a faint smile before slowing to steer them around a pothole so big that it was more like a crater.

"I will cherish the image of you rolling down that hill for a long time."

"Glad you'll remember me so fondly when this is all over."

His words tugged at unfamiliar heartstrings. She really liked being with him. Sure, they'd spent the last two days stuck in the office, searching the internet, tracking down county records and making phone calls. But with Adam making her smile and bringing her treats and working so hard by her side, she'd actually enjoyed it.

And fortunately, no animals had turned up dead while they did their research. Though there had been a couple reports of shots fired out in these hills last night. It was a good thing they were driving out here today.

"We made it." Adam accelerated over a rise in the road and there they were, at the top of the ridge. "Looks like quite a view from up here."

"Let's stop and check it out." Gracie was out of the Jeep the moment Adam set the brake. Her stomach could use a break from the bouncy, jolting Jeep. "This is incredible."

They had to be at one of the highest points in this whole section of the Coast Range. When Gracie looked west toward the ocean, she could see layer upon layer of tree-covered ridges. It was sometime after lunch and the sky was a hot, hazy blue. She spun around, arms outstretched, trying to take it all in. "If I owned this land, I'd build a tiny cabin here. Or a sleeping platform. Something where I could lie down and watch the stars and wake up to the sunrise over all these hills."

Adam watched her with a wary smile, like

he couldn't figure out if he should run far away or join in her reverie. "It's pretty nice," he finally said.

Nice. Maybe nature just wasn't his thing. But it was hers. Out in wild places like this, Gracie felt energized and alive.

"I think we'd better keep going. I have to get back to town in time to pick up my kids at four o'clock."

She might have a bit of a crush on him, but that was all the more reason to note how different they were. She was on cloud nine enjoying this beautiful spot, while Adam kept his eyes on his watch.

Gracie followed him back to the Jeep. Adam started the engine. The dry, dusty fire road took them along the ridge top. Occasionally, through the hodgepodge of oak, madrone and toyon trees that grew alongside the road, Gracie could see out over more wooded ridges and grassy hills.

"I think this road follows the side of the ridge and crosses that saddle over there." Adam pointed to where the road dipped just a little in the distance then rose again to connect to another ridge. "And surprise, surprise, it's going to put us right up on above Will Bateman's barn."

"I just wish we could figure out who his nephew is," Gracie said. "If we could get his name, we could probably figure out if he's the owner of that black truck."

"I've got all the local agencies watching out for it," Adam said. "If he's still driving around without license plates, they'll have a perfectly good reason to pull him over and get his information."

"I hope they find him soon." Gracie looked out the window at the gnarled trees and thick shrubs. They were a testament to nature's survival skills—drought tolerant, fire adapted, tough from trunk to twig.

The Jeep crossed the sunbaked saddle, went over a rise and then dipped into a more sheltered section of the ridge. The chapparal plants gave way to fir trees here, that took advantage of the extra shade.

"Wait." Gracie's stomach lurched at the sight of a deer carcass tossed against a tree trunk, just downhill from the road. "Adam, stop the car."

He slowed the Jeep to a halt. "What's wrong?"

"Someone took a deer back there." Gracie grabbed her camera from the floor of the Jeep and yanked it out of the case. She shoved open the door and jogged back a few yards. Behind her she heard the motor go silent, then Adam's heavy footsteps crunched the earth behind her. "There it is." She stopped and pointed, distaste curdling in her stomach.

"Those jerks." She could hear thick disgust in Adam's voice, mirroring her own. "They left the entire body."

"Trophy hunting. Out of season." Gracie took a photo. "I don't see any footprints. There are too many fir needles here."

"Let me check." Adam studied the dusty road. "You've got to be kidding." He knelt down by the wheel of the Jeep. "A cigarette butt."

"Someone was smoking up *here*?" Gracie shook her head in disbelief. "There won't be any wildlife for them to poach if they burn down the forest. Will you collect it as evidence?"

"Of course."

"And will you try to figure out exactly where we are on the map as well?"

"Yup." Adam went to the Jeep and Gracie approached the carcass to get some close-up photos of the poor, discarded buck. Her heart raged at the loss, at the lawbreaking, at the waste.

But if there was one positive aspect to this sad situation, it was that they now had a concrete clue. This was a message that they were on the right path. Even if they never found any more evidence than this, they could trace the buck's DNA to whatever taxidermist's shop was processing the head. Then they could find whoever did this and bust them for hunting off-season. It wouldn't be justice, in her opinion, but it was something.

Gracie returned to the Jeep and opened the back door. She pulled out the small cooler chest she'd filled with ice packs, as well as the plastic case that held her collecting kit.

Adam came around the side of the Jeep to meet her, map in hand. "I've got the coordinates and marked the map. Does this look right to you?"

He'd drawn the letter B, for buck, on the map. Gracie studied the fine lines representing the topography, then looked at the landscape around them. "I think you've got it right. And we *are* really close to Bateman's property." She pointed to the wide-set lines signifying the long narrow valley that was the county road.

"Yup. I really think we're onto something here." He glanced at the buck again. "I sure hope we are. This is just so wrong." Then he pointed to her cooler. "What's in there?"

"A DNA sample kit."

He grimaced. "I figured that was your lunch, when you loaded it in."

She couldn't help but smile, though it was bleak humor. "Nope, nothing tasty in here." She tilted her head toward the dead deer. "You want to join me? I could use some help."

"I have a feeling I'm not going to like this aspect of your job."

"It's definitely not the scenic part." Gracie took the sterile container out and resealed the zip lock bag. "Can you hold this bag for me?" He took it and they walked back to the carcass. Gracie pulled a scalpel out of her kit and sliced through the hide over the animal's shoulder muscle. "This kill is so fresh it barely smells yet. I bet these were the shots that were called in this morning."

"Probably." Adam's voice sounded strained. Gracie looked over at him. He was kneeling on the far side of the buck, looking a little green around the gills. "Are you okay?"

He swallowed hard and nodded. "There's a reason I chose law enforcement over ranching."

Gracie couldn't resist teasing him a little. "Just be glad there is muscle tissue intact. Otherwise, I'd have to take samples from the organs."

Adam made a small gagging noise and Gracie realized she'd better take pity on him. She held out her free hand. "Here, I'll take that bag. You wait at the truck."

"No, I'm fine. I can handle it. Just don't say *organs* again."

"I won't. I promise." She focused on her work, slicing out a couple samples of the muscle tissue and depositing them carefully in the sterile container. When she finished she glanced at Adam. He looked less mottled, but he was still pale. "How are you doing?"

"Better. But I think I'm done here, unless you need me."

Gracie put the lid on the container and zipped it into the plastic bag. "Would you mind putting that in the cooler chest?" She handed the bag to Adam, noting that he accepted it between just two fingers.

She needed to give the poor guy an easy way out. "I can retrieve the bullets on my own. Why don't you do a more thorough search on the road?"

"Will do."

Gracie didn't miss the note of relief in his voice. "I'll be finished in a few minutes," she told him.

Adam nodded and headed back up the slope toward the Jeep. Gracie pulled in a deep breath, steadied her hand and her stomach, and got to work. Only when she was completely finished, with her kit and samples put away in the back of the Jeep, did she let herself grieve. She didn't know why some animal deaths affected her more than others. This buck's death felt more unfair than most.

She was leaning against the front grill, picking at an old sticker on her water bottle, when Adam came into sight around the bend in the road. "Are you all done?"

Gracie nodded, casting about for something to say. She couldn't come up with anything.

"Are you okay?" Adam joined her at the front of the Jeep. "You look upset."

Gracie took a deep breath and exhaled, trying to steady herself. "I should be used to this by now. And most of the time I can handle it. But once in a while, finding an animal really gets to me. This poor buck. He's been working so hard to survive up here in pretty inhospitable terrain. Most of the creeks dry up in the summer. There are mountain lions, wildfires and about ten thousand ways he could break a leg on these steep ridges. But despite all that he was thriving, from what I could tell. And then these stupid people..." Gracie put a hand over her eyes to mask her tears.

"Hey." Adam scooted closer and draped an arm carefully around her shoulders. "I get it. Our jobs can be really upsetting. It's okay to cry. It's better for you than holding it in."

"I'm not sure if I want to cry or punch something, I'm so angry." She scrubbed at her face with her wrist. "And I shouldn't be crying all over you."

He gestured to the hot, dusty fire road in front of them. "Where else are you going to do it?"

That made her laugh, though it sounded more like a sniffle. Gracie gave in to the comfort he offered, letting her head rest against his shoulder. She closed her eyes, savoring this unexpected moment, tucked against him. If she could do this every day, she'd probably be a much more relaxed person.

"How are you doing down there?"

She lifted her head. How long had she been leaning on him? She didn't think she could doze off on her feet, but it felt like she'd drifted off to a very peaceful place. "I'm sorry if I overstayed my shoulder welcome."

"Nah. You're good. I'm just checking on you."

His deep voice, so close to her ear, sent shivers over her skin. She tilted her head up to see his face, wanting to thank him for supporting her. He was looking down at her, a serious expression in his dark brown eyes. A faint growth of stubble ran along his jaw. Instinctively she brought her fingers up to trace it.

Adam closed his eyes and tilted his head toward her touch, reminding her of a big cat. "Gracie," he whispered when he opened his eyes. "I'm supposed to keep you safe."

"I feel safe." Safe and blissfully content, as if in his arms, she'd found the exact spot she was meant to be. The idea jolted her out of her reverie. She slipped out from under his arm. "Thanks, Adam. I feel a lot better now."

"Good." Adam walked a few steps away, as if he had to bring himself back down to earth, too. "We should probably get going. I think we should drive a little farther along this road. Maybe we can find a trail that leads down the hill toward Will Bateman's land."

"Let's give it a try. But I know you also need to get back in time to get your kids. We can always beg your brother for his Jeep again if we need to come up here another time. I'll even clean the manure next time." She was babbling, trying to drown out the unexpected intimacy in a flood of words. "Let's go."

She climbed into the Jeep and buckled her seat belt, opened her window, sipped her water. Kept herself too busy to say anything while Adam got in and started the engine. They bumped and rattled farther along the ridge lost in their own thoughts, their easy banter silenced by whatever had happened back there.

It was just an odd moment, Gracie decided. A random flare of chemistry. Her butterflies taking a lap around her heart. Or it could have been their shared sorrow and anger about the buck. Or maybe just plain old loneliness.

Whatever it was, it was unprofessional, and it shouldn't happen again.

ADAM GLANCED AT his watch as they sat at one of the few stoplights in Shelter Creek. He was barely going to get to day camp in time to pick up Jack and Penny. It had taken a while, and some crashing around in the bushes, but he and Gracie had eventually found a narrow path that snaked down the steep ridge. They couldn't know for sure unless they hiked it, but it seemed pretty likely that the path would end up at Will Bateman's barn.

It wasn't proof of poaching, but it did mean that it would be pretty easy for someone to start from that barn, hike up to the ridge, walk the fire road and shoot that buck.

The light still hadn't changed. Adam glanced at his watch again. "Would you mind if we picked up my kids before I take you to your car? Their day camp ends in three minutes."

"I don't mind at all. You can't be late."

"Thank you, by the way."

She gave him a puzzled look. "For what?"

"For helping Penny at the party last week-end."

"You already thanked me."

"Yeah, but you should know what a difference you made. She keeps talking about how you ran up and helped her. And that you told her that getting scraped up isn't anything to be ashamed of. It just means that you were having an adventure."

"I'm happy that she's feeling better."

"She's going to be really excited to see you today. I hope you don't mind a seven-year-old's undying affection."

Gracie laughed and Adam had to remind himself that he was supposed to be watching the road, not her pretty smile. "I've never had that before, but I suppose I can learn to deal with it."

"And she's very proud of the new hole in her pants. She says it's her souvenir." He smiled at the memory of Penny's pride when she pointed it out to him. "I told her it was a nice souvenir, but in the future we'll go to the gift shop if she needs one."

That got another smile out of her. And he couldn't help it, he wanted to see Gracie smile again and again. They'd both been pretty quiet after what had happened, or almost happened, up on the ridge. He'd wanted to give her comfort. Then he'd wanted to kiss her.

The feeling had gotten so strong, it seemed to fill up the air between them. He was pretty sure she'd felt it, too.

Adam pulled his truck up to the curb in front of the community center. Several kids were milling around on the sidewalk. He could see Jack messing around on some kid's skateboard in the parking lot, with no helmet of course. He sighed. They'd have to talk about that tonight. Again. *No helmet, no wheels* was Adam's motto. He thought it had a nice ring to it, *and* it could save his kids from brain damage as well.

But Jack wanted so badly to look cool. And apparently helmets weren't cool. Maybe after Gracie left, Adam would organize some school presentations and community events to try to change that dynamic around here.

"Why is Penny all the way over there?" Gracie pointed to where his daughter sat huddled on a bench, far away from the other kids. "I don't know much about kids, but she doesn't look happy."

"I'll go see." Adam parked the car as fast as he could.

"Can I come with you? I mean, unless I'd

be intruding? I don't want to sit here doing nothing if she's feeling sad."

He studied her for a second, sensing her warmth and honest emotion. "You're a good person, Gracie. I hope you know that." He got out of the car quickly, before he said anything more. The back of his neck felt hot and he couldn't bring himself to even look at her as they walked up the sidewalk toward Penny. Because now he knew that it wasn't just a random spark between them up on the ridge today. He really liked Gracie. Liked her way too much. She was the whole package—smart, motivated, strong, tough, kind, generous and beautiful.

It wasn't welcome news. He couldn't get involved with her. They had to work together. And she'd be moving on soon anyway.

Adam shoved the thought aside so he could focus on his daughter, forlorn on the bench with a yellow piece of paper clutched in her hand. "Hi, honey, are you sad? What's going on?"

Penny thrust the paper at him and crossed her arms, leaning back against the bench and looking away from them. A lump rose in Adam's throat when he read the words on the flyer. *A Performance for Moms and Dads*.

He'd like to have a word with whoever wrote this flyer. As a sergeant, he got to know all kinds of families in the area. A whole lot of kids were from single-parent homes, or were living with grandparents or another relative.

But for now, he just had to help poor Penny, who looked like she had about a gallon of tears pent up behind her eyes. "Are you worried about the performance?"

His daughter nodded. "It's this Friday. We're singing some songs. But you'll be working and Mommy's never here. It says it's for families, and I don't have one."

"Ouch." Adam looked down at the pavement for a moment to compose himself.

Gracie had put her fingertips to her lips and was looking from him to his daughter with such compassion that he thought she might cry right along with Penny. He'd never have guessed that under her prickly exterior she had so much empathy.

Adam knelt in front of his little girl and put a hand on her knee. "Penny, you have a family, and we love you very much. I'll get off work early to see your performance. And we can ask Aunt Sara to come, and maybe even Uncle Wyatt."

"He won't come," Penny said. "He never goes to kid stuff."

Adam couldn't really argue with that. "Sara and I will be there. Don't worry. And I will let your mother know about the performance as well."

"She definitely won't come."

Adam had heard Jack speak about Tanya in that tone many times, but it was the first time he'd heard Penny sound so bleak. Worry threaded through his veins. He hated that although he had no control over what Tanya did, or didn't do, he still had to live with the aftermath of her indifference, every single day.

Penny was quiet for a moment, then she looked at Gracie, then back at him. "Daddy, can Gracie come? She's my friend."

Adam tried to give Gracie an out. "Gracie is a very busy person. It might be hard for her to take time off work." The last thing he wanted was for his work partner to feel pressured to hang out with his child.

"Is that true, Gracie? Are you busy? We're singing two songs and there will be an art show, too. You could see my painting of my Pony of the Americas, Comet."

Gracie blinked a couple times and sent a questioning glance toward Adam. "I am happy to come and watch, as long as I'm not crashing a family event."

"My teacher read a book about families today," Penny said. "It was about how there are all kinds of families. It said sometimes families aren't always moms and dads and relatives. Family can be other people, too."

This was a little awkward, but Adam had to try hard to hide his smile. He had no doubt that Penny was going to law school someday. And that she'd do really well there. "You are more than welcome to join us, Gracie. But only if you have the time."

Gracie sat down next to Penny on the bench. "You're sure you'd like me to be there?"

"Yes!" Penny's smile was wide with delight and showcased her two missing teeth.

Adam loved Penny's smile, but her reaction to Gracie worried him. Was this all because she missed her mom so much? He didn't mind that Penny wanted to spend time with Gracie, but there was a hint of desperation in his little girl's actions.

"Then I'll be there." Gracie held up her hand. "Give me a high five?"

Penny high-fived her and Gracie stood up. "I'm going to walk back to the station, Adam. It's only a few blocks and I'd like to stretch my legs. Will you and Penny drop off my stuff there on your way home?"

"Sure."

She looked from him to his daughter, thoughtfully. "Thank you for inviting me to your performance. I'll see you soon, Penny."

"On Friday."

"Yes, on Friday."

Adam watched as Gracie walked off down the sidewalk. He wondered how she really felt about Penny's affection. She was so gracious about it. Another one of the things he admired about her. But he had to stop listing those things, or his admiration would grow even more, and then he'd be in real trouble.

Enough about Gracie, or his admiration, or desperation, or whatever was going on with him today. He had to get the kids home, bathed and fed, and figure out how to help Penny feel more secure.

"Come on, Pen, let's go round up your brother before he breaks a bone on that skateboard."

THAT EVENING WHEN Penny was tucked into bed, Adam sat down next to her. "Sweetie, I think you might miss your mom a lot. You can tell me about that, you know. Anytime you want to talk about anything, I am here for it."

Penny looked up at him from her pillow with a quivering lip. "She never comes to see us."

Adam's entire chest ached and something akin to panic rose in his throat. All he wanted to do was protect his children from harm, but he could not protect them from this. "She does come sometimes. But I know it doesn't feel like enough. It's okay to miss her and to feel sad."

"How come she doesn't want to see us?"

Adam took a shaky breath and swallowed hard. "I think your mom is trying to understand herself a little better right now. She's trying to learn about herself. And learning takes time."

"When she's done learning will she see us more?"

He smoothed her wavy mass of hair back from her forehead. "I don't know for sure, but I hope so. And we can also keep inviting her to come. *I'll* keep inviting her. I promise."

"Okay. Thanks, Daddy." Penny yawned and nestled down under her covers. She seemed to have had fun at day camp, but her fears about the performance must have worn her out. Still, Adam had one more thing he had to say.

"Penny, I know you like Gracie a lot. So do I. She's really nice. But we also have to remember that Gracie doesn't live in Shelter Creek. She's only going to be here for a little bit, to help out some wildlife. We don't want to get so used to having her around that we get really sad when she goes away."

Penny yawned again. "Okay, Daddy," she mumbled. "I won't get used to her. But I still like her." In moments her breathing evened out and her lips parted slightly. She was asleep.

Adam turned out the bedside light and closed Penny's door silently behind him. He took a deep breath and let it out. Penny wasn't the only one who had to remember that Gracie wasn't staying. As soon as he'd said the words to Penny, he'd known they applied to him.

He had feelings for Gracie. Real feelings. He wanted to hold her again, not just because she was scared or sad, but because he loved the way she fit right into his arms, as if she belonged there.

But feelings didn't have to become actions. Theirs was a temporary connection that would disappear once they caught the poachers. The emotion between them needed to stay just as it was. Unspoken. And recognized for what it was. Useless. Whatever it was that he and Gracie shared might feel important and special, but it could never be anything more that it was now.

CHAPTER TEN

ADAM GLANCED OVER his shoulder. Gracie was right behind him, moving lightly and easily on the trail despite the big backpack strapped to her shoulders. They'd left her SUV at a turnout about a half mile down the county road. Now they were making their way cross-country to Will Bateman's barn.

"I still don't understand how you are going to install cameras around the barn without a warrant," he told her. They'd been arguing about this ever since they left the station, and she still wouldn't give him a satisfactory answer.

"You have to trust me," Gracie retorted. "It's all figured out."

"If it's all figured out, then why can't you tell me what's going on?" Adam stopped and turned to face her. "We said we'd be a team. That we'd think before we act. I need to know that you've thought this all out."

She nodded. "I have."

"So why are you keeping me in the dark here?" The annoyance he felt was almost welcome. It was the wedge between them that they so desperately needed, after the intimacy they'd found up on the ridge yesterday. Bickering was better than holding her close in his arms. Well, not better, but a whole lot more professional.

She pushed her floppy bangs out of her eyes and glared at him. "I promised I wouldn't tell because Maya may have bent the truth a little to make this happen."

"You dragged Maya into this? In what way, exactly?" He didn't like being kept in the dark. Especially when any mistakes she made could reflect on him and his career.

"She's doing a study on bobcats for the Shelter Creek Wildlife Center. Too many people are using rat poison and other rodenticides. Bobcats are eating the poisoned rodents and it's making them sick."

"And what does that have to do with Will Bateman?"

Gracie worried her lower lip for a moment before confessing. "Maya went to visit Will Bateman, and the other people who live on his lane, earlier this week. She told them that she suspected that there was a bobcat den near the old barn. She asked if she could have her assistants set up cameras to observe the bobcat and assess its health, as part of her study. They agreed."

Adam ran a hand behind his neck, trying to take this all in. "But we're not scientists."

"I am." Gracie flashed him a bright smile. "Gracie Long, PhD in wildlife biology, at your service. And this morning you are simply Adam Sears, my trusty research assistant."

He had no idea Gracie had her PhD. That was impressive. And this was actually a pretty good plan. "Are there really any bobcats near this barn?"

Gracie's nod had a touch of triumph to it. "Maya has been coming out to observe for the past few days. She spotted one yesterday evening, hunting in the field between the barn and the road."

"And did it look sick?"

"Not yet. But if we don't observe it, we won't know how it's doing." Her smile was all innocence. "This way, if it becomes ill, we might notice that via the cameras. Then we can trap it and try to help it heal."

"I appreciate how hard you've worked to make this mission legitimate."

She flashed him a sweet smile. "Thank you. Also, Will Bateman and his neighbors have promised not to use rodenticides anymore. So that's another good thing to come out of all this."

He couldn't argue with the plan. Except… "If you're observing bobcats, shouldn't the cameras be focused on the ground, not the barn?"

"Of course. But if one or two of them happen to get bumped, and they tip upward just a little bit…" Gracie shrugged. "Wildlife observation is an imperfect science."

Adam started laughing. "You're incorrigible."

"Yes. And ingenious. Now come on, assistant Adam. We have some serious wildlife conservation to do today."

It only took another ten minutes of walking to reach the woods directly behind the old barn. Adam could see the sagging shingle roof from between the trees.

Gracie spotted it, too. "Adam, wait."

He stopped and waited for her to catch up. "Is everything okay?"

She nodded. "Just a reminder. We might be doing some legitimate science, but we don't want anyone to see us installing the cameras. Especially not Will, since we've already met him."

"You're right. That would be bad."

They both stood silently for a moment, listening hard for any sound from the barn. There was a blue jay screeching in the woods behind them. A truck went by with a low roar on the county road below. Adam's own heart was drumming hard in his ears. But he heard no voices near the barn, no cars on the nearby lane.

They left the trail and picked their way carefully down a gradual slope littered with leaves and branches. They stopped when there were just a few trees between them and the cleared land around the barn. A wild hazelnut bush provided extra cover.

Gracie unzipped her backpack and Adam did the same. The motion sensitive cameras they carried should turn on if anyone came in between the woods and the back door of the barn. And, of course, if a bobcat stopped by. Still crouching, they moved forward, picking their way quietly to the very edge of the woods. This was where they could be spotted. This was where it could all go wrong.

Gracie positioned the first camera downhill from the barn, at the edge of the field. This was their most honest choice. They'd be able to observe the resident bobcat's hunting grounds.

They put the next camera near the downhill side of the barn. After they lashed it to the trunk of a young fir tree, Gracie bumped it just a little with the toe of her boot. The lens tilted up, giving them a nice view of the barn. "Oops!" She winked at Adam and they moved uphill to install the final camera.

The sound of a car driving up the lane had them both jumping back into the woods and dropping flat on their stomachs. Heart in his throat, Adam peered around a wild blackberry thicket and saw a blue sedan passing in front of the barn. He glanced at Gracie, half expecting her hand to be on her head in the signal for panic that they'd agreed on. She looked back at him with wide eyes and pale skin, but then she rolled onto her stomach and army crawled toward the edge of the woods. Adam heard the click of her camera as she tried to get a photo of the car going by and knew that her fears hadn't taken over this time.

After the car was gone, Gracie collapsed in a heap, rolled onto her back in the fallen leaves, and stared up at the trees, her hand on her heart. "It's pounding," she whispered as she looked up at Adam with a smile. "But I'm still breathing."

That smile. The open trust in her bright eyes. The way the forest light dappled her skin. She was so beautiful when her prickly armor fell away. Now *his* breath was gone. Adam was the one who needed a signal, to put a hand on his head and call for help. But no one was coming to his rescue. His only hope was to look away before he was totally dazzled. He needed his head back on his shoulders. In that moment when she'd dropped her guard, she'd been a wild, luminescent creature and all he'd wanted was to reach for her.

Three deep breaths.

Gracie rolled back onto her stomach. "Let's set up the last camera and get out of here. That car was too close for comfort."

Adam was happy to have something to do. He pulled the third camera out of his backpack and they moved quietly through the trees. Gracie attached the camera to the base of a tan oak, whose leaves hid it well. This camera would give them a view not just of the back door of the barn, but also around the uphill side.

When they were finished, Adam motioned Gracie farther back into the woods. "Let's go."

She looked longingly at the barn. "You know, it would be easy to unscrew the hinges on that back door."

He laughed softly. "Absolutely not."

She gave an exaggerated sigh. "I don't know how you have so much patience."

"And I don't know how you've ever gotten a case through court with your methods."

"Hmph." She was all indignation as she led the way back into the woods, but then she lost her dignity and made a goofy face at him.

Adam followed her through the woods, deliberately falling a bit behind Gracie so he could think. He was a logical guy who'd always done the logical thing. And the logical thing was to ignore any feelings he had about Gracie. They were opposites. They were work partners. There was no room in their situation for the emotions he'd felt for her just now.

There was no place for the longing he'd felt up on the ridge.

Gracie was complicated when he needed to keep things simple. She was difficult and he needed easy.

Adam just hoped she didn't smile up at him again, the way she had by the barn just now. Logic and good sense could only take him so far. There were some things in the world that were irresistible, and Gracie's relieved smile, on a sunny day, on the forest floor, just might be one of them.

GRACIE SAT BEHIND the wheel of her car and searched for her courage. It was Friday afternoon, and she needed to get into the community center to watch Penny's performance like she'd promised. But that meant seeing Adam.

She'd managed to avoid him all day. Maybe it was wrong, but she'd told him she had to drive to Sacramento to take care of some paperwork. Really, she'd taken Rio back to the fire road where they'd seen the mother bear and her cubs. She honestly did want to check on them and she was thrilled when she got out her binoculars and spotted them foraging in a patch of huckleberries downhill from the fire road. But she was also desperate for a break from her partner.

When she'd rolled onto her back in the leaves by the barn yesterday, Adam had smiled down at her with so much warmth and relief in his eyes, he'd melted the last of the tension right out of her. But there was something else. A sense that he had something to tell her but couldn't bring himself to say it.

And just like when they were up on the ridge, she'd wanted so badly to close the space between them. To take his hand, to lean against him, to feel the energy that at times seemed to vibrate in the air between them. And yes, she'd wanted to kiss him.

Which was why she'd gone looking for bears today. She and Adam were so different; they wanted different things in life. She had to get over these feelings for him because they would take her precisely nowhere.

The clock on her dashboard told her she had just two minutes to get inside. She grabbed the little bouquet of miniature roses she'd bought from the florist and hurried into the community center. She jogged past the kids' art show in the empty lobby and into the small auditorium packed with parents, all waiting for the performance to start. She slipped into the back row of seats, feeling a bit like an imposter.

She was instantly aware of Adam. He was seated in the second row, near the aisle. A woman with light brown hair pulled into a messy bun was next to him. Maybe that was his ex-wife. It would be great for Penny if her mom was here.

The show started with a cute song about ladybugs. Penny wasn't in that performance, but in the next song, about trees, she was there, flapping a pair of felt bird's wings with gusto as she pranced among kids holding up construction-paper branches. Gracie had to snap a photo—Penny was just too cute.

Next, Penny's group sang a very pretty folk song about a river. This summer camp must have a nature theme. Then the ladybug kids came back on stage, but this time they were wearing paper butterfly headbands and they sang a song about leaving their cocoons.

That was it. Short and sweet. The kids all came back onstage and took a few bows. Gracie stood applauding enthusiastically with all the parents, surprised to find a couple tears on her face. Her level of pride in Penny's achievement was way out of proportion to their actual relationship.

Maybe it was just that kids singing nature songs were so cute, it was bound to touch even a cynical heart like hers.

Gracie sat back down to wait for Penny. Adam and the woman he was sitting with did the same. Gracie studied Adam's broad shoulders, and his thick dark hair that was usually hidden under a cowboy hat when they were together. She was here as a friend, but what if they were more than that? What would it be like to date a man like Adam, who wouldn't take a relationship lightly? Who would treat the person he loved with respect and care?

Gracie had never dated anyone like that. Maybe because men like Adam lived in cute towns like Shelter Creek and had settled, organized lives, while she was rarely in one place for long.

A herd of excited children stampeded out from behind the stage. Penny emerged from the pack and threw herself into her dad's arms. Then she hugged the other woman, too. When she spotted Gracie making her way down the aisle, the little girl jumped up and down and waved wildly. "You came!"

"It was a great show. I'm really proud of you." Gracie handed her the little bouquet. "These are for you."

Penny's blue eyes rounded. "They're so pretty!" She turned to the tall woman standing next to Adam. "Look, Aunt Sara. I got flowers!"

Oh. This was Adam's sister, the rancher. Gracie hadn't been looking forward to meeting Adam's ex-wife, but her heart ached for Penny. She was probably really disappointed that her mom hadn't come to see her.

"Those are great-looking flowers." Sara offered a friendly smile. "You must be Gracie."

"It's nice to meet you."

"I heard about how you helped Penny after her fall at the barbecue. Thanks for that."

"I'm glad I happened to be there."

"My hands are all better now." Penny displayed her palms. "Except this one is making a scar."

Gracie could see the raised white mark. "Another souvenir."

"I didn't think of that." Penny grinned. "And I won't outgrow this one."

"But maybe we can slow down on our souvenir collection for a while." Adam said. "They're only special if they're rare."

Gracie laughed. "That is very good advice."

Adam smiled back. "How was Sacramento?"

"It was okay." She hated that she'd lied. But her time in the woods today had given her a little more perspective. Maybe she and Adam were as mismatched as could be, but they could still have a friendship. She could try to focus on that from now on.

"Glad you survived. I was a little worried because I know how much you hate paperwork."

Ugh. He was being kind and she was fibbing. "At least I got to come here and see Penny afterward."

"And we appreciate it. Don't we, Penny?" He tickled his little girl lightly in the ribs, eliciting a delighted giggle.

"Yes. Thank you, Gracie." Penny looked up at her dad. "Can I give her a hug since she brought me flowers?"

"If it's okay with Gracie."

They all looked at her expectantly. Gracie's face heated. This whole loving-family thing was pretty foreign to her. "Sure. It's fine."

Penny came at her full force and wrapped her arms around Gracie's waist. "I'm glad you're my friend, Gracie."

Gracie patted Penny's back, not quite sure

how to hug someone who was so tiny. "I'm glad, too."

Penny released her and went to her dad to tug on his arm. "Can Gracie come with us when we move the cattle on Sunday?"

Adam glanced at Sara. "I'm sure we could use an extra hand."

Sara nodded. "Sure. The more the merrier. Want to join us, Gracie?"

Gracie tried to read Adam's expression, wondering what he thought of the idea. "You should come," he said. "I'll text you the directions."

"It's been a long time since I've helped move cattle. That would be fun."

"Yay!" Penny jumped up and down. "We can ride together and you can meet Comet, my POA, and I can meet your horse. Daddy said her name is Rio. That's river in Spanish."

Gracie wished she could bottle up some of Penny's enthusiasm for life and take it with her everywhere. "It will be nice to meet Comet." Gracie glanced around, noticing that the auditorium was emptying out. "I'd better get going."

"We're having pizza now, if you'd like to join us," Adam offered. "We just have to get my son, Jack, off the basketball court first."

It was tempting, but scary, too. Joining in a family dinner seemed a lot more intimate than watching Penny sing, or joining a cattle drive. "That's very nice of you, but I'm cooking for Maya and Caleb tonight." She blew Penny a kiss and waved goodbye to all of them. "Thank you for inviting me, Penny. Congratulations on your songs. It's good to meet you, Sara."

Gracie hurried away up the aisle, ready for the cozy safety of her car. She was glad she'd said no to pizza. She was already struggling with her feelings for Adam. Seeing Penny's performance had increased her affection for his sweet little girl as well.

Friendship. That was the only thing that made any sense for her and Adam. But deep down, Gracie knew it wasn't that simple. Both father and daughter had wandered right past the boundaries she set up so carefully between herself and other people, and found a path that led straight to her heart. She was going to have to find a way to protect herself around Adam *and* his family. Otherwise, her heart might break more than once when it was time to say goodbye.

CHAPTER ELEVEN

ADAM PUSHED THE gate open and used the chain to hook it back against the fence so it couldn't swing shut again. Then he returned to where Bodie was standing so patiently, swishing at a fly with his tail. "Come on, Bode, you ready to move some cattle?" Adam put his foot in the stirrup and swung up into Bodie's saddle. The late-afternoon sun was hot on his back and he shoved his straw hat down to try to block more of the glare. "Let's go."

He eased Bodie into a lope and started across the wide field to where Wyatt, Sara, Gracie, Penny and Jack were all waiting to help move the cattle. The herd had grazed down their July quarters and Sara wanted them on fresh pasture so the old field could regenerate.

Bodie loved it when he got to help with the cattle and Adam had to rein him in so he didn't approach the herd at a full gallop.

When they got closer, he slowed the gelding to a jog, which Bodie turned into more of a prance. "Easy, friend. We won't get invited back to this party if you scare all the guests." He managed to get his horse to a walk by the time he reached the end of the pasture where Sara and the kids were waiting.

"Thanks, Adam," Sara said. "Let's get these cattle moving. Gracie, would it be okay if you and the kids take the back of the herd? Since you grew up doing this, they can learn to bring up the strays from an expert."

"I don't know about that—it's been a while," Gracie said. "But yes, it will be fun." She looked so natural on Rio, completely one with her horse. She'd brought a coil of rope with her and it hung ready on her saddle horn. Adam was kind of hoping they would have some strays in the back. He'd like to see Gracie's cowgirl side.

Sara fixed Jack and Penny with a stern look.

"Will you both listen to Gracie?"

"Yes. Plus, we've already done this a lot." Jack looked a tiny bit resentful. Maybe he'd been hoping to feel more grown up by being in charge at the back today. Or maybe it was because he'd never met Gracie before today, whereas Penny already knew and adored her.

Gracie turned Rio toward the back of the herd. "Are you two ready?" She eased Rio into a trot and the kids followed, the three of them keeping to a single file line around the edge of the herd.

"She's a fine rider," Sara said, when Gracie was out of earshot. "The real deal."

Gracie was the real deal in more ways than Sara knew. Even though Adam kept telling himself that he and Gracie had to keep their relationship simple, his brain wasn't cooperating. He must have woken up half a dozen times last night. He'd wanted morning to come just so he could see her again.

It was silly. They were just moving cattle and wouldn't have much time alone together. But Gracie was planning to head north this next week to work on their poaching case from the Department of Wildlife office up there. She was becoming more convinced that their poachers were the same ones she'd been chasing up in Mendocino County. This was probably his last chance to see her for the week. And he really liked seeing her.

"You're staring at her, you know," Sara

said, shaking her head. "Don't get all hung up on her. She's not sticking around."

Adam watched as Gracie, Jack and Penny started trotting in a circle, as if they were in some kind of formation. That was probably Gracie's idea. She'd want to make things interesting until the cattle got moving. Waiting was not her strong suit.

"She could decide to stick around."

Sara's eyebrows rose in a skeptical expression Adam knew well. "What are the chances?"

He let out an audible sigh. "Not great."

"I'm not trying to be a downer, but I worry about you getting involved with her. What about the kids? Especially Penny? What if she's heartbroken when Gracie leaves?"

Adam grimaced as Sara's words amplified his biggest worries. "I don't want to see Penny hurt either. But isn't it pretty common for little girls to pick someone like Gracie to idolize for a while? She might be sad if Gracie leaves, but she also might be glad she had that connection."

Sara shrugged. "I hope you're right. Are you ready to date again?"

"I have no idea," Adam said. "I've never

dated. I asked Tanya to go steady during homeroom in seventh grade and that was it." It was a flippant answer but how could he tell Sara what he really felt? That on some deep level he knew that Gracie mattered to him a lot. That last night he'd lain awake wishing that she lived in Shelter Creek, and they could have the chance he already knew he wanted.

Adam caught sight of Wyatt on the other side of the field, waving to get their attention. Then he raised his arms in an exaggerated shrug, as if to ask what was taking so long.

"Such a patient guy." Sara punctuated her sarcasm with a wry smile. "Let's get going."

"Where do you want me to be?"

Sara motioned toward the gate he'd just come from. "Will you lead us through? After we get up this lane and out into the next field, I'll need you to support Wyatt along the side of the herd."

"Keep an eye on the kids for me?" Adam was always a little nervous about them helping with the cattle, even though they had been born and raised on this ranch. "Make sure they're listening to Gracie."

"Don't worry so much. Remember how many times we fell off our horses? They'll be fine." Sara reined her horse around and went to ride alongside the herd.

His sister was right. All three of them had started riding before they could walk. By Penny's age they had been roaming the ranch on their own. He was probably way too protective of them—especially now that every single parenting decision fell on his shoulders.

Bodie jogged along, happy to be out front of the cattle. Adam took a moment to relax into the horse's rhythmic gait and take in his surroundings. The dirt lane he followed would lead them up and over a hill to the steeper pastures that Sara and Wyatt had left alone since early spring. The cattle would love it up there this fall, with fresh forage and some huge old oaks for shade. As a bonus, the afternoon winds that scoured these hilltops would help keep the flies away.

Adam glanced back to check on the herd's progress. Most of the cattle were through the gate now and funneling nicely into the lane behind him. The kids were still back in the pasture, riding close together, waving their coils of rope to keep the cattle moving forward.

Gracie rode behind them, probably letting them feel in charge.

In her enthusiasm, Penny got a little too close to a heifer and it bolted away from the herd and back into the pasture. Gracie and Rio were after it in an instant, Gracie leaning forward in the saddle, rope in one hand, reins in the other.

Adam's jaw dropped at the sight. She was pure cowgirl, pulling Rio up and around to turn neatly on her hindquarters when the heifer suddenly veered right. The ornery gal was heading toward the shrubs at the far corner of the field where it would be harder for Gracie to guide it back to the herd.

In a flash Gracie's arm came up, her rope spun over her head and cut through the air to land neatly around the heifer's neck. She must have trained Rio for this somewhere along the way, because the mare slid to a stop, forcing the heifer to stop, too. Gracie backed the mare up a few paces to tighten the rope, then calmly led the heifer back to the herd and let it go.

Adam knew, right then, that he didn't stand a chance. These feelings he had for Gracie weren't going away. They were only going to grow. Adam knew it with the same certainty that he knew it was sunny out today.

As he watched, Jack trotted Peter Parker over to ride alongside Gracie. Adam didn't need to see the expression on his son's face to know that Gracie had just won Jack over, too. Anyone who could ride and rope like that was a hero in Jack's eyes.

After about fifteen minutes, the lane opened out into another wide pasture. The cattle were a little more restless here. Wyatt and his big quarter horse, Chevy, took off after a stray. Adam turned Bodie around and urged him back alongside the herd, to help with Wyatt's side until his brother returned. Wyatt's rusty red cattle dog, Sparky, was helping as well, racing back and forth to keep the cattle in place, his tongue lolling in delight.

After a minute or two, Wyatt and Chevy appeared out of the brush, hustling a disgruntled-looking brown heifer back into the fold. Sparky took over for Wyatt, staying right behind the heifer to make sure she didn't bolt again. Wyatt rode up alongside Adam. "Thanks for the help."

"Of course. Do you still need me over here?"

"As long as that miscreant stays put, I'm

good. But while you're here…do you think you could pick up the pace in the front?"

"You want me to get us going faster? That's going to take everybody's help." Adam eyed his younger brother suspiciously. "What's your hurry?"

"It's nothing. I'd just hoped to stop by and see a friend this evening, that's all."

Worry flared. "It's Sunday. You're not going to the bar again, are you?"

Wyatt grinned. "That's my sheriff's sergeant big brother talking. No, I was hoping to stop by the high school field for a few minutes."

As far as Adam knew, Wyatt didn't have much interest in sports beyond rodeo and the occasional football game on TV. "Don't tell me you're joining the softball league? How come you'd never join my team?" Back when he'd been team captain, he'd asked Wyatt to play many times. That was before Tanya left and he'd stepped away to be a full-time parent.

"I'm not joining a league," Wyatt said. "I ran into Summer today. She invited me to stop by. Her son is playing in the school's off-season baseball league."

"Ah. Summer." Adam urged Bodie into a

trot to stop a small brown heifer from striking out on her own.

"Nice move," Wyatt said. "I always said you'd be a good rancher."

Adam laughed. "You and Sara have that covered. Don't change the subject. Are you dating Summer?"

"Nope." Wyatt tilted the brim of his hat down, as if he were trying to obscure his expression. "We're just friends. We talk when we run into each other around town. That's it."

"Is that all you want it to be?"

Wyatt glowered at him from under the dusty brim of his hat. "Am I under interrogation? I'm just going to swing by for a few moments. Show some support to a single mom whose son is kind of a handful these days, from what she's told me."

"Isn't that kind of you." Adam grinned. "So charitable. Come on, Wyatt, admit it. You've always had a thing for Summer."

"Speaking of 'things,' how are things going with Gracie? She's got some pretty awesome moves on that horse of hers."

"Don't change the subject." Adam took the rope from his saddle horn and waved it at a few sluggish cattle who'd slowed to an amble. "She grew up on a ranch, so she knows her way around cattle."

"And she saves wildlife and likes your kids and she's great-looking to boot. Why are you not dating her? You must be blind."

"We're *colleagues*. I can't get involved with someone I work with." Adam glared at Wyatt like it was his fault.

"But you won't be working together very long, right? So, if you like her, I say go for it. I can already tell she's way better for you than Tanya ever was."

"What are you talking about?"

"You've been happier lately. Taking the kids out for an evening ride, making pizzas on the grill the other night."

"Your cabin is all the way on the other side of the property. How did you know about that?"

Wyatt shrugged. "Jack told me. Next time I'd like an invite, by the way. Anyway, you look different, too. More relaxed."

That had Adam laughing outright. "Gracie Long does *not* make me feel more relaxed. She argues all the time, she breaks all the rules we're supposed to follow at work—" He saw the triumph in Wyatt's smile. "What?"

"You've got it bad for her. I can tell. And she sounds like exactly the kind of person you need. Someone to shake things up a bit." Wyatt laughed softly. "Someone the opposite of Tanya."

Gracie couldn't be more different from Tanya. His ex-wife had been all about creating a certain image—driving a particular car, wearing particular types of clothes. Gracie was all about passion and emotion and justice. The image of her lying in the leaves, laughing up at him, reappeared in his mind and he closed his eyes for a moment, willing it to go away.

"Look at you, all lost in thought… You're making a mistake if you don't make a move." Wyatt gestured toward the herd. "And speaking of moving, can we *please* pick up the pace?"

Adam saw his chance and took it. "You mean hustle these cattle so you can reunite with your high school crush on the high school bleachers? Sure. I'll go tell Sara that you have plans with a woman tonight, so we'd better get this drive over with in record time."

"Don't tell Sara—"

Adam ignored his brother and rode away

laughing. He and Wyatt were supposed to be adults now, but maybe you were never too old to mess with your brother. He urged Bodie into a lope so they could get out in front of the herd again. Wyatt might deny it a million times, but he'd been sweet on Summer forever. If he had a chance with her, they needed to get these cattle moving.

CHAPTER TWELVE

"GRACIE, OVER HERE!" Maya waved at her from the sunny iron bench where she sat next to her grandmother, Lillian. Next to them was Emily, the veterinarian who Gracie had met when she came to check on Caleb's horse, Amos. Emily waved at Gracie and went to fetch an empty plastic chair. She set it down next to hers.

It took a few moments for Gracie to weave her way across the busy patio at the edge of the Shelter Creek Farmers Market. "Thanks for the chair, Emily."

"Good to see you." Emily raised her paper coffee cup in greeting.

Maya held out her arms and Gracie went to give her a quick hug. She'd never been much of a hugger before, but Maya and her grandmother were always hugging each other, and now they included Gracie. She hadn't had much choice but to get used to it.

"You found us," Lillian said, patting Gracie's back gently as they embraced.

"Yes. Maya gave me good directions. She said to look for masses of people with coffee cups in their hands." The patio in the back of the Shelter Creek Tourist Office transformed into something called Coffee Corner during the Saturday farmers markets. Surrounding the patio were two market stalls featuring delicious baked goods, and four different coffee carts, all competing to fuel up the citizens of Shelter Creek. "This is pretty impressive."

"How was your week up north?" Maya put a hand on her growing belly. "I couldn't help but worry about you, working on your own, chasing your poacher. I think Adam was worried, too. I ran into him on Wednesday and he said you hadn't checked in with him yet."

"He was supposed to be enjoying a week off work with his kids, before they go back to school." A touch of guilt clouded Gracie's mood. The truth was, she'd been avoiding Adam. She didn't want to miss him the way she had. She didn't like the way he was always on her mind. So she forced herself not to call him until work demanded it. "We spoke later in the week. I got a great lead from a colleague up there."

"That's good news," Maya said.

Gracie smiled, still almost unable to believe her luck. "We're getting really close to solving this case, I think. A man up in Humboldt County was caught baiting deer so he could easily shoot them on his property. He ratted out one of his closest hunting buddies, saying the other guy talked him into it."

Maya grinned. "And let me guess. The man he ratted out was the nephew of a certain someone who lives off the county road?"

Gracie nodded. It hadn't taken her more than a half hour on the computer to identify Chuck Bateman, who supposedly talked his friend into baiting deer, as the nephew of Will Bateman. And she'd been able to determine that he'd recently purchased a big black pickup truck. "I can't say more, but I think we're getting closer to putting one more poacher out of business."

"This is all very mysterious," Emily said. "I hope you solve this case really soon so you can fill me in on all the details."

"I shouldn't be talking about it anyway,"

Gracie said. "I didn't mean to leave anyone out of the conversation."

"That's okay." Emily's easygoing demeanor put Gracie at ease. "How are you enjoying Shelter Creek?"

Gracie glanced around. Fiddle music from a bluegrass band playing somewhere in the town square wafted over the crowds of people milling around. There were a huge number of stalls and tables displaying food, crafts and more. "It's…busy. I haven't spent too much time at town events like this."

"This place can be overwhelming sometimes," Emily said. "It used to be such a sleepy town. Now it's gotten all fancy, and we get so many visitors." She lifted up her cup. "One good thing is, the coffee is way better now."

"And you'll need the caffeine today, right?" Maya grinned at her friend. "Don't you and Wes have your monthly wedding planning meeting with your mother today?"

Emily's smile was accompanied by an eye roll. "Yes. But Wes is getting out of it by taking urgent cases at the clinic. So, it will be just me and Mom." She turned to Gracie. "My mom is obsessed with this wedding. You'd think she was the one getting married!"

"It's so sweet that you're including her in the planning," Lillian added.

"She's way better at it than Wes and me," Emily confessed. "When we have free time, we just want to work with the horses."

"Congratulations on your engagement." Gracie tried to sound enthusiastic. Fluffy dresses, fancy cakes and bridesmaids had never really appealed to her.

"Gracie, how are things going working with Adam?" Lillian patted Maya's arm. "Maya has been telling me a little about your investigation. It sounds like you two make a good team."

Gracie glanced at Maya, who looked away with an all too innocent expression. Gracie hadn't told her friend, or anyone, about her growing feelings for her partner. But from the look on Maya's face, she just might suspect something. "I think it's going okay. I haven't seen him all week, but we're making progress on the case."

She left out the fact that she'd missed him a lot. And that she'd missed Penny and Jack, too.

Gracie had loved hanging out with the kids

last Sunday. After they'd finished with the cattle, she'd stayed at their house for an early dinner. Adam had barbecued chicken, and Gracie had helped him put together a couple of salads. They'd eaten out on the deck, but Gracie had enjoyed a tour of the house, courtesy of Penny. It was a spacious modern farmhouse, with cozy furniture that begged you to curl up and relax.

After dinner they'd made ice-cream sundaes and played volleyball on the trampled grassy area that served as the backyard.

"Adam is a good man," Lillian said. "I'm glad you ended up working with him."

Gracie had never been very comfortable sitting around chatting like this. The urge to get up and move was overwhelming. The last thing she should be doing was thinking about Adam and what a good man he was. He was a good *friend*. A good *colleague*. And just because she wanted him to be more than that, didn't mean it was a good idea. She turned to Maya. "I was thinking I'd cook a yummy dinner tonight. But I need to shop for it. I'll see you all later?"

"Yes, please go shop and then cook me dinner," Maya joked, waving her off.

Gracie smiled at Emily and Lillian. "Would you like to come over for dinner? If it's okay with Maya, that is?"

"That would be fun," Maya said. "And then you could meet Emily's Wes. He's a great guy."

"That would be really nice," Emily said. "Just tell us when, and we'll be there."

"I'd love to join you," Lillian said.

"Then we have a plan. I'd better go stock up." Gracie waved goodbye and traipsed off into the market. She might not be great at small talk, but at least she could cook. Tonight would be a nice way to connect with Maya's friends and grandmother, without feeling like she had to be the life of the party.

It was fun to wander through the colorful stalls bearing the names of the farms selling their produce today. None were familiar, so Gracie made her way to the closest stall, happy to learn that Safe Haven Farms had beautiful, sun-ripened, organic tomatoes.

She bought a couple pounds, then wandered until another vendor caught her eye. It was just a simple table covered in jars of honey. The beekeeper, an older woman who introduced herself as Charlotte, was happy to explain her different varieties. She started with the colors and the flavors, then went on to describe the plants the honey came from, and the characteristics of the bees who lived in her hives. Ten minutes later, Charlotte was still talking, and Gracie was shifting her feet and stifling her third yawn.

Then she saw Adam and her sleepiness disappeared. She waved and her heart leaped when he spotted her and jogged over.

"Welcome back." His broad smile was exactly what she needed to see. "I missed you, partner."

She'd missed him way too much to respond in kind. Her blush would give her away. "How was your week off with the kids?"

"Fun. And tiring. Four more days and they'll be back in school. And as much as I'll miss them, my life will be a lot more manageable." Adam waved to Charlotte. "Gracie, is my beekeeping friend giving you a lesson in sweetness?" Adam pointed to one of the brilliant golden jars on the table. "Get her wildflower honey. It's delicious."

Charlotte beamed up at him. "Adam Sears, you are too kind."

"Just speaking the truth. How are you doing today, Charlotte?" Adam reached his hands across the table and Charlotte took them in her own. "I'm better, now that you've stopped by."

"How is Nathan's back?"

"Getting better now. He's up and about." Charlotte gave Adam's hands a firm squeeze and let him go. She smiled at Gracie. "Adam came out to help us when my Nathan fell off a ladder not too long ago." She shook her head. "I told Nathan not to fix the shed roof himself, but he didn't listen. Good thing Adam was so quick to answer my call. He had Nathan in the back of his truck in no time. He took him down to the clinic and got him all fixed up."

Gracie nudged Adam with her shoulder. "You didn't tell me you're such a hero."

When he glanced down at her, his face looked a little flushed. "Just doing my job."

"Now, where are those kids of yours?" Charlotte craned her neck to look beyond them.

Adam pointed and Gracie saw Penny and Jack, standing in the next stall looking at some handmade wooden toys. "Penny! Jack! Come on over for a moment."

Penny pelted over and bounced up and down in front of Gracie. "You're home!"

"I am. Now stop wiggling for a minute so I

can see what an almost-second-grader looks like." Gracie knelt down so she could see her little buddy's face more clearly. "Hmm...you look very wise. I'm sure you're all ready for the first day of school."

The little girl giggled, just as Gracie hoped she would. "I know my teacher's name now. Mrs. Ortega. Everyone says she's really nice."

"That will make your new school year extra special, then." Gracie stood as Jack approached. "Hey there. How are the last few days of summer treating you?"

"Pretty good," Jack said. "But I don't feel ready for school to start." He frowned. "Summer goes by so fast."

"I remember that feeling. But I also remember that it was kind of exciting to start a new year."

"I guess." He looked at her with hopeful eyes. "Want to come out and go riding with us soon? Maybe you could help me with my roping."

"Jack—" Adam gave Gracie a flustered look.

"No, it's fine. I'd be happy to."

"He's been a little obsessed with roping ever since he saw you in action when we moved those cattle," Adam said.

Gracie smiled at Jack. "It's a useful skill to have when you live on a cattle ranch."

"My dad ropes," Jack said. "But not like you."

Adam laughed. "That is true. I don't think anyone I know ropes as well as Gracie."

Now she was the one getting flustered.

"I haven't said hi to you yet, Charlotte." Penny went around the table to give Charlotte a hug. Gracie watched as the older woman closed her eyes as if to absorb the sweetness and save it for later.

"Hi, Charlotte." Jack went to her table and they bumped knuckles.

"Do you two still like honey sticks?" Charlotte pulled two thin straws out of a jar on her table.

"Yes, please." Penny held out her hand eagerly for the stick.

"If it's okay with your dad?" Charlotte gave Adam a mischievous smile. Gracie had a feeling this was their usual routine to tease the kids a little.

"Well, I don't know." Adam crossed his arms over his chest and looked at his kids skeptically. "I'm not sure they like sweets that much."

"Dad!" Penny bought right into it. "*Of course* we do."

Jack looked like he might be a little too cool for this game, but when Adam said, "Oh…okay then." Jack took the honey stick with a big smile. "Thanks, Charlotte."

"You two be good now."

"We're always good." Penny held her honey stick up to the light to examine the golden hue.

Gracie caught Adam biting his lip as if he were trying not to laugh. "*Of course* you are," he said with a wink at Charlotte.

"I'll take a bottle of that wildflower honey, please." Gracie handed Charlotte the money.

"We're going to the bounce house next," Penny announced in an abrupt change of subject. "Will you come watch us bounce, Gracie?"

Adam intervened. "Gracie probably has a lot to do today."

"I have to finish shopping, but I can watch for a few minutes." Gracie wanted to make Penny happy, but she was aware—as much as she tried to ignore it—that she was also trying to have a little more time with Adam.

"Yay! Come on!" Penny took Gracie's hand and they started across the town square. A few bounce houses were set up on a lawn at the far edge. "I want to bounce in the castle one," Penny said. "Look, Jack, it even has a slide."

The kids kicked off their shoes, Adam paid their entry fee, and they disappeared into the rubbery depths of the houses.

"We didn't have these when I was a kid," Gracie said. "They look fun."

"They love them. I spend a lot of time standing around watching them jump. It's one of the torturous joys of parenthood."

"Sounds exciting."

"It is what it is. What do free-wheeling, childless people like yourself do on the weekends? I can't even remember anymore."

"Well, I'll work if any poaching tips come in. But assuming it's quiet…" Gracie tried to picture the rest of her day. "I'm going to finish shopping here, then I'll take Rio for a ride this afternoon. And go for a run, too. I also want to start cooking early, because I'm making a big dinner tonight. Tomorrow I'm thinking of going rock climbing or for a hike, and of course I'll exercise Rio again." She trailed off when Adam's smile turned into a chuckle. "Are you laughing at me?"

"You never slow down, do you? That's a really full weekend."

She shrugged. "Hey, life's short. You've got to take advantage of the time you've got." It was one of the resolutions she'd made lying in that hospital bed. Not that she had much trouble doing a lot of things in a day. It was slowing down that was hard. "Why? What are you doing this weekend?"

"The kids and I will go for a ride later today, then probably watch a movie tonight. Tomorrow they've got an afternoon playdate with Josie, the receptionist at the office. She has a son Jack's age and she loves having Penny over. They do arts and crafts, stuff like that."

It all sounded so comfortable. "What do you do when you get time to yourself like that?"

"It rarely happens." He shrugged. "I guess I'll help out on the ranch. Or do some chores."

"That's it?" She shouldn't have blurted that out. This was why she couldn't do small talk. Her manners only lasted so long. "I'm sorry, that was rude. It sounds like a very nice weekend."

His laugh was so loud, a passing couple turned to look at them. "You are not a good liar. You think I'm boring."

"I didn't say that!" Gracie rolled her eyes. "You are entitled to do chores in your free time. You're a father, so I'm sure there are plenty of them."

"Yes, there are." His laughter died down and she thought she caught just the faintest hint of regret in his eyes. It must be hard for him, as a single parent, to even think of taking time off. He looked at her curiously. "What would you do if you were me, and you had a free afternoon?"

It only took her a moment to decide. "I'd do something fun, exciting and maybe a little ridiculous, to balance out all the times when I had to be responsible and mature."

"Like rock climbing?"

"That could work. But maybe something a little more exciting. How about skydiving?"

He shook his head. "No jumping out of airplanes—I've got two kids to raise."

"Makes sense. Let's see…" Gracie tried to think of something else that fit her fun, exciting and ridiculous description. "I know. Zip-lining."

"Zip-lining?"

"Yeah, why not?" It was actually the perfect solution. "It's fun, and it's not something you'd normally do. It's exciting, but you're not at the mercy of a parachute. Plus, Maya said there's a company that has zip lines in the redwoods, toward the coast from here."

"Oh yeah, I've seen their signs on the road." Adam waved to his kids, who were trying to get his attention from the top of the bouncy slide. "Do you want to go with me?"

"What?" Gracie wasn't sure if she'd heard him right.

"Zip-lining. Tomorrow afternoon."

"You're seriously going to take my suggestion?"

He grinned, looking more relaxed already. "I think you make a good point. It's been a long time since I did anything out of the ordinary like that." Then his smile broadened to a grin. "Well, except the days I've spent out in the woods with you."

"That's just an average day at work," she protested.

"For you, maybe." His questioning look was just a little shy. "So what do you think? Shall we try it? I could stop by Maya's place and pick you up at two."

Gracie only hesitated for a moment. "Okay, it's a date." Oh no, what had she just said? "I mean, not a *date* date. It's an agreement, to meet. And go zip-lining." Her face was getting warm, and it wasn't from the sunny morning.

"I think I understand what you mean." His voice had a quaver in it. He was trying hard not to laugh at her.

"All right. Well, I'd better get shopping. Say goodbye to the kids for me?"

"Sure."

"I'll see you tomorrow."

He tipped his hat brim her way. "See you at two."

Gracie turned to go and collided with a very tall person. "Oof!"

She stumbled back just as a soft female voice said, "Oh no!" and gentle hands closed over her shoulders to steady her. Her rescuer was a pretty woman about her own age, with long dark hair. She looked at Gracie with honest concern. "Are you okay?"

Gracie's face was on fire and she figured she'd be a lot better if she could sink into the pavement and disappear. "I'm fine."

Then Adam was there, with the tall man she'd crashed into at his side. "Gracie, are you hurt?" Adam's expression was a cross between amusement and worry. "Not too many people can have a collision with this big guy and stay on their feet."

Adam was trying to be nice, but it didn't do much to ease Gracie's embarrassment. How could she be so clumsy? She looked up at the tall man she'd walked into. He was dressed like a rancher, in a cowboy hat, jeans, T-shirt and boots. "I'm really sorry about that," she told him. "I should have looked where I was going."

He gave her a warm smile. "Don't worry about it. I bet people run into each other every few minutes at this market, it's so busy." He held out a hand. "I'm Jace. A friend of Adam's."

Gracie shook his hand. "I'm Gracie. A colleague of Adam's."

"You're the one who's got him chasing after poachers." Jace flashed a megawatt grin. "Good for you. The guy needs a change of scenery."

"I'm right here," Adam reminded them.

Gracie burst out laughing. "Yes, you are." She glanced from him to the woman who'd caught her. "I owe you one. Thanks for catching me."

"Not a problem," the woman said. "I'm Vivian. I work at the Wildlife Center with Maya. You're staying with her, right?"

"I am." Gracie recognized Vivian's name.

"Nice to meet you. I've heard Maya mention you a few times."

"We work really closely together." Vivian's smile was so sweet, it put Gracie at ease. "I'd love to talk with you about your work sometime. I do education and outreach for the Wildlife Center. I want to put together some information for the public about coexisting with bears. We're not that used to seeing them around here."

"I'm happy to help," Gracie promised.

"I suspect that your kids are in the bounce houses, too," Adam said to Jace.

"Alex and Amy? Absolutely." Jace turned to Gracie. "They're my niece and nephew, but we raise them."

"We parent Jace's oldest niece, Carly, also," Vivian added. "She's almost eighteen and she volunteers at the Wildlife Center. Maybe you'll meet her there."

"That would be nice." Gracie looked behind her to make sure she wouldn't plow into anyone else, then took a step back. "It's very nice to meet you both, though I wish I'd managed it in a less violent way."

Jace laughed. "No, this was better. Memorable. Now we'll never forget each other."

"True." Gracie smiled at him. What a nice

guy. Then she turned to Vivian. "You can reach me at Maya's house any time you'd like to chat about bears."

"I'll be in touch soon," Vivian said.

Gracie waved to Adam and wandered away into the crowded market in a daze. She and Adam were going zip-lining. And she'd babbled something about dating to him. Then she'd crashed right into his friend.

The gazebo was ahead of her and folding chairs were set up all around it. There must be a concert planned for later. Gracie dropped down into one of the chairs and took a deep breath. Then another. She had to pull herself together. This wasn't like her. Gracie Long did not get all ditzy around men. She didn't have crushes on colleagues or wish for things that she couldn't have. She didn't get jittery and say embarrassing things about dates that weren't really dates. Except today she'd done all of those things. Adam Sears might like to play by the rules, but he was breaking all of hers, every time he looked her way.

CHAPTER THIRTEEN

ADAM STARED UP at the enormous redwood trees rising above him. Why, exactly, had he thought this was a good idea? He'd always loved hiking among the silent, majestic giants. But right now they weren't offering their usual soothing solace. Maybe because today's zip-lining plan was going to put him right up in the treetops, and never had the forest canopy looked so far away.

Gracie had made it seem so appealing at the farmers market yesterday. Her love of a good challenge must be contagious—a virus that infiltrated his system, until suddenly he was wearing a harness around his waist and legs, and another on his chest and shoulders, contemplating crossing a wobbly suspension bridge with huge gaps between the boards.

Apparently, the word *zip-lining* didn't mean just zip-lining at Redwood Wonderland. Guests could only access the zip line by completing a wacky-looking obstacle course, set high up in the redwoods that grew alongside a steep gorge.

"Doesn't this look awesome?" Gracie looked up at him, her face lit with an excited smile. Even the scratched-up yellow helmet she wore couldn't dim her beauty. When she dropped the tough facade she wore like armor, she was all lively energy and warm compassion. Her big blue eyes combined with her delicate features to make her seem almost other-worldly. She could be a fairy or an elf, native to these woods. "Are you ready for this?"

"Absolutely." Though Adam wasn't quite sure if he meant their upcoming adventure or something else. Something more, with her, if she'd have him. It was almost all he could think about, lately. He'd missed her last week, when she'd been away. Being on vacation from work had probably made it worse. He'd had too much time to think about her, and about the chemistry he felt between them. About the way she smiled at him, and how good she felt when she leaned into his arms.

Gracie motioned to a bearded young man approaching with his own harness and helmet on, and a bundle of rope under one arm. "This is Dez. He's going to be our guide today."

"Adam, right?" Dez held up his hand for a high five, so Adam returned it, feeling old all of a sudden. This kid looked twenty at most. His wide blue eyes and shoulder-length blond hair made him seem especially carefree. Adam glanced at Gracie, brows raised. They were going to trust this guy with their lives?

She responded with a smile. "This is going to be good for us."

"Sure." Pride conquered his last reservations. When Adam looked up at the course, he could see kids not much older than Jack climbing around up there. If they could do it, so could he.

"It will be great." Dez looked Adam up and down. "Gracie said you're a sheriff?"

"A sergeant," Adam clarified.

"Awesome, man. Glad to have you here today." Dez motioned for them to follow him. "You two already went through the safety orientation, so we just need to get clipped into the course and we'll get started." He led them to the deck next to the suspension bridge.

It took Dez a minute to untangle the bundle in his arms. But eventually he revealed three ropes that had carabiners attached to each end. "These are lanyards. We have a safety cable that runs over your head as you go through the course. One end of the lanyard attaches to your harness." He demonstrated by hooking a carabiner to the belt of his own harness. "The other end attaches to the safety cable. That way, if you lose your footing, you're not going anywhere."

"See?" Gracie nudged Adam gently with her elbow. "It's perfectly safe."

"I like your energy, Gracie. Let's get you hooked in." Dez helped her secure the carabiner to her harness and attached the other end to the safety cable. "Go ahead and sit down in your harness. Let the wire hold your weight so you can see how it feels if you take a tumble."

Without hesitation Gracie grasped her rope in her gloved hands and sat, lifting her feet off the ground. She bounced in the harness, laughing like a kid on a swing. She found her feet easily and grinned at Adam. "It's a lot like rock climbing."

Adam tried to look nonchalant as Dez clipped his lanyard to the cable above his head. His heart rate was up and sweat prickled the back of his neck. But that was good, right? He was out of his comfort zone. That was the plan.

"All right, Adam, you're set. Go ahead and sit down."

Adam didn't let himself think about it, just sat down in his harness and let his feet go out from under him. He spun and bobbed wildly on the safety cable, his outstretched legs forcing Dez to jump out of the way. Then he scrambled awkwardly, trying to get his feet back under him.

When he finally stood up, Gracie had her hand over her mouth, trying to pretend she wasn't laughing hysterically.

"Be nice." He readjusted his harness and shook out a pant leg that had gotten all hitched up.

"I am nice. I brought you here, right?"

"So you could laugh at me. I see through your plan." But he was grinning now. He must have looked pretty funny, all akimbo in the harness.

"Laughing *with* you. We're partners, right?"

"You guys are partners?" Dez gave the air an incongruous fist pump. "All right! This is a great place to do some team building." He patted Adam on the back. "Don't worry about the whole bouncing-around thing. Big guys like you always fall hard."

Was that meant to be comforting? Fortunately, there wasn't much time to think about it. Dez led the way out onto the bridge. "Hold on to the railings and watch your feet," he advised. "But don't look down either. You know what I mean?"

Adam would have laughed at Dez's conflicting directions, but he was too busy trying to balance. The bridge sloped upward as it crossed the ravine. With its missing steps and rope railings, it was like trying to climb a staircase with a mind of its own. It bounced and tilted every time any of them took a step. After a few moments where Adam thought they were all going to be thrown off like disappointed bull riders, Dez stopped and looked back at them. "Okay, team, do either of you have any ideas that might make this situation go a little better?"

Ah. Here came the teamwork lesson. "Let's step at the same time," Adam suggested.

"Great idea," Dez enthused. "Gracie, anything you want to add?"

"Let's walk on opposite feet. So you and I, Dez, should start on our right foot, and Adam should start on his left. It might help the bridge stay more upright."

"I like your thinking." Dez nodded vigorously. "Do you agree with your partner, Adam? Because we need to build consensus in order to work well together."

Adam might be able to handle the ropes course, but he wasn't sure he could take much more of Dez's earnest, team-building dialogue. "Yeah, sounds good."

"All right," Dez said. "We have a plan. Adam, say, 'One…two…three…step' when you're ready."

Adam put his weight on his right foot, freeing up his left to step when the time came. "One…two…three…step." They all stepped. And it worked. The bridge wobbled a little, but it didn't shimmy and buck like it had. He continued counting that way and they quickly reached the wooden platform on the other side of the ravine.

"That was great," Dez said. "I like how you came up with a creative solution and implemented it together. That's something you can take back to the office with you."

"Thanks, Dez. We'll be sure to keep that in mind." Adam was so close to laughing that he couldn't even look at Gracie. If self-help books had heroes in them, Dez would be perfect.

"The next challenge is an individual course." Dez led them across the platform to something that looked like a tightrope made from a thick steel cable. "But we can keep the positive team energy going by offering advice and encouragement. Watch your partner and really pay attention to their strengths."

Adam glanced at Gracie and caught the sparkle of laughter in her eyes before she quickly looked away.

"This is called a single line bridge," Dez told them. "See the higher cables on either side? Those are for your hands." Dez side-stepped onto the lower cable and held onto the cable in front of him with both hands. "Since you're newbies, I recommend that you shuffle sideways, like this." He took tiny side steps along the cable one way, then the other, and hopped back onto the platform, nimble as the blue jay flitting in the branches above him. "Who's next? Gracie?"

Gracie nodded. Lower lip caught in her teeth, she stepped out onto the cable with her body turned sideways. She gripped the upper wire with her hands and lurched forward. "Everything wobbles," she gasped.

Adam instinctively took a step toward her, but Dez put a hand on his arm. "She's got this," he murmured. Then he raised his voice for Gracie.

"Keep your body nice and straight," Dez advised. "Don't put much weight on the wire under your hands. It's there to help you, but the trick is to stay balanced over your feet."

Adam could see Gracie straighten, as if she were steeling her spine for her next move. But she didn't go anywhere.

"Are you okay, Gracie?" Dez glanced at Adam when she still didn't respond.

"Gracie?" Adam moved to the edge of the platform, so he was as close to her as possible. "Do you need help?"

"I'm summoning courage," Gracie said in a shaky voice. "Which is harder than it looks." Her face under her helmet looked small and pale and her legs, sheathed in black leggings, trembled.

"You can do this," Adam said, pushing down his own worry. This day was supposed to build their confidence, not send her into a panic. "Can you use the number three trick? Three deep breaths, remember? Focus on three things you see, or hear. Feel the cable under you."

Dez looked at Adam with admiration. "Great idea, man. I'm filing that one away."

It took a moment, but Gracie's breathing slowed, her shoulders squared and she gave Adam a tentative smile. "Thanks, partner. I'm okay now."

"Great comeback, Gracie. Well done." Dez might be annoying sometimes, but he had the perfect calm, enthusiastic voice for this. "So, here's what you need to do. Pull your stomach muscles in and straighten up your torso to get your weight over your feet."

It didn't take her long to get the hang of it. She sidestepped carefully along the rest of the cable until she reached the platform on the other side.

"Nice work," Dez called over to her. "I like how you overcame your anxiety there." He turned to Adam and whispered, "Compliment her."

"What he said." Adam motioned toward Dez. "I'm proud of you."

She took a mock bow. "Your turn, Sergeant."

Adam stepped sideways onto the cable, catching his breath as it swayed underneath him. "Stay over your feet," Dez said. "Put all your focus on your next step."

Well, that he should be good at. Taking one more step—it was all he'd been doing since Tanya left. He remembered what Dez had told Gracie and tightened his abs and tried not to hunch over the cable he was clinging to for dear life.

"You can do it, Adam!"

Gracie's encouragement reminded him that she was watching. He took a step. Then another. Maybe it was all the times he and his brothers had walked along the top rails of the fences when they were kids, but for some reason this didn't seem too difficult. He smiled, remembering how Dad would get mad at them and give them lectures on the cost of replacing wooden fencing. But here at Redwood Wonderland, his fence-balancing escapades were finally paying off.

Soon he was standing on the next platform with Gracie. "We did it!"

She raised her hand for a high five and he clapped his hand to hers. She had a smear of dust on her cheek and she looked adorable, but she didn't return his smile. "I almost lost it there."

"But you didn't." He put gentle hands to her shoulders. "It's okay to have fears. I have plenty. We're learning to conquer them, or at least tame them a little, right?"

She looked up at him with solemn eyes. "What are you afraid of?"

"Not being there for my kids. Making mistakes and messing them up somehow." It was easy to tell the truth out here, so far off the ground, with the redwoods rising to the skies around them. "Not having the guts to reach for something special when it comes along."

She nodded, not taking her gaze from his, stealing his breath like he was still on that single line bridge. "I worry about that, too."

"How's the law enforcement team doing?" Dez practically skipped across the cable to join them. "Let's give each other some more compliments on that last obstacle. Go ahead, Adam."

He was still processing Gracie's words, trying to play it cool despite the hope doing loops around his heart. He released her shoulders and took a step back, realizing there was no way he could be cool with such a goofy, smitten grin on his face. "There are so many compliments to choose from."

She rolled her eyes, but she was smiling, too. "Just pick one."

"I'm glad we became partners."

"Really nice, Adam. We guys have to learn to be honest with our emotions. Gracie?"

She looked up at him, seeming suddenly shy. "I like that you don't judge me. And that you've stuck by me even when I haven't made it easy."

"Oh sweet," Dez exclaimed. "Really positive. Way to spread the love, you two. Are you ready for your next challenge?"

It was another suspension bridge, less wobbly than the first. But they had to step on ropes woven together like a basket, except the basket had extra big holes that they could fall through if they weren't careful.

Thankfully Dez lightened up on the team-building talk so they could just enjoy the challenge and the fresh air and the forest around them. The course took them up an inclined redwood log and traversed a ladder bridge hung high in the treetops. The best part was completing each challenge with Gracie. They cheered each other on and helped each other out. A sense of possibility lingered between them, and Adam knew he'd never felt this way with Tanya. Theirs was a teenage romance that they'd both hung on to and tried to keep alive. This connection with Gracie had a life of its own.

"That was the last challenge," Dez told them as they clambered from a shaky rope ladder onto a wooden platform perched high on the trunk of a redwood tree. "You two have rocked it today. Such impressive teamwork and bonding."

"We are impressive, aren't we?" Gracie looked up at Adam. "We've come a long way."

"We sure have," he murmured. They leaned against the soft, thick bark of the redwood's trunk, the dense forest stretching out all around them. Beyond its borders Adam could see the grassy dry hills and oak groves surrounding Shelter Creek. They'd ridden trails, hiked hills, driven roads and now, climbed trees. With every mile traversed by Gracie's side, Adam's life had changed for the better.

"It's beautiful." She slipped her hand into his and he held on tight.

Dez arrived on the platform and pointed to a rope net strung between them and another platform about ten yards away. The net was made of thick, rough rope, each strand over an inch across. "Why don't you two crawl on out there and take a load off? After this, it's just the zip line all the way back down, and then we're done."

Although the ropes of the net were thick and unyielding, the holes in between the ropes were…well…holes. With a few hundred feet of space between them and the ground. They weren't big holes, there was no way they could fall through, but it still took Adam a moment, and a few deep breaths, before he could crawl out there. He took his time, gripping the ropes so tightly his knuckles were white. When he reached the middle of the net, he turned over gingerly and lay on his back.

Gracie quickly crawled across the net and flopped down on her back next to him, as carelessly as she might lie down on a sandy beach. "This is so neat!" She looked over at him with a dreamy expression in her eyes. "Pretend you're in a hammock."

Adam took a deep breath, trying to relax and ignore the long distance between his back and the ground. A couple of crows were calling nearby and he could hear the distant laughter and excited shrieks of the group behind them on the course. This was an afternoon he'd never forget. "How did you get so adventurous?"

He could feel Gracie shrug in the shift of the net. "Growing up with my older brothers, I guess. I was always trying to keep up with them. Trying to prove that I was one of them."

Adam opened his eyes and looked over at her, but she was staring up at the sky. "How come you're not still there, if you were trying so hard to be one of them?"

She pursed her lips, quirked them to the side. "I realized it would never happen. They'd always treat me differently because I'm a woman. And they'd always have expectations, on some level, that I'd be like my mom. The perfect ranch wife. Making their meals, doing their laundry… That wasn't the job I wanted on a ranch."

He smiled at the thought. "I can't imagine you in that role." Gracie's family couldn't have known her at all if they expected that from her. "How did you get into wildlife protection?"

"I always liked the wildlife around the ranch—the coyotes, the rabbits. It broke my heart when my dad or brothers would just shoot them on sight. We'd argue, and I'd bombard them with all kinds of information about why shooting them was a bad idea… I guess it was my calling even when I was little."

"That's nice, that you had a calling. It must have made your path pretty clear."

"Isn't law enforcement your calling?"

"I never really thought about it that way. I knew I didn't want to ranch full-time. Tanya and I married right out of high school. I needed something steady, so I could earn enough to build us a house, have kids, all that. Joining the sheriff's department seemed like a good choice."

"Do you still like it?"

No one had ever asked him that. "I do. Maybe it's become my calling over time. I like helping people. I like solving problems. I want to keep my community safe." He gave her hand a squeeze. "I even like working with you."

She rolled onto her side to face him. "Really?"

"Mostly," he qualified, unable to keep a straight face.

"Meanie," she chided quietly. Her gaze searched his, more serious than before, and she leaned a little closer, just a fraction of movement. But Adam felt it like a shift in the wind.

"Nah. I'm not a meanie," he murmured,

unable to look away from her. He brought his hand up and lightly brushed his fingertips over her cheekbone. Her eyes went a little wider at the sensation. "I'm good for you. I keep you grounded."

She mirrored his gesture, tracing the line of his jaw with her fingertips. "And I'm good for you. I wake you up."

She did. On the job, in the woods, here in the sky—these were the times, lately, when he'd felt most alive. She'd helped him find a new sense of himself. More than Adam the dad or Adam the jilted ex-husband or Adam the dutiful sheriff's sergeant. Somehow Gracie had tapped into a conduit wired to the innermost part of him. The part he'd never thought to nurture, he'd been so busy providing for everyone else.

He trailed his fingers across her cheekbone to free a lock of her long bangs, which were plastered against her skin by the helmet. "I'm glad you came along and woke me up."

Gracie's fingers on his jaw stilled. She rose onto her elbow, her lips parted just slightly. The longing Adam had been trying to ignore distilled into raw craving. He slid his hand gently behind Gracie's neck, hoping it might encourage her to lower her mouth to his.

They'd been waiting for this. He was sure now that they were meant for this. She brought her mouth to his and kissed him, her lips brushing tentatively over his. Adam slid his fingers into her satin hair and returned the kiss, exploring the curve of her lips, the whispers of her breath, the depths of his heart.

The sound of Dez clearing his throat brought him back to reality. Gracie pulled away and flopped onto her back on the net, her hands covering her face.

"Sorry to interrupt," Dez said. "It's zip line time."

"We'll be right there." Adam looked over at Gracie. "Are you okay? I didn't mean to embarrass you in front of Dez."

Gracie took her hands away. Kisses and mischief added sparkles in her pretty blue eyes. "It's a little embarrassing. But hey, Dez kept saying that he wanted us to have a better connection."

Adam laughed. "You're right. We probably made his day."

"His whole week." Gracie sat up. "Ready to zipline?"

"Are you sure there isn't another way down from here?"

Gracie's smiled. "I think the elevator is out of order."

He loved that she understood his dorky dad-like humor. "I guess it will have to be the zip line then." He rolled over onto his stomach and looked through the gaps in the net at the forest below. A couple of songbirds flew below them. "This is pretty amazing, isn't it?"

Gracie rolled onto her stomach, too, and pressed her face into the net. "It sure is. Thanks for doing this with me today."

He tilted his head to look her way. "Anytime."

She peeked up at him with a shy smile. "Did we really just kiss?"

"We did."

"Did we like it?"

"We did." He laughed softly. "At least, *I* did. A lot. I hope you did, too."

"I did."

"Um…guys?" Dez was sounding a little frustrated now.

Gracie pushed herself up onto all fours and started up the sloping net. "You're zip-lining first, you know."

"Me? Why?" Adam crawled alongside her toward the platform.

"Because I went first on almost everything else. Now it's your turn."

"I was being chivalrous. Ladies first, and all that."

She stopped crawling to laugh at him. "I'm sure Dez would have a few words to say about that. He'd want equality in our team, and no assumptions based on gender. Haven't you learned anything today?"

"I have, actually." A lesson bigger than he'd imagined. That it was dangerous to kiss Gracie. Because now he wanted to kiss her every single day for the rest of his life.

When they'd crawled onto the last platform, so high in the sky that Adam was surprised they didn't need supplemental oxygen, Dez gave his final pep talk. "You two obviously did some intense bonding on this adventure. Nothing like a high ropes course to bring a team together."

Gracie slid her hand into his and Adam wove his fingers through hers, relishing her touch. He could not wait to kiss her again. But first he had to fly through the air in a harness at a really high rate of speed. No big deal.

Dez fitted Adam's harness to the zip line and showed him where to put his hands, and how to use the brake if he got going too fast—which seemed pretty likely. The zip-line cable ran from the top of this tallest tree, growing on this highest ridge, out over the treetops and down into the ravine where the course started.

"No more teamwork, now," Dez said. "This is just you, man, on your own. Just you and the sky."

Adam glanced at Gracie and she blew him a kiss. "You and the sky," she repeated.

"My pal Wendell will be waiting at the bottom to help you stop and get you off the line. Start using the brake just as you enter the trees." Dez grinned. "It prevents whiplash at the end."

"So reassuring," Adam said.

Dez clapped him gently on the shoulder. "Just messing with you. Wendell has a safety brake. You'll have a smooth stop no matter what. Are you ready to go?"

Adam took one last look at Gracie. "See you at the bottom."

She waved. "Have a good ride."

Adam gave Dez a nod and let go of the brake. Gravity took care of the rest and he was flying feetfirst, the forest and the sunlight and the bright blue sky a blur of light and color around him. The whine of the zip line and the whoosh of the air filled his ears. It was mesmerizing, all-consuming, a quick visit to another reality where he was just a guy whooping and hollering when the adrenaline took over, laughing as he dipped into the trees and applied the brake, breathless when his feet hit the ground and the guy named Wendell caught his shoulders and helped him stand up.

Adam stepped off the deck and onto solid ground, grateful for the crunch of soil and gravel below his feet. He unbuckled his harness, stepped out of it and looked up at the green canopy of trees. There was some kind of magic up there. He wasn't the same man he'd been when they'd started up that first wobbly bridge.

It was kind of funny, though. During the whole ropes course, he'd been worried about falling off one of the obstacles. But instead, he'd taken a different kind of tumble, one that was even more risky. He'd been teetering at the edge for a while now. But up there in the trees he'd lost his balance and fallen head over heels in love with Gracie.

CHAPTER FOURTEEN

"I AM REALLY glad I finally have a chance to see the famous Shelter Creek Wildlife Center." Gracie looked around Maya's spacious office. Large windows looked out over an oak forest behind the building. "This is nice. Is this entire building brand-new?"

Maya nodded. "We started out working in a trailer on this site. But Eva, who I met through my grandmother, is a powerful force behind this center. She found us donors from wine country, San Francisco and even Silicon Valley. So now we have a wildlife hospital, recovery rooms, an education center, and we've been expanding our outdoor pens so animals can rehabilitate in their natural environment."

"All in just a couple years. That's amazing." Gracie trailed her hand over a row of biology textbooks. "I remember these."

"They're still good reading, if you want to borrow one."

Gracie needed a book on human psychology, not wildlife biology. She'd woken up from a nightmare again last night. The same nightmare she'd been having more and more frequently, though it morphed into different settings each time. But the theme was always the same—a man, a gun, a helpless feeling. A shiver crawled along her spine, a trace of the terror the dreams always left behind. "May I have a tour? Or are you too busy?"

"Not at all. Monday afternoon is a good time to visit. Nice and quiet." Maya stood up from her chair. "I'd love to show you around. I'm so glad you got off work a little early today."

"The truth is, we're stuck right now. I'm almost positive Chuck Bateman is our poacher, but he keeps moving around. When I was up north last week, I followed up on a few leads about him, and then found out he was on a trip to Oregon." She sighed. "He probably went up there to terrorize some more wildlife."

"Ugh." Maya winced. "I really hope you catch him. Let me know if I can help in any way."

"You already are helping with those cameras at his uncle's barn," Gracie reminded her.

Maya led the way out her office door. "Yeah, but we're not seeing anything except one healthy, happy bobcat, a bunch of raccoons and a skunk or two."

"Fine by me. If my hunch is right and Chuck uses that barn to store parts of the animals he's poaching, I'd rather he wasn't going there to add to his stash."

"Me, too. But if you don't have proof that he's using that barn, you can't get a warrant to search it." Maya sighed. "It would be so much better if you could catch him in the act, right as he's trying to poach." Maya stopped in her tracks. "I know! Maybe you can use that robotic bear I've heard about. The one that looks so real the poachers will actually shoot at it?"

Gracie pressed her hands together as if in prayer. "That is my biggest hope. But there is only one robot-bear in the whole state right now. The department only lets us have it if we're pretty sure we know where and when the poachers are going to try to take a bear. That is why I have to try to figure out Chuck's future hunting plans." She paused, reality sapping her enthusiasm. "And that's not easy to do."

"I can imagine. But I know that you and Adam will get out ahead of him eventually."

"Thank you." Gracie crossed her fingers. "I just hope no one else is using Robo-bear when we do."

"Let's take your mind off it for a moment or two." Maya pushed open a heavy door. "This is our hospital."

"Oh wow." The hospital was perfect. Big steel tables to work on, surgical lamps overhead, oxygen tanks, glass-front cabinets stocked with supplies… "This is so nice."

"We've helped a lot of animals in here." Maya looked around proudly. "Emily, the vet, does our surgeries and advises us on animal care. Trisha, who you met at the barbecue, acts as our vet tech. Though I don't know how long that's going to last. She has two kids now and their ranch keeps her busy."

"She's the one married to the Texan who I saw at your barbecue."

"Yes, Liam." Maya fixed her with a wry look. "The one you didn't actually meet because you disappeared that day."

Gracie made a silly, grumpy face at her

friend. "And I've said I'm sorry a whole bunch of times."

"I'm just teasing you. I know it can be hard to be at a party where you don't know anyone." Maya smiled. "However, if you get to know my friends, I'm sure you'll really like them. And then it will become clear to you that Shelter Creek is the best place on earth and you should stay here forever."

Had Maya just read her mind? Ever since her and Adam's heart-melting kiss yesterday, Gracie's thoughts had been stuck in an endless loop. She was falling for Adam, unable to stop thinking about him, wandering around in a happy, confused daze. But he lived in Shelter Creek and her life was on the road with Rio, chasing poachers up and down the state.

She voiced her doubts. "I can't stay here. What would I do about my job?"

"You could work here," Maya said quietly.

"Work here? At the wildlife center?"

"If you wanted to stick around Shelter Creek." Maya's cheeks flushed a little. "It might sound silly, but I feel like you belong here. And you'd be perfect for the job. You've got so much energy, and you're a trained biologist. We need someone who can do field-work for us. You could also educate the people around here about how to manage the bears we're starting to see. You could advise our town council and park service on conserva-tion projects. And I really need help in my work with the agricultural community. There is a lot of important stuff you could do here, if you're interested."

It was such a kind offer. Why did it make Gracie want to turn around and run the other way? "That is so nice of you, Maya. I'm flat-tered that you think I might be a good fit. But I'm not sure that I'm ready to settle down yet. I've never worked in one place for very long." She was babbling. Trying to put words to a discomfort she couldn't even define.

"I know it would be a big change. But it might be a good change."

"Maybe." Suddenly Gracie's vision of her career went from crystal clear to muddy. The job Maya was offering came with many perks, including time with Adam. But she couldn't base a career decision on something so new and tenuous. Especially when she'd never imagined her life any differently than what she already had. The kiss, this job offer, it was too much to take in.

Maya must have sensed her distress. "Do you want to see some cute baby raccoons? They're in the other room."

"Baby animals? Yes, please." Gracie followed Maya across the hospital area and through a side door. This room held several clean, empty kennels waiting for animals in need.

"Look over here," Maya said quietly. She led Gracie to a big kennel set into the wall. It was all made of a cream-colored plastic except the door, which had the typical metal bars of an animal crate. Inside, Gracie could see a few tiny raccoons curled up under a three-sided plastic house, their bodies nestled down in a thick bed of wood shavings.

"There are four of them," Maya whispered. "They were pretty hungry and dehydrated when a local plumber brought them in late last week. He found them hiding under someone's house."

"They're snoozing," Gracie said. One of the raccoons woke and looked up at her with an indignant expression on its little bandit face.

Gracie took a step back. "Sorry," she whispered, then grinned at Maya. "It's so cute!"

"Aren't they just perfect?"

"They are. But I feel bad that I woke it up. We should let them rest."

They left the raccoons and passed through the hospital on the way to the lobby. "By the way," Maya said. "You haven't told me how the zip-lining went. Did you have fun with Adam?"

It was impossible to keep her feelings a secret. The moment Maya mentioned zip-lining, Gracie smiled. And couldn't stop smiling. Whatever was happening between her and Adam, and they hadn't put any name to it, was based in such a feeling of happiness and gratitude, she couldn't help her expression.

Maya laughed. "I guess it went pretty well?"

"It did. He's a really great guy." Her voice went all dreamy on her. She cleared her throat.

"Not such a stick-in-the-mud after all?"

Gracie shook her head. "I was wrong about him."

"Your face is going to match my favorite red sweater soon," Maya teased. "You really like him, don't you?"

Gracie's stomach felt queasy, admitting it. "I do. A lot."

Maya clapped her hands together in delight. "That's a good thing. When was the last time you fell in love with someone?"

Gracie shook her head, her stomach roiling now—as if by confessing her feelings they'd suddenly flooded her whole system with unfamiliar emotion. "Never."

Maya's eyes widened. "Okay, so this is a big deal, right? These feelings for Adam?"

"Yes. And I don't know what to do about them." Gracie scrubbed her palms over her face as if she could wipe away all of her uncertainty. "I just don't know if we have any kind of future."

Maya set gentle fingers on Gracie's wrist. "My job offer is serious. We could really benefit from you working here. Think about it."

"I will." It was hard to talk to Maya about Adam. She and Adam hadn't even talked much about that kiss yesterday. Maybe it only happened because they got caught up in the magic of that treetop moment. Though Adam had asked her to go to dinner with him later this week. And his touch, when he hugged her goodbye yesterday, had been full of warmth and feeling.

The anxiety in Gracie's stomach was turning into an ache. She'd make herself sick if she didn't stop worrying. This thing between them was brand-new and barely blooming. How could it grow strong if she got all hung up on wonderings and what-ifs? Maybe she should just set her fears aside and follow her feelings to see where they led. That made the most sense. She'd never been someone who could resist the lure of a new adventure.

CHAPTER FIFTEEN

ADAM CROSSED THE parking lot toward the sheriff's station, balancing four paper coffee cups on a flimsy cardboard tray. Hopefully the double shot of espresso in his cup would jolt him into Monday morning work mode. But even all that caffeine might not be enough to keep his mind on his job. That kiss with Gracie, up in the redwood forest just eight days ago, had changed everything. He was a new man, wide awake and full of hope. Each day glowed with promise, and last week's workdays were enlivened by the secret smiles and new connection he and Gracie shared.

And the weekend had been even better. On Friday night they'd met at Emilio's Restaurant for their first real date. They'd practically closed the place down, they had so much to say. Every time Gracie smiled or laughed, Adam felt like he'd won some kind of prize.

He had a new goal in life. To make her smile like that, every day.

One date hadn't been enough for either of them, so Gracie trailered Rio over to the ranch on Saturday for a trail ride with him and the kids. Last night she'd come over with pizzas, and they'd had a fun family evening.

He'd reached the door of the station. This was it. Time to concentrate on work. But all he really wanted was to see Gracie again. Pulling the glass door toward him, Adam carefully edged his way through, worried he might drop the coffee. Josie looked up from her desk and gave him a wave.

"Good morning, Josie." Adam set a paper cup containing her favorite skinny mocha on the receptionist's desk.

Josie looked up from her computer and clapped her hands together. "You brought me coffee? Why?"

He shrugged. "It's Monday. Our kids are starting their first full week of school. We made it through summer vacation and I thought we should celebrate."

The truth was, he tried to do nice things for Josie as often as she'd let him. She was such a giving person, always wanting to help others. But he knew she had her own troubles underneath her cheerful facade. Her husband was finishing his second deployment to Afghanistan and planned to leave the army afterward. Adam often saw Josie holding tight to the small gold cross she wore around her neck.

"I guess that is something to celebrate." She regarded him with narrowed eyes. "Does your excellent mood have something to do with a certain beautiful and brilliant wildlife agent?"

Adam froze. "Why would you think that?"

"Because this is Shelter Creek. Someone saw you and Gracie eating an early dinner in the window of Emilio's on Friday night. Hand-holding was reported."

"Ah." She was right. There had been handholding. And some of the best kisses of his life when they said good-night on Maya and Caleb's porch.

"There are no secrets in this town." He took a sip of his own coffee.

"You know how it works. Someone gets a piece of gossip and they share it at the hardware store, or the feed store, or at the Creek

Café. It doesn't take much to get the whole town buzzing."

"Is there any other gossip you want to share before I disappear into my office and stare at my computer screen?" He and Gracie were in an investigative rut. They needed Chuck Bateman to make a move, and instead no one had heard a peep from him in over a week.

"Oh yes. Last night, Gracie was seen picking up a whole lot of pizza at that take-out place near the old livery barn. *Way* more pizza than she could eat alone. And in that order was a plain cheese pizza. And we all know what that means. Kids. And who has kids? You."

Gracie came through the front door carrying a rolled-up piece of pizza wrapped in a napkin. "Good morning."

"Is that pizza for breakfast?" Josie asked, her voice all innocence.

"Oh yeah, this stuff is so good. It's from that take-out place by the livery barn—" Gracie looked at Adam. "Why are you laughing? Lots of people eat pizza for breakfast."

Josie leaned back in her chair and folded her arms across her chest. "I rest my case."

"What case? Oh, never mind." Gracie gave

Adam a warm smile and started for the conference room.

"What's the hurry?" he called after her.

"A friend of mine left me a voice mail. He says he has a tip. I need to call him." The door of the conference room slammed shut behind her.

"So did you have a fun pizza night?"

There was no use playing innocent with Josie anymore. She was a gossip shark. "We had a great time. Pizza out on the deck and then a nice walk up to the barn so the kids could say good-night to their horses." And then he and Gracie sat out on the deck and looked at the stars and talked and laughed.

"It's great to see you looking so happy," Josie said.

The conference room door swung open so fast that its hinges shrieked. Gracie charged out, waving her phone wildly. "Adam, we have what we need. I think we're going to get him. Meet me in the conference room?" She jogged down the hall to poke her head into Dean's office. "Captain Dean, do you have time for a quick meeting in the conference room?"

When all three of them were seated around the table, Gracie explained.

"I have a friend, Scott, another wildlife agent, who I've worked with in Mendocino and Humboldt Counties. He just called to tell me that he caught a guy poaching up near Crescent City a couple days ago. And this guy agreed to give evidence against some of his buddies to lessen his own charges, which are numerous because he had a whole assortment of eagle feathers on his property, as well as bald eagle carcasses."

"Lowlifes," Adam muttered. What kind of person poached the national bird?

"This guy told Scott that he frequently hunts with a friend named Chuck Bateman. And a few weeks ago, Chuck told this man that he'd almost bagged a bear and her cubs."

"Chuck is our guy." Adam leaned forward and put his elbows on the table. "How can we get him?"

Gracie held up a hand to signal him to wait. "Apparently Chuck has a friend down here, someone named Bernie. They have a plan to try for those same bears again real soon. And *that* is how we are going to catch our poachers."

"He didn't say when, though." Dean tapped his pencil, looking thoughtful. "Let's get all the information we can on that unmarked truck Bateman is driving. Then we can put out a call to all the agencies around here. I'm sure they'll be happy to keep an eye out and let us know the minute Chuck Bateman crosses the Sonoma County line."

"If we figure out who Bernie is, we can have someone keep an eye on his house." Adam said. "When he and his buddy Chuck get their guns ready, we'll know that it's poaching night."

"A friend of Chuck's might be likely to have a criminal record," Dean mused. "Let me ask Josie to see what she can find."

While he was gone, Adam looked at Gracie with new admiration. "I have no idea how you handle this job," he admitted. "I am really stressed out right now. I keep thinking we're going to mess up somehow and they'll get to the bears when we don't expect it."

She nodded, her sympathetic smile a balm. "You have to remember that this is a battle in a long war. We'll do our very best to win, but there is no guarantee." She glanced at the open doorway and then reached across the table for his hand.

Adam wrapped his fingers around hers, relishing their connection. "These last couple days with you have been some of my best days," he said softly.

Her smile widened. "I agree. The very best." Dean's footsteps echoed in the hall and she released his hand.

"Stop with the lovey stuff," Dean said as he walked in. He surveyed their shocked faces with a satisfied grin. "Yeah, I know. Everyone knows. It's Shelter Creek." He tossed a piece of paper on the table. "I think we might have found Chuck's local hunting buddy. His name is Bernie Voors. He's got past citations for hunting out of season, taking more animals than his permit allowed, unlicensed firearms, reckless driving, trespassing…"

"That's got to be him," Adam said. "Let's keep an open mind, but can we get someone to watch Bernie's house for the next few days? It sounds like they are planning to hunt those bears soon."

"I agree." Dean scribbled idly on his notepad. "There's a pretty vital detail in all this we're not talking about. How are we going to catch those guys? We need proof of their plans, or they can just say they were out for a drive."

"It's difficult to catch poachers in the act," Gracie said. "But because we know exactly where Chuck is going hunting, and *what* he's hunting for, we have an opportunity to trap them. I called the Sacramento office right after I heard from Scott. We now have a two-week lease on the one and only Department of Wildlife robotic bear." She flipped open her laptop with a flourish and showed them a photo on the screen. "It looks like a black bear, and it can even move like a bear. We put it out in the woods and hide. If they shoot at it, we arrest them for attempted poaching. And then—" she glanced at Adam "—we can finally search that barn."

"A decoy." Dean looked more excited than Adam had seen him in a long time. "This is going to be fun."

"If it all goes well. Someone from Sacramento is going to drop it off here tomorrow morning. It's big. Dean. Does this office have a garage or a shed we can store it in?"

"We do." Dean wrote *garage* on his notepad.

"There's one more part of this I can't quite

figure out," Gracie said. "There's just a one-lane fire road out there that follows the side of the hills. There aren't many places where we can pull our vehicles over and hide them. But we're going to need transportation to get out there. For us and the bear."

Adam tried to puzzle it out. "If they see our vehicles, or think anyone else is out there, they'll just head home."

Dean frowned. "This is concerning. We want some back up out there, but we can't have a lot of vehicles."

The answer hit Adam over the head. "The mounted sheriff's unit. They can keep their horses concealed until we need them."

Dean shook his head. "I just saw a bulletin this morning. They've all been assigned to the Mount Shasta area. A missing person's case."

Adam tried to ignore a momentary pang of nostalgia. In his earlier life, he'd have been out there with them. Then disappointment set in. Mounted deputies would have been the perfect solution.

"Is it possible to create our own mounted patrol?" Gracie looked at Dean. "Don't a lot of people volunteer with the sheriff's department?"

"They do," Dean said. "But we can't put them in any known danger."

"What if they were just there to block the road in case our poachers tried to escape? We could give them those really bright flashlights that you all use. All they'd have to do is shine them in the poacher's eyes if they tried to drive away and escape."

"This could work." Adam sat up in his seat and started ticking names off on his fingers. "The three of us. Caleb. My brother Wyatt and my sister Sara. Jace. Liam. Emily and her fiancé, Wes."

"Also Aidan Bell." Dean looked at Gracie. "He's a rancher who's married to my sister, Jade. A great horseman as well."

Adam looked at Gracie and Dean, hope rising in his heart. "It's a good plan. They're all totally at ease on a horse, they're not afraid of much and they'll keep our plan a secret, so nothing leaks out to Chuck or anyone else."

"That's a lot of people on horseback," Dean said. "If we divide them into two patrols, then no matter which way our suspects flee on that fire road, they'll be stuck." He grinned.

"We're going to bring in our very own Shelter Creek cavalry."

"Armed with flashlights," Gracie said. "The biggest, brightest flashlights they can carry."

"I think we might be geniuses." Dean said. "Or something close." He wrote the words *big flashlights* amongst the scribbles on his note pad. "You'll each have to be in charge of one patrol. Since you both have the power to make an arrest. I'll come out there on horseback, too, so I can move back and forth easily if either patrol needs backup. Maybe I can round up a couple of our other deputies as well."

"We'll need someone to take charge of the decoy," Gracie said. "They'll need to hide close by to control it."

It only took Adam a few seconds to figure it out this time. "Who around here is used to being out in the wilderness? And knows firsthand how a bear would move? And they're not afraid of anything?"

"Maya's pregnant," Gracie protested.

"We'll have to get the robot bear out there in a truck," Dean said. "We'll have a deputy drive it and she can ride with him. Or Vivian, the other biologist, could do it, if Maya can't.

"You two better get busy," Dean said. "You've got a lot of plans to put in place. Operation Robo-Bear is officially underway. Let's meet again tomorrow, same time, same place, and you can report on your progress." He grinned at Gracie. "I cannot wait to see that bear."

CHAPTER SIXTEEN

"GRACIE, THIS BEAR is amazing." Maya moved one of the dials on the remote control and the bear raised its paw. She moved another and its head swayed to the side.

"It's really realistic." Gracie put a hand on its back. "They even covered it in a real bear pelt."

"Don't you think it's a little creepy?" Vivian wrinkled her nose as she studied it. "Kind of like a taxidermy bear, except it can move."

"I think it's sort of cute." Maya lowered the front paw again.

"This is a strange way to spend a Friday night," Vivian said.

Gracie smiled at her. "It depends on what you do for a living. This is fairly average for me." She looked around at the site they'd chosen for the robotic bear. It was where the dry creek bed met up with the fire road. Almost exactly where the poachers had fired a shot that very first day she'd worked with Adam. "Do you think putting the bear in the same spot is too obvious?"

Adam shook his head. "It's going to be dusk or dark when they come by. I doubt they'll know exactly where they took a shot before."

Dean nodded. "I think it will be an instant reaction for them. See the bear, pull the trigger." He slid the robot bear's wooden base a few inches farther into a wild hazelnut thicket. "What do you think, Gracie? Does it look right?"

Gracie backed up a few paces to get a better look. "I think we're good."

"Are you sure Chuck Bateman and his friend Bernie are coming here tonight?" Maya was trying to make the bear nod. It did look kind of cute.

"We've been having someone watch Bernie's property all week," Adam told her. "Chuck Bateman crossed into Sonoma County on Wednesday. He's been staying at Bernie's since then. We got word that they were cleaning rifles and loading up Chuck's big black truck this afternoon."

"But still, there's no guarantee that they'll show up," Gracie reminded her.

Vivian surveyed the hillside above the fire road. "Gracie, where do you think we should sit to operate the remote?" She glanced at Maya, who was still playing with the bear. "Not that I'll ever get a turn with that thing."

"I heard that," Maya called. "My bad, Viv. Come try it out."

"Why don't you two go up behind those fallen logs?" Gracie pointed to a spot near the creek bed, several yards away from the road. "The remote should work at that distance, and it will be impossible to see you there, as long as you stay down."

"Perfect. Let's test it out." Maya started gathering her things. Deputy Calhoun, young and new to the department, knelt to help her. He'd driven Maya, Vivian and the bear out here tonight, and was going to stay with them for added security.

Gracie couldn't help but pull out her phone and snap a few photos of the scene around her. Not just the incredible robot, but all the horses and riders who'd agreed to be a part of Operation Robo-Bear. They'd all trailered their horses from Shelter Creek to a Forest Service station along the county road. Then they'd ridden out here in a big group, using a forest service trail that met up with the fire road.

The Shelter Creek cavalry was an impressive sight. Caleb, Sara, Jace, Wyatt and Adam were going to be ready to block the fire road to the west of the robotic bear. Aidan, Liam, Wes and Emily were all going to accompany Gracie and wait east of the bear. Both groups would hide their horses in the wooded gullies that divided the hills out here. The poachers wouldn't know it, but they'd be surrounded the moment they got to the fake bear.

Caleb rode up on Amos, with Jace just behind on a sleek chestnut quarter horse. "It looks like everyone's ready," he said to Gracie. "It's getting close to dusk. We should get everyone into position." Caleb was ex-military so they'd put him in charge of forming the two groups and figuring out where along the road they should be stationed.

Gracie nodded. "Does everyone have their flashlight?"

"Yup," Caleb said. "And each platoon has two communications officers."

"He means people with walkie-talkies," Jace clarified, grinning at his best friend.

"Perfect," Gracie said.

"Okay, folks, I just heard from Deputy Leary," Dean called out. "He's been watching Bernie's house. Our two vermin loaded up guns, spotlights and a whole bunch of beer. They're on their way."

"Let's be ready for them." Caleb swung Amos around and Jace followed. They called out to Aidan, and the tall cowboy on the striking buckskin gelding waved an arm in the air to help round up his riders.

"We'd better join our groups," Gracie told Adam. They held hands as they walked quickly to where Rio and Bodie were standing close together, nibbling at the grass by the side of the fire road. Gracie gathered her reins, swung up into her saddle and blew Adam a kiss.

Caleb was already leading his group of riders away at a brisk trot. Adam practically vaulted onto Bodie, blew Gracie a kiss back and took off at a lope after them.

Gracie and Rio caught up with Aidan and the other riders. They jogged down the fire road together and she had a chance to thank them all, and to chat with Liam, Aidan and Wes, all of whom were new acquaintances.

It was fun to see Emily and Wes riding together, exchanging loving smiles. They really seemed meant to be.

When they reached their designated hiding spot, they dismounted to lead their mounts carefully into the uneven terrain of the gully. "Let's make sure we're pretty far back in these trees," Gracie reminded them. "This is our one chance to trap these guys."

They waited in silence punctuated by the jingle of bridles and the occasional stomp of a restless hoof.

Just when Gracie was worrying that maybe Deputy Leary had made a mistake, and Chuck Bateman and his buddy Bernie were really just heading out to party, she heard the sound of an engine in the distance.

"Here we go," Wes muttered.

"Hold your reins tightly," Liam advised. "That engine is loud. We don't want anybody spooking."

"Can't wait to catch these jerks," Emily said to Gracie. "They deserve whatever they get tonight."

The engine noise grew louder, grinding through the quiet forest. "Get ready to lead the horses out as soon as they've gone by," Aidan said quietly.

The truck had floodlights above the cab. They all instinctively turned their faces away as the vehicle roared by.

"Let's go." Aidan led the way back to the fire road and they all mounted quickly, soothing their horses, who were feeling their riders' nerves.

"Get ready for a shot or two when they see the bear," Gracie warned, gathering Rio's reins closer. "Easy girl," she soothed her mare. "You're okay."

Gunfire cracked open the night.

"Go," Aidan commanded.

They trotted their horses around one bend and then the other. When the truck's taillights came into view Aidan held up his hand and they all stopped. Gracie could see Adam's group of riders walking down the road toward them, illuminated by the truck's enormous flood lights.

"Pull up," Aidan commanded, and they all slowed their horses and moved into formation, side by side, blocking the fire road. Caleb, on the opposite side of the truck, motioned for his group of riders to do the same.

Captain Dean and Deputy Calhoun were carefully approaching either side of the truck with guns drawn. The young deputy looked really nervous. Just then Adam rode up behind him on Bodie, his gun out as well, so balanced and powerful in the saddle that for a moment Gracie forgot she was also supposed to be helping with the arrest.

She pulled out her gun and asked Rio for a trot. The obedient mare moved quickly to Dean's side of the truck, unfazed by the commotion. Rio had helped arrest poachers many times before.

"You are being detained by the Sonoma County Sheriff's Department and the California Department of Wildlife," Dean called out. "Chuck Bateman, Bernie Voors, you are outnumbered and surrounded. Leave the vehicle slowly, with your hands up and visible at all times."

There was a pause and then the doors opened. Gracie recognized Chuck from the driver's license photo she'd pulled up from his records. "Close the doors behind you and put your hands on the roof of the vehicle," Dean ordered.

It was a good thing Dean was here. Gracie's breath was getting shallow, her heart was picking up its pace. She backed Rio up a few steps to give herself some breathing room.

Chuck noticed her movement and glared up at her. "What is this, the Wild West?" he sneered.

"Watch your mouth, Bateman." Dean had the handcuffs on him in seconds. He patted the poacher down and started to read him his rights.

Swallowing hard, Gracie tried three deep breaths. But her lungs felt stiff, and her hands started to shake so hard it was difficult to hold the reins. It was over. They'd caught the poachers. Why wouldn't her heart slow down?

Adam rode Bodie over to join her. Rio gave a low nicker of welcome. "We got them. We did it." Then his voice softened. "Gracie, what's wrong?"

She didn't want to say what was wrong. Not with so many people around them, and Chuck Bateman so close. She put her hand on the top of her head in the signal she'd hoped she'd never have to use.

Adam reined Bodie in a circle and guided the horse to stand beside Rio. He reached for Gracie's hand. "Can you take three deep breaths?"

Gracie tried again and this time she could breathe a little bit deeper. She squared her shoulders and tried to pay attention to the feel of the leather reins in one hand and the warmth of Adam's fingers in the other.

"I'd skip the listening part," Adam said. "All you'd hear is Chuck over there, cursing a blue streak."

She laughed. In the middle of her panic attack, he made her laugh. Her heartbeat calmed.

Adam was smiling at her, but she could still see the concern in his eyes. "Do you need something to look at?"

"I've got you." Gracie focused on his dark eyes, his slight smile, the way he sat so easily on Bodie's back. Three out of the many things she loved about this man.

Adam gave her hand a reassuring squeeze. "You might also look at our friends." All the riders were still lined up across the fire road, on either side of the truck, watching Dean and Deputy Calhoun finish the arrest. Gracie's heart filled with gratitude, that all these people made such an effort to ensure that she and Adam caught their poacher.

"Look at all you've accomplished here tonight. You did this, Gracie. You caught the bad guys."

She could breathe again. She could even smile at him a little. "*We* caught the bad guys. Together. With a lot of help from our friends."

"Sergeant Sears." Deputy Calhoun's voice crackled through the radio.

"On my way," Adam replied. He looked at Gracie. "He'll need me to keep an eye on Bernie while he goes to get the vehicle he hid away somewhere. We have to transport these fools and get them booked."

"Wait, if you transport those guys in our only vehicle, how will we get Robo-bear back to the station?"

Adam grinned and pointed to Chuck Bateman's fancy new truck. "We'll borrow his keys and Robo-bear can ride in the back. Seems kind of fitting, doesn't it?"

"He'll look grand." It was a relief to know there was such a simple solution for the robot. Gracie just wished some of the other dilemmas in her life could be solved as easily.

CHAPTER SEVENTEEN

ADAM LEANED ON the wooden rail of the pasture fence and watched Jack race by on his horse, Peter Parker, spinning his rope as he went. Jack had begged Wyatt to step up his roping lessons after he'd watched Gracie rope that heifer a couple weekends ago. Wyatt had finally promised him an hour every Sunday morning, in exchange for Jack's help cleaning a few extra stalls.

"Your kid is getting better at this," Wyatt said. "Slowly but surely."

"I really appreciate you mentoring him."

Wyatt grinned. "Who else is going to do it? Your roping arm is so rusty I'm surprised it hasn't fallen right off."

"I don't practice as much as you," Adam pointed out.

Wyatt laughed. "You can't use that excuse anymore. Gracie doesn't work on a ranch either and she was on fire when she roped that heifer." He nudged Adam in the ribs. "What the heck does that goddess see in you, anyway?"

"Ouch." Adam glared at his brother. "You're a grown man. How can your elbows still be so pointy? And I don't quite know what Gracie sees. I'm just glad she sees it."

"Speaking of which…" Wyatt pointed toward the driveway. "Isn't that her SUV and trailer parking right now?"

It was. Adam hadn't expected to see her. After their exciting Friday night catching poachers, and an exhausting Saturday morning search of Will Bateman's barn, he'd figured she'd want to stay home and rest today. Especially after the heartbreaking collection of items they found in that barn. Chuck Bateman had been poaching for a long time. The only scrap of hope in that gruesome search was the knowledge that everything they found could be used against Bateman in court.

Adam glanced at Wyatt. "I wonder if she's hoping to ride Rio here today."

"Get her to take over the roping lessons," Wyatt said. "She's as good as I am, and probably a better teacher."

"I'll go see what's up." Adam walked across the cropped grass to the driveway. By the time he got there, Gracie was leaning on her car, jingling her keys in her hand, waiting for him.

"Thank you for coming over. I didn't know if we'd get to see you today."

She pushed herself off the truck and wrapped her arms around his neck. He pulled her closer and held her tight. She seemed to want to stay in his arms, so he relaxed into holding her, inhaling her soapy scent with just a hint of flowers, enjoying the feel of her smooth soft hair against his cheek. But he knew her well enough to know that something was wrong. "What's up?"

She stepped back and worried her lower lip between her teeth for a second, as if she were gathering her thoughts. "I love what we have together, Adam. It's the most unexpected thing that's ever happened to me. But I don't think I'm ready for it yet."

"Yet," he repeated, instantly needing to know what that meant.

"You saw me at the arrest the other night. I could barely hold myself together. I couldn't control my fears."

"You used your magic number. You took breaths. You calmed yourself down."

"*You* calmed me down."

"That's okay, too. I'll be here for you. I want to help you feel better in any way I can." He studied her expression. It was one he hadn't seen in a few weeks. The shuttered eyes, the tough exterior, she was giving nothing away. And then it hit him. She was leaving. In fact, it seemed like part of her had already left.

"I need to figure myself out. I need to get back out there, take on new assignments and find my courage. It was what made me successful at my job before. I have to get back to the person I was before the attack."

It was difficult to make sense of what was happening here. Adam had woken up today so full of hope and excitement for their future. Now all of that was crumbling away with every word she said.

"You can work on all that stuff here, Gracie. Caleb mentioned that Maya offered you a job at the wildlife center. Why don't you take it? It would be less stress, you'd be working with all kinds of wildlife and it would give us a chance to see where this thing between us goes."

"I don't want that job. Not now."

"Oh." This was the knife to the heart. All the other stuff—about fear and what had happened to her—he knew that they could find a way through it. But she'd been offered a fantastic job, in her chosen field, that would let her stay right here with him, and she didn't want it. "I don't understand. These feelings between us, I know they're new, but they're also big. They're life-changing. We both know that. We've both felt that."

"I still feel it. This isn't about love, Adam. If it was just about love I'd be with you every minute. I never knew I could feel the things you make me feel. I want to keep feeling them, but I can't make that my priority right now. I wish I was different. and I could stay here and take this job and be your love and just be…I don't know…a regular person."

"What is stopping you? Explain it to me in some way I can understand. I'm standing here, wanting to fight for you. For us. But you're not telling me who the enemy is."

A tear ran down her cheek and then another, and her lower lip trembled. "It's *him*, Adam. That poacher who attacked me. He beat me into the dirt and left me for dead, and the whole time he told me that he could do it because I'm a woman and I'm weak and I have no business doing a man's work. When I first tried to arrest him, he *laughed* at me." She was pushing her words out between sobs now, and Adam realized that this was the untold story, the part that no one knew—not the doctors who'd patched her back up, not Maya—the part that she'd been hiding inside all this time.

His own tears slid down. "Gracie, that man was deranged. He was out to destroy you. Whatever he said to you has nothing to do with reality or who you are. He was spouting evil from some corrupt place inside of him. None of those words were even about you."

"Maybe that's all true. But he took things from me that day and I can't seem to get them back."

Adam took a step toward her, wanting to hold her, to be the one to protect and heal her. "Gracie, there is counseling for this stuff. You can get help. And I want to be here, to support you through that, in every way I can. You don't have to keep carrying this all by yourself."

Gracie straightened her shoulders and swiped at her tears with her sleeve. "Yes, I do. The other night, even surrounded by you and Dean and so many strong people, I was on the edge of panic when I tried to help arrest Chuck Bateman. It doesn't matter how many people want to help me, or who stands beside me. If I want to get better, I have to learn to face this on my own. I have to learn to find my courage somewhere within. That man tried to make me feel so scared and weak that I'd give up and curl up and die. If I walk away from my career now, because he made me too scared to handle it, then he's won. And I won't let him win."

He'd never known how deeply she hurt. Or the kind of pain she was carrying. Love was supposed to heal, but his love wasn't enough to heal her.

"I don't think chasing poacher after poacher is going to help you fight this, Gracie. It seems to me that you're trying to get a cut to heal by picking the scab again and again. But I haven't lived with the kind of hurt you're carrying, so maybe I can't understand it. But just consider, please, that you might have this equation backward. You're telling me that if you stay, if you change your life so you can have love and family and friendship and a great job in a special town, this psychopath will have won. That just doesn't make sense to me."

She'd leaned back against her car again, restless and fiddling with her keys like she had the first day they'd met. Adam knew she was listening as best she could, but he had the sudden image of her pain built up like a fortress wall around her, so thick and dense it muffled the impact of his words. Maybe the only way for her to heal was to break through that wall on her own. But that didn't seem right to him.

He took a step toward her and held out his hand. Reluctantly she put her fingers through his. "Gracie, if you go this route, aren't you giving up all the good things you could have in life, just to disprove the nonsense some sick man spouted while trying to kill you? Is that really going to be your life's journey? Because it seems to me that if you do that, you're letting that man control not just that one day of your life, but every day from now on."

That was all he had for her. He let go of her fingers and waited, hoping that his words had broken through. That she'd step into his arms and they could start to heal.

She looked at him for a long moment, her eyes pink-rimmed and dull. "I love you so much, Adam. I love Penny and Jack, too. I'm sorry I'm like this. I'm sorry I have to go."

CHAPTER EIGHTEEN

USUALLY, SMALL SIERRA highways lifted Gracie's spirits. These old roads, overlooked by most after the big freeways were built, combined California history with so much natural beauty. Pastures gave way to vineyards as the highway wound up the foothills, and eventually the vineyards were replaced by meadows and pines. A pristine river, tumbling over granite boulders, accompanied the road for a bit. Gracie passed a town with the ruins of an old mill, where miners used to pan for gold.

Gracie had always enjoyed driving this road with the windows open, singing along with her favorite country music just as loud as she could. But today there was no trace of the elation she used to feel in this part of the mountains. Today she was empty of any identifiable feelings except an aching sadness that sat in her stomach like a lump of clay.

For the five nights since they left Shelter

Creek, she and Rio had stayed at a boarding ranch over in Grass Valley. Gracie knew the owners well—she and Rio had bunked there many times—and it was a good place to be quiet. She'd thought it would help, to sit in her own small cabin and relax. Mostly she'd cried, trying to reconcile her feelings for Adam and his kids with her own calling to fight poaching. She'd read a couple of the paperbacks from the cabin's bookshelf, and she'd taken Rio out for long, slow rides around the ranch.

Gracie had been certain that a few days on her own would help her feel better about leaving Shelter Creek. It hadn't. Then she'd figured that when her boss called her with her new assignment, her energy and enthusiasm would return. But he'd called, and she was still so tired.

She was supposed to be driving north, almost to Oregon, to patrol a remote section of coast there. Someone had been poaching in the protected herds of elk that roamed the fields and forests by the ocean. But this morning, when she'd loaded Rio in the trailer and started on her way, a voice inside her had told her *no*. That there was something she needed to do first.

So here she was.

Gracie navigated a few more turns and pulled off the road into a gravel lot. The last time she'd been here she was barely conscious, on a stretcher, being loaded into an ambulance after a hiker had come upon her lying by the side of the trail. Later she'd learned that the hiker had thought her dead at first.

She parked her SUV and commanded her pulse to settle down. She needed to do this. If she could visit the place where she'd been attacked and confront her fear, maybe she could find some peace. Maybe the panic attacks would stop, and she could get back to being her old self—tough, confident, independent, happy to be on her own.

Fifteen minutes later, Gracie had her mare saddled and they were on their way. Taking Rio was a good choice. When Gracie was attacked here, she'd been on foot. Riding her mare provided a sense of control and power that Gracie hadn't had that day. Plus, the mare's ears, pitched forward to take in the new sights and scents, were a cute and comforting sight. Her soft hoofbeats, threading through meadows dotted with yellow mules ears, made a reassuring sound.

Suddenly, much sooner than Gracie had expected, she saw it. The huge granite boulder that rose out of the earth like a monolith. And there was the fallen pine she'd hidden behind for what felt like hours, until the poacher had emerged from the woods behind the boulder. She'd confronted him and he'd jumped on her, hands reaching for her neck.

A shudder ran up Gracie's back and over her shoulders, leaving her chilled though the day was heating up. Rio sensed her tension and moved restlessly, jogging a few paces sideways. "Easy girl," Gracie said for both of their benefit. "Easy." She pressed her calves into Rio's sides, encouraging the mare forward until they were next to the boulder. That granite face was the last thing Gracie remembered seeing, until the terrified hiker had put a hand on her shoulder and brought her out of her stupor.

She swung her leg over Rio's back and dismounted. "We're okay," she told her mare, giving her a few firm pats on the neck. "We've got this."

Her heartbeat echoed in her ears. Gracie took a deep breath, took comfort in the strength of Rio's muscles under her hand. The scent of pine was all around, spicy with a hint of sweet.

Her pulse slowed and Gracie led Rio to the log. She put a hand on the rough bark and peered over to where she'd hidden the day of the attack. New pine needles had fallen, and a chipmunk had left a stash of half-chewed pine cones. There was no hint that she'd been here.

Of course not. It had been months ago.

Taking another steadying breath, she walked Rio back to the foot of the boulder. She knelt down and scooped up a handful of soil from the spot where she'd fallen. Tiny pebbles ran through her fingers. Dust rose in a small poof and drifted away. All that was left in her hand were a few dried pine needles. No blood, or pain, or fear.

It was a relief to see it. Gracie scooted around and sat with her back against the boulder. Rio nudged her cheek with her soft nose and blew horsey breath on her forehead. It felt good to smile. "Settle down, you goof," Gracie told her, and Rio sighed, cocked a rear hoof and took a three-legged rest.

Gracie tilted her head back and looked up at the bright blue sky. A jay called somewhere out in the scrub and another answered with a discordant screech. On a branch above her, a chipmunk was munching on a pine cone. Life was moving on here for everything except her. She'd thought that going back to her old job was the only way to prove she was okay. But all it showed was that she was still trapped by her attacker, fighting him, reacting to him—letting the fear he'd instilled and the pride he'd destroyed dictate her decisions.

The realization seeped in slowly, bringing with it new clarity and energy. Gracie stood and stretched and went to Rio's head. "Are you awake, sleepy girl?"

Rio answered with a gentle nuzzle to Gracie's shoulder.

"We're not going to drive north, Rio. We're not going to take that job. Someone else is going to have to save the elk this time. We're heading back to Shelter Creek."

Rio looked at her with mild interest, as if to say, *It's about time you figured that out.* Gracie swung up onto her back and they trotted back the way they'd come. As soon as she had cell phone reception, she'd give Maya a call. If she and Rio got on the road now, they could be back in Shelter Creek by dinnertime.

THE PERSON WHO came up with the idea for a Friday-night school fundraiser at the pizza parlor must be both brilliant and a sadist. Brilliant because the school was going to make a lot of money tonight. A sadist because the place was packed with kids and families, and it was so, so loud. Adam tilted his head to try to hear what Jack was saying.

"You want soda?"

Jack shouted again. "Tokens!"

"Oh, *tokens*." Adam pulled out his wallet and handed his son a five-dollar bill. "Don't spend it all in one place."

"What?" Jack cupped a hand to his ear. "What did you say?"

Adam kept it simple this time. "Have fun."

"Love you, too, Dad." Jack waved the fiver at him and dashed off through the crowd to find his friends in the maze of arcade games in the adjacent room. Adam shook his head, smiling at their miscommunication.

A small hand tugged at his sleeve. "Daddy, it's loud in here." Penny looked tired and rightly so. It had been a long week and it was close to her bedtime.

"Why don't you tuck your head against me and read the book you brought with you?" Adam patted the sleeve of his jacket. "Or I can tie a napkin around your head to muffle the noise."

"Daddy!" But Penny was smiling as she got out her book and cuddled against his side.

Adam looked around idly at the remnants of pizza scattered on paper plates. The congealing pepperoni and limp crust were a pretty good metaphor for how he was feeling right now. He wanted to be a good dad, all enthusiastic and friendly on school pizza night, but mostly he just wanted to go home and crawl into bed and sleep off the longest week of his life.

Gracie wasn't here. She'd been gone for five days and it seemed a lot longer than that. And there was a good chance she wasn't coming back. Once again, life was bashing him over the head with the same lesson. That love wasn't enough. It wasn't enough to make Gracie want to stay. It wasn't enough to make Tanya spend time with their kids.

Funny how Tanya and Gracie had both left

Shelter Creek and he was still here, carrying the torch for love. Love for his kids, which had him enduring this deafening evening. Love for Gracie, which kept him hoping that she'd change her mind.

If you love someone let them go. It was a cliché, but it had been echoing in his mind all week. Gracie needed to be free, to travel, to do her work. He could love her, but he couldn't keep her, and it was up to him to learn to accept that.

It was a tough lesson. He wasn't nearly there yet. He was at the sad, mad, depressed, grumpy and exhausted stage of setting her free.

"You look like you could use a hand here." Josie scooped up the mess on the table and dumped it in a big black garbage bag she was carrying.

Adam took a big breath so he could make his voice carry. "Did you get stuck on cleanup duty again?"

She shrugged. "Brendan is in the arcade with Jack. I might as well make myself useful." She gave Penny a wave. "How are you, sweetie? Is that a good book?"

Penny nodded.

"So how was your first week back on your old beat?" Josie shoved a stray strand of hair out of her eyes. "I barely saw you all week. You must have been busy."

"There was a lot to catch up on." He'd been trying to *keep* himself busy. Asking Dean for extra work, responding to every call whether the other deputies needed him or not, taking extra time with his paperwork. Anything was better than thinking about how much he missed Gracie.

"We're looking forward to Jack's birthday party tomorrow. Let me know if you want us to bring anything." Josie gave a little wave and went on to the next table.

Jack's birthday. How could he have forgotten that the party was tomorrow? He'd ordered a cake already, thankfully. He might have talked Wyatt into giving the kids roping lessons, but he wasn't sure if his brother had really said yes or just changed the subject and wriggled out of the conversation.

He had to get out of here. He couldn't think straight with all this noise and he had a lot of thinking to do if he was going to throw a fun party tomorrow. His boy was going to be twelve. That was a big deal. Plus, this time last year, Tanya had recently left, and they were all too stunned and upset to throw a party. Adam had to get it right this time. He lifted up the arm he'd draped over his daughter. "Penny? Can you sit up?"

Reluctantly she closed her book and scooted over on the bench. "Is it time to go?"

"Yeah. I just remembered that it's Jack's birthday tomorrow. We have a lot to do to get ready."

Penny nodded and he took her hand as they made their way to the arcade.

It took a few minutes to pull Jack away from his game, but finally they stumbled out the pizza parlor doors and into the blissfully quiet night. It was a relief to be able to hear himself think, but unfortunately Adam's thoughts went straight to Gracie. Where was she right now? Was she glad to be gone and on her way to somewhere else? Was she relieved to be on her own again?

Adam looked up at the dark sky as he and the kids crossed the parking lot. If this were a country song, he'd take some comfort in the knowledge that Gracie was under it, too, maybe looking up right now, thinking about him.

But he was no songwriter, and he needed

to toughen up. He'd been fine on his own before Gracie showed up in Dean's office. He hadn't even liked her that much at first. Gracie went off to find her former self and maybe he should do the same. Though Adam wasn't sure it was possible for him to go back to who he was before. He was pretty sure he'd left that guy behind in the forest, on a quiet trail, when he'd been out riding Bodie with Gracie and Rio by his side.

CHAPTER NINETEEN

GRACIE HIT THE brakes when she saw the cars crowded in Adam's driveway like a wayward herd of cattle. Maybe this was a bad idea. Gracie had assumed that the only adults at Jack's party would be Adam and maybe Sara, trying to keep track of a bunch of preteen boys. It hadn't occurred to her that all the kids' parents would be hanging out, too.

She backed her SUV carefully away down Adam's driveway, gripping the steering wheel tightly to stop her hands from shaking. Maybe it would be better to just go back to Maya's house now. She could stop by Adam's tomorrow and drop off Jack's present.

Gracie guided her truck onto the road and over to the wide gravel margin. She shut off the engine and pressed her forehead to the warm plastic of the steering wheel.

She'd never been a coward. She couldn't run away just because there were cars in the driveway. She had to see Adam, tell him she was back to stay and convince him to give her another chance. But he would need more than words to know she was serious. If she went to the party Adam would *see* that she'd remembered Jack's birthday and he'd know how much she cared for him and his family.

Plus, she missed Jack and Penny. And what if Penny was feeling left out, surrounded by all these older boys?

"Come on," she muttered into the silence of the cab. "This is ridiculous. You can go to a twelve-year-old's birthday party."

Except this wasn't just any twelve-year-old. This was Jack, who she adored and who she wanted to know better.

She lifted her head and glanced in the rearview mirror, rubbing at the faint pink steering wheel imprint on her forehead. *Great.* She pulled her bangs forward to hide the mark.

Gracie grabbed Jack's gift—a new set of reins she'd picked up at the tack and feed shop in town. They were a nutty brown, but black on the back side, with tiny brass studs along the section of rein adjacent to the horse's neck. She thought they looked cool and hopefully Jack would, too.

Outside the car, Gracie patted her jacket pocket to make sure she had Penny's gift as well. It wasn't Penny's birthday, but it seemed strange to only get something for Jack. She'd found Penny some cute purple socks with white horses all over them.

Gracie started up Adam's driveway on foot, willing her mind to notice her surroundings, instead of picturing what might happen when she saw Adam again. But it was hard not to dream that she'd open the door, his surprise would be replaced by a smile and his arms would open, welcoming her home. Gracie shut her eyes for an instant, imagining the feeling of being wrapped up in his embrace. The solid warmth and strength of him that seemed to speak to something so deep inside her. He was what she needed to be whole, when she'd never even realized she'd been missing such an important piece of herself.

She quickened her pace, hoping to outpace the fear that dogged her heels. What if she were too late? What if he no longer felt the same way? By the time she'd threaded her way through the cars and stepped onto his porch, she was winded. She leaned against one of the stained-wood columns to catch her breath and find her resolve.

"Gracie."

Her eyes flew open and heat flooded her cheeks. "Sara. Hi."

Sara had one booted foot on the bottom porch step, a paper grocery bag in her hand. "You're here."

"I am." Gracie gestured with her wrapped gift. "For Jack's birthday."

"Just for his birthday?" Sara came up the steps to stand beside her. Her striking green eyes were kind, but she wasn't smiling.

"To stay. I'm taking over Maya's job at the wildlife center. At least until she's ready to come back to work after the baby is born."

A slight smile reached Sara's lips. "No kidding? You're sure?"

"I'm very sure." Gracie pushed her prickly need for privacy aside. "I love him, Sara. I love the kids. I wish I hadn't left."

Sara's mouth quirked to the side in wry acknowledgment. "I think my brother might feel the same way. Does he know you're back?"

Gracie shook her head. "I was standing here getting up my nerve."

"Oh, come on. Where's the tough woman

who had my brother shaking in his boots when he first had to work with you?"

Trust Sara to give her a kick in the pants and get her smiling at the same time. "I don't know if that tough woman has ever had so much at stake before."

Sara's shoulders rose in a dismissive shrug. "When I'm competing and the stakes are high, I just focus harder. I try to be clear on exactly what I want and then I bring my best self to the moment." She shrugged. "I don't know much about love, but I know that." She put her hand on the front door. "You ready to get in the ring?"

"Sure." Gracie's heart was racing faster than it had the night they'd caught the poachers. But she'd faced that down and she could do this, too. She returned Sara's smile as best she could and followed her into the entry. Adam's hat and coat hung on the wooden pegs along the wall, greeting her like old friends. If she'd been alone, Gracie might have buried her face in his coat, inhaling Adam's fresh-air scent and all the comfort it gave her. Instead, she followed Sara into the kitchen.

"Ice cream," Sara said, setting the bag on the counter. "None of us are very good at this birthday-party thing. We remembered to order Jack's cake, but we forgot the ice cream."

"Did you remember candles?"

Sara pulled a small packet out of the grocery bag with a sheepish smile. "Luckily they had some hanging right next to the ice cream case."

"You got lucky." Gracie gestured to the pints of ice cream Sara was unloading on the counter. "Can I help you?"

"Yeah, will you grab a couple of trays? They're in that cabinet to the left of the sink."

Gracie put her gift down on the counter and went to get them. She handed the two bamboo trays she found to Sara. "Want me to grab some plates? Or bowls?"

Sara loaded the cartons and a few large spoons onto the trays. "Nah. We've got paper plates and some plastic silverware outside. If it hasn't blown away yet. The breeze is really picking up. Something else I didn't consider when Adam said he wanted to have the party outside."

"Breezy or not, outside seems like the right place for a bunch of twelve-year-old boys."

"Ha." Sara picked up one of the trays. "You

got that right. Maybe next year Adam can take them all hiking or something. They have so much energy!"

Gracie tucked Jack's gift under her arm and picked up the other tray. She followed Sara through the house to the back door. Everything looked so familiar—the big red couch in the comfortable living room, the dining room table with the chairs all pushed in neatly for once—and yet she didn't belong here anymore. She'd left, and now she was a stranger, a tentative visitor hoping to be allowed back into this family she'd so recklessly walked away from.

"It's a cowboy party." Sara glanced back as they reached the back door. "Wyatt is teaching them all to rope. It's pretty funny."

Gracie followed her out onto the back deck. A bunch of adults Gracie didn't recognize were sitting around in lawn chairs, talking and laughing. Then she spotted Josie, the receptionist at the sheriff's office, sitting among them. That's right, her son, Brendan, was friends with Jack. Josie saw her and waved, and Gracie smiled and nodded to return the greeting.

There was a hint of barbecue smoke in

the air and used paper plates were scattered around, threatening to take flight in the breeze. Gracie set her tray and Jack's present down on the closest picnic table and went to collect the plates before they blew away, smiling a greeting to the guests who thanked her. Someone had put a garbage can against the wall of the house. She was shoving the garbage inside when a voice behind her sent goose bumps over her arms. "You came all the way back here to take out the trash?"

She turned to face him, wiping her palms on her jeans. "I have a big mess to clean up. I figured I'd better get started."

For an instant she was sure he was going to smile. A tiny spark of hope flickered to life way down inside her. "I hope I'm not out of line, crashing the party like this."

He shrugged. "You had an invitation."

Gracie tried to find some warmth and welcome behind the wariness in his eyes. "I brought a gift for Jack. It's a new pair of reins."

"He'll like that. Come on over and see him. Penny's around here somewhere, too. They'll be glad you're here."

But was he? Gracie followed Adam, grabbing Jack's gift as she passed the table. They went out onto the cropped grass, stopping a few yards behind where the kids were sitting and listening to Wyatt as he demonstrated how to coil a rope. The boys had their backs to them, but Wyatt must have seen Gracie because his eyes went wide under the brim of his hat and he dropped a length of the rope, making the kids laugh.

"That's about how I felt when I saw you on the deck just now," Adam murmured.

"How do you feel now?"

He didn't answer right away. Gracie studied his face, wishing it looked more familiar. She was used to seeing warmth and humor there. Without it, Adam felt like a stranger all over again.

"I guess I'm confused."

Gracie nodded, trying to keep that glimmer of hope alight. At least he hadn't said 'angry.' Or that he just didn't care. "*I* was confused," she said as quietly as she could. "I shouldn't have left. It's not what I really want."

He glanced at her then, his dark brows drawn together. "What do you want?"

"What we had. What we could have. You, me and the kids."

"Why?"

"Because I love you. And I love them. You, and all of us together, that's what feels like home to me." It was a relief to say it. To admit that one feeling, one overwhelming emotion, took precedence over everything.

He turned toward her, and she thought he was going to reach for her, but he put his hands at his sides.

"Gracie?"

She looked down and there was Penny, standing to one side of her, eyes big, fingers twisting together like they did when she was anxious.

Gracie knelt down so she could be face-to-face with Penny, her heart melting in her chest at the sight of Penny's adorable face, scattered with wayward freckles. "Hey, Penny, how are you?"

Penny threw her arms around Gracie's neck. "You came back. I knew you would."

Gracie wrapped her arms around Penny's little back and held her tight, tears washing her eyes. "Thanks for believing in me," she said, releasing the sweet girl from her embrace. She put her hands to Penny's shoulders. "Let me look at you." She waited a moment, pretending to look Penny up and down. "Yup, you've grown in the past week. I'm sure of it."

Penny laughed. "You don't know that."

"Are your pants shorter than they were?"

Penny looked shocked. "They are!"

Gracie stood up and gave her an exaggerated shrug. "See? I know stuff." She reached into her jacket pocket and pulled out the small parcel. "I realize it's not your birthday, but I brought you a little present. I figured it might be hard to see your big brother get a bunch of loot."

"You didn't have to do that." But Adam was smiling at her and that was worth a lot more than the price of the socks. And Penny bouncing up and down in glee was absolutely priceless.

"It's nothing big."

Penny ripped open the paper and pulled out the socks. "I love them! Thank you, Gracie." She gave Gracie a huge smile.

"You are very welcome."

Adam held out his hand to Penny. "Do you want me to hold those for you?"

"Yes, please." Penny handed him the socks and the crumpled paper. "Gracie, did you get a present for Jack?"

"Of course."

"I'm going to go tell him." She dashed off to where the boys were getting ready to take their turn at roping the stumps Wyatt had set up in the field.

Gracie tapped her fingers against the leg of her jeans, trying to find an outlet for the tension inside. She'd just declared her love when Gracie showed up. Adam was busy shoving the socks into the back pocket of his jeans. The toes hung out like a purple pony bandanna.

He caught her staring and smiled. "I'm glad you're back."

"Gracie!" Jack came jogging up behind Penny. "You made it to my party!"

"I did. Happy birthday." Gracie raised her hand and Jack gave her a high five. "Looks like you're having a nice celebration." She handed him the gift. "I hope this adds to the fun."

"Awesome." Jack tore the paper with Penny-like enthusiasm and lifted out the reins. "No way." He held them up for Adam to see. "Check these out, Dad."

"Classy." Adam smiled at Gracie. "Good choice."

"I do manage to make them once in a while."

He gave a huff of a laugh. "*Once* in a while."

"Thanks for the reins," Jack said. "They're really nice, Gracie. And thanks for coming to the party." He glanced from her to his dad as if he wanted to say more, then shrugged. "Dad, can you hold these for me? It's my turn to rope soon."

"Sure." Adam winked at Gracie. "Apparently I am the receptacle for all items my children don't know what to do with."

Jack gave Gracie a shy smile. "See you around?"

"Absolutely. Have fun. Rope well." It was such a nice feeling to know that she didn't have to say any more now. She'd be here in Shelter Creek. They could see each other all the time.

"I want to rope," Penny said.

"Well, come get in line." Jack gestured to her. "Let's go."

Penny jogged eagerly after her big brother.

"I know you have to host this party," Gracie said to Adam. "And if you want help, I'm happy to stay. And maybe we could talk more? When you have a chance."

He looked at her, really looked at her finally, and the wariness was gone. "We'll talk." He reached for her hand, took it in his own and gave it a gentle squeeze. "I missed you."

She was grinning. She must look silly, but she couldn't help it. They were words she'd been desperate to hear. "I'm glad you missed me. But I'm sorry you *had* to miss me."

He let go of her hand slowly, as if he were prolonging the touch of their fingers. "We'd better focus on the party for now. That ice cream you and Sara brought out will melt soon. I should go find the cake."

"Sara got candles. I think she left them on the kitchen counter."

Adam winced. "Candles. Oops. Glad she thought of them."

He turned to go and stopped instantly. A woman was coming toward them. She was petite with neatly combed blond hair that almost reached her shoulders. On one arm was a pink leather purse and on the other an enormous gift bag.

"I made it." She smiled at Adam with a breezy confidence. "Surprise, surprise."

"You told me you couldn't come. I told the kids you weren't going to be here."

"My schedule opened up." The woman looked at Gracie, her perfectly arched brows raised. "I'm Tanya. Jack and Penny's mom."

"I'm Gracie. A friend. Nice to meet you." It was hard to focus on Tanya when Gracie could feel the tension radiating from Adam's body, even with a few feet of space between them.

"Make sure you tell the kids how long you're staying," Adam said to Tanya. "No open-ended statements. No getting their hopes up for anything more than you're sure you can give."

Tanya opened her mouth as if to retort, then shut it again. She took a visible breath and nodded once. "I'll go find them now. Nice to meet you, Gracie."

She walked off toward the kids. Gracie moved to Adam's side. "Are you okay?"

He shook his head. "They were so upset that she wasn't coming. I had to console them and now…here she is."

Gracie tried to find words that might help him feel better. "That sounds really tough, for you and the kids. Is there any hope that she's here because she is trying to change?"

"Maybe. Or maybe she'll try harder for

a while, and then disappear again. Get distracted. Change her plans. And the kids will get hurt, and there's nothing I can do about it."

They stood together, watching the kids with Tanya. Penny was hanging on tight to her mom's hand and talking a mile a minute. Jack was standing a few feet from her, head slightly down, as if he didn't know what to think.

"This can't work," Adam said quietly.

"What can't?"

He turned to face her, the lines around his mouth etched deep. "You and me, Gracie. I love you, but that can't matter. Not right now. The kids already have their mom coming and going from their life. They can't rely on her or expect anything from her. That's a big emotional mess for them to deal with."

Gracie stilled, trying to absorb the impact of his words. "You're saying you don't want to be with me?"

"I *want* to be with you. It's what I wanted before you left—what I want for myself the most, even now." His voice gentled. "Gracie, I'm sorry. If it was just us it would be different. I could be patient while you figured out if small-town life is going to work for you. But I can't do that to the kids. I can't invite you into our lives and have you walk out again. Not when their own mom is doing the same thing."

The love she could see in Adam's expression made it worse. If he was just being mean, she could be angry, and at least anger would propel her out of this party before she broke down and embarrassed them all. But here he was, raw and hurting, loving her in one breath, insisting they didn't have a future in the other. All that left Gracie was heartbreak.

"Right." She dug her fingernails into her palms, needing the pain to hold herself together. "I understand." She tried to give him a smile, to summon the tough facade that used to come so easily, but her lips were trembling. She nodded instead and walked away.

Gracie managed to keep herself together as she wove her way past the other guests. But as soon as she made it to the side of the house she broke into a run. The tears she'd tried to hold back spilled over and poured over her cheeks. She stumbled through the cars and down the driveway, blindly seeking the shelter of her SUV.

But when Gracie climbed into the driver's seat and slammed the door, she didn't feel any better. The tears still slid down. The sobs still hurt her chest. She started the engine, wanting to be as far away from Adam as possible. But as soon as she pulled out onto the road she had to accept that she was in no shape to drive.

The truth was, hitting the road wouldn't work anyway. It didn't matter how many miles she put between her and Adam. This was something she couldn't outrun. She cut the engine, leaned her cheek against the cool window and let the tears pour down.

CHAPTER TWENTY

IT WAS SHEER relief to say goodbye to the last of their guests. With a final wave to Jack's departing friends, Adam shut the front door and looked down at his son. "Well, what do you think? Was turning twelve okay?"

Jack wrapped his arms around Adam and gave him a quick, rare hug. "That was fun. Thanks, Dad."

"You're very welcome. Make sure you say thanks to Uncle Wyatt and Aunt Sara when you get a chance. They really chipped in today."

"I will. The roping was so cool."

"It was. I think a few of your friends are going to give you some competition if you decide to join the high school rodeo team. Cole was pretty good with a rope out there. So was Tommy."

"He's Tom now, Dad. Remember?"

Adam laughed. "No. I don't remember. Because it seems like yesterday that you and Tommy were running around on the deck playing with your toy trucks."

"*Try* to remember."

"I'll work on it." Adam put a hand on Jack's shoulder, and they walked through the living room and into the dining room. "I'm going to start cleaning up. Do you want to go outside and talk to your mom? I think she and Penny are out there having seconds on the cake."

"I can help you clean."

Adam stopped in his tracks. "Say that again?"

Jack shrugged. "Just seems like it was my party, my mess… I should help."

"Are you feeling okay?" Adam put a palm to Jack's forehead.

"Dad!"

Adam looked closely into eyes so like his own. "Is this about your mom?"

His son shrugged. "Maybe. She said she wasn't coming today. Then she just walked in like it's no big deal."

Adam wished he could fold Jack into his arms and hug the hurt and frustration right out of him. But emotions didn't work that way and Jack probably wouldn't appreciate all that hugging. "I know it's confusing. But in the end, she did come to see you."

"I guess. I just wish she'd show up more. Why does she have to act like this?"

"I can't answer that. But she might, if you ask her. It's okay to tell her how you feel. She's still your mom."

Jack rolled his eyes. "Yeah, right."

"She's made a lot of changes in her life this past year. But that doesn't mean she loves you and Penny any less. Could you try spending some time with her, since she's here?"

"I can try. But I don't think I should have to pretend like everything's all perfect, just because she finally decided to visit."

Adam's heart hurt. He wanted so badly to be able to put a Band-Aid on this, to fix it all for his kids. "You don't have to pretend anything. Just be honest, but also respectful."

"She doesn't respect us. She's always canceling."

"Respect isn't a trading card, or a gift exchange," Adam said. "Showing respect is just the right thing to do." Jack nodded in response, but Adam wasn't sure what he was thinking. "I'm proud of you, son. It's been a rough year and you've handled it all like a champ."

"Thanks, Dad." Jack took a step toward the back of the house and then paused. "Is Gracie going to be around more? Seems like everything is a lot more exciting when she comes over."

Adam tried not to take that too personally. "She says she wants to live in Shelter Creek now. But Gracie has a lot to figure out, too. She's used to moving around a lot. I guess we'll have to wait and see what happens."

"Is she going to be your girlfriend again?"

When Adam opened his mouth to protest, Jack gave another of his preteen eye rolls. "Oh, come on, Dad. It's obvious that you two were dating. And that you're all crazy about her. Anyone could see it from miles away."

Adam studied his son. "What do you think about that?"

"I like her. She's really cool. It's fun when we all hang out."

Adam had kept his emotions shoved far down today. He'd forced himself to focus on Jack's party and Tanya's unexpected arrival. Now the image of Gracie, devastated when she left the party, wrenched at his heart. He'd panicked when Tanya had showed up out of the blue, right after Gracie had done the exact same thing. "But what if we all hang out a lot more, and then she decides to leave and take a job somewhere else? I don't want you kids to feel bad about that."

"You mean like *Mom*?" Jack's brows went up as if he couldn't believe his dad's stupidity. "It's totally different. I mean, Gracie is nice and all, but she's not our mom." He stepped forward and put a hand on Adam's arm, just as Adam had done with him so many times. "It's okay, Dad. We'll be fine. And maybe if you don't mess it up too much, she'll decide to stick around."

Adam opened his mouth to speak, then closed it again. When had his little boy become this wise, and wisecracking, young man? Jack gave him a last pat on the arm. "I'd better go outside, speaking of Mom."

"Okay. Thanks for the talk." Adam watched his son walk away, noting the slight swagger in Jack's stride.

"He gives good advice." Sara was leaning on the kitchen door frame. "Sorry, didn't mean to eavesdrop, but I was doing dishes in there."

"And I'm sure you have some advice, too."

"How did you guess?" She stepped into the dining room and folded her arms across her chest. "I don't know what you said to Gracie today, but I saw her running by the kitchen window in tears, so it couldn't have been good."

"I told her we couldn't be together. I was worried the kids would get attached, and then be hurt."

"I think Jack just resolved that issue for you. The real question is, do you love her? Really love her?"

"God, yes. I just… She's just…" How could he explain his feelings for Gracie? She was fire and strength and softness. She was brave and beautiful and tough and funny. "I love her. But she—"

"Left," Sara finished for him. "Yes, she did. But she came back only a week later to tell you that loves you. She gave up the job that she enjoys and almost died for to live in *your* small town, where she still doesn't know that many people. Doesn't that pretty much show you her feelings? Or are you really that obtuse?"

Apparently, he was. The image of Gracie's

eyes, so full of hurt and loss today, would haunt him for a long time. "I don't even know what to say to her, I've messed this up so badly." Knowing Gracie, she was probably over at Maya and Caleb's ranch right now, packing her SUV to leave. "I wish I could go talk to her now, but I have to figure out what's going on with Tanya."

Sara rolled her eyes, looking an awful lot like Jack for a moment. "*She* was a surprise today."

"Yup." Adam glanced. "I just hope it's a sign that she's ready to act more like their mom again."

Sara folded her arms across her chest. "I'll believe it when I see it."

"I'm skeptical, too." Adam admitted. "But I can't give up. The kids want their mom in their lives. If I can get her to commit to a predictable visitation schedule, it would be so good for Penny and Jack."

"I admire your optimism," Sara said. "You go talk to Tanya. I'm going to rinse a few more dishes and then saddle up my mare and check on the cattle. I need to go far away from here, or I'll be tempted to walk out your back door and give your former wife a piece of my mind."

"That would not be very helpful." Adam smiled at his sister. "Thanks for being such a great auntie to my kids. And for saving Jack's birthday today."

Sara grinned. "Let's put ice cream and candles on the list for Penny's birthday party, so we don't forget again."

"Does anyone give out awards for most disorganized party planning?" Adam laughed, remembering his panic when he realized he'd forgotten the ice cream. "Because we could win, hands down."

Sara was still laughing when she walked out his front door. Adam wandered out back. Tanya was sitting with Penny, who'd lined up her favorite stuffed animals on a bench and was showing them to her mom. Jack was nearby, trying to rope a stump again. If someone snapped a photo of them right now, they'd look like an average family. But a photo couldn't show you broken hearts, or tattered trust. A photo couldn't measure how much there was to heal and mend.

Despite all their broken parts, Adam still believed in his family. It might look different now that he and Tanya were divorced, but it could still be a source of strength for all of them. He'd learned from Gracie that if something was worth saving, you threw yourself into it 100 percent. She hadn't given up on saving those bears, and he wouldn't give up on salvaging his family.

Adam squared his shoulders, clapped his hands three times and made sure he had everyone's attention. "Family meeting. In the living room. Everyone needs to be there in five minutes." He smiled at Tanya's shocked expression. "You, too," he told her. "Especially you. It's time we all face this situation head on, together."

GRACIE PICKED UP the mugs of tea she'd made and brought them out to the porch where Caleb sat on the steps rubbing Einstein behind the ears. Hobo was perched on the railing, his tail twitching as he peered out into the darkness of the yard. It was a gorgeous night. Cool but not cold. The fog hadn't rolled in yet and the stars hung bright in the sky. "Mind if I join you?"

Caleb turned to look at her. "Sure. I'd like the company. And the tea." He scooted over so there was room on the steps for her. He was such a big guy. When she'd first come to stay here, Gracie had been a little intimidated by his tattoos and rough-edged demeanor. But he was so kind, now he felt like an old friend.

He smiled up at her when she handed him his mug. "Peppermint," she told him.

"You made this for Maya, didn't you?"

"Yup," Gracie admitted. "But she was too tired to drink it. She went up to bed."

His smile was a little rueful as he set the steaming mug on the porch floor. "That's the weird thing about pregnancy. I miss my wife. She can't stay awake long enough to have a conversation at the end of the day."

"Her pregnancy book says she's supposed to feel better in the third trimester," Gracie said. "And after that you'll have a baby. Maybe you should enjoy your solitude while you can."

He nodded. "You have a point."

"Except not tonight," Gracie qualified. "I could really use your company tonight." She sat down on the step beside him. Einstein leaned in to give her cheek a nuzzle. "Hey, you big goof. Watch the tea." She put the mug on the step next to her, hopefully out of Einstein's way.

"Maya mentioned that you're going to look for a place in town. You know you're welcome to stay with us as long as you like."

She nudged him with her elbow. "That's so nice of you, but you two don't need me hanging around! This is your last chance to be alone together before the baby comes."

He nudged her gently back. "I'll miss your cooking, though."

"That's easily solved. I'll bring you food. I like to cook and it will help me feel better about Rio staying here. Maya won't let me pay a boarding fee."

"You are definitely not paying a boarding fee. But you can pay me in that potato soup you made a few weeks ago. And those spare ribs we had once? Oh, and the roast chicken. That was really good."

It felt good to laugh after such a sad day. She'd been so sure of her feelings, and of Adam, and of their love. To have it acknowledged, then taken away an instant later, was shattering. This must be why she'd avoided relationships for so long. On some instinctual level she must have known that if she ever gave someone her heart, she was risking annihilation.

She'd always tried to be so tough. Today she'd learned that she wasn't. Not on the inside. Not when she offered her love, and her whole life, really, only to have it handed back to her with a polite *No, thank you. Now is not a good time.*

Her eyes stung and she blinked hard. How could she have any tears left after today? Perhaps when it came to Adam, she had an endless supply.

"I'm glad you'll be taking on some of Maya's work at the wildlife center," Caleb said. "She has to start slowing down."

"I'm happy to." Gracie laid her cheek on Einstein's furry neck. That was the other piece of this disaster. She'd committed to work at the wildlife center and now all she wanted to do was leave Shelter Creek so she'd never have to see Adam again. "I can stay until she's back from maternity leave, at least."

He glanced down at her in surprise. "But I thought you and—"

Gracie quickly shook her head.

"You're kidding." Caleb clapped his palm

to his forehead. "You went out there today and he wasn't on board?"

Gracie shook her head again, not trusting herself to speak.

"I've known Adam pretty much my whole life," Caleb said. "He's always been so steady. He can't have changed his mind about you guys."

"He says I'm just not a good idea right now." She hated the way her voice shook.

"He must have his head on backward." Caleb said. "I should have a talk with him."

"Please don't." Gracie picked up her mug, the warmth offering a fragment of comfort. "He has his reasons. He's trying to protect his kids."

"From you? That makes exactly zero sense." Caleb put an arm around her shoulders and gave her a quick squeeze. "He'll come around. If he doesn't, I'll kick his butt."

He had her laughing again. This man was a godsend. "You are not going to kick his butt. I don't want him if you have to beat him up to make him love me."

"Oh, he loves you. Even I can see that." Caleb set his mug down and scooted around on the step to face her. "I'll tell you something else. What you two have? It is very different than what he had with Tanya. Those two were like an old married couple when they were in high school. I never saw Adam laugh or get excited about much. He's always been a great sergeant, but outside of work it seemed like he was on autopilot. With you, he's a different man. A way better one, if you ask me. It's like he's finally come alive."

"Alive enough to realize that I'm way too complicated."

"Are you?"

Gracie looked down at her mug, watching the steam rise and disappear into the night. "I come with my own set of issues," she admitted.

"Are you talking about what happened to you? When you were attacked?"

"Partly." She looked up from her mug to see Caleb watching her intently. He counseled veterans. He'd been through battles. "You know a lot of stuff about people's problems, right? Like when they come back from war and have PTSD and all?"

"I know a fair amount," Caleb said. "First-hand, and from other veterans."

Gracie's skin felt tight and hot. There was

still time to head this conversation off, to change the subject and move on. But maybe this was a small window opening up for her, after Adam slammed the door today. It would be hard to be happy without him, but maybe she could find some peace.

The realization she'd had when she'd hiked into the site of her assault echoed inside her. Everything had moved on. Everything but her. "I feel kind of weird even asking this, but do you think it's possible that I have some kind of PTSD?"

"I'm no doctor… I can't diagnose you. But I don't see why you wouldn't. Some guy attacked you, out in the middle of nowhere, and came pretty darn close to killing you. That seems like a pretty big deal."

"I guess it is. But other people have been attacked, too. People have had car accidents and other scary stuff happen to them. Are they all walking around all messed up inside?"

"Some are, for sure." Caleb smiled slightly. "I know you won't want to hear this because you're like me. You pride yourself on being strong. But not everyone who goes through something traumatic gets PTSD. Those of us who do…well, they don't entirely know why it happens. Genetics, maybe."

"Great. Lucky us."

"If you don't mind me asking, what's going on?"

There was that stinging behind her eyes again. Her voice was shaky. "I don't know. Mostly I'm fine. But I'm always a little on edge, like I'm expecting something bad to happen any moment. It's hard to relax and just be."

He nodded. "Sounds familiar."

"And I jump right out of my skin if I get startled by anything—like a loud noise or a deer jumping across my path. Then it's like my heart can't calm down. It just gets going faster and faster, and it's hard to breathe."

"A panic attack." Caleb looked at her with concern. "Have you talked to a doctor about any of this?"

All Gracie had to do was look at him. He laughed. "Of course you haven't. Does Adam know?"

Gracie nodded. "He's had to calm me down a few times."

Caleb smiled. "I imagine he's actually pretty good at that."

"He is. Adam is so kind and understanding. He's—" He wasn't hers anymore.

"Are you open to some advice?" Caleb picked up his mug and took a sip. It was cute to see him drinking tea when he looked more like someone who'd be downing a six-pack on his porch.

"I am. I think I'd better figure this out." Especially if she was going to go back to her old job once Maya was ready to work full-time. No way was she going to stay in Shelter Creek and watch Adam live his life without her.

"You've got to see a doctor. Get a physical and make sure you don't have anything going wrong up here." Caleb tapped a finger to his temple. "You were hit in the head really hard. Your first step is to make sure no new damage has shown up."

"Yikes. Okay." Gracie took a sip of her tea and let the warm, spicy liquid ease some of her stress. "Then what?"

"If nothing is physically wrong, you need to see a psychiatrist. There are medicines to help stop panic attacks. And there's all kinds of therapy you can try."

"Therapy?" Gracie couldn't hide her disdain.

Caleb smiled slightly. "Don't knock it until you try it. I wouldn't be here with Maya, and a baby on the way, if I hadn't accepted some help. And some of that help was therapy."

It was really hard to imagine Caleb sitting in a therapist's office telling someone all his troubles. "I keep thinking that as time goes by, my memories of the attack will fade. Then they won't feel so real anymore."

"I guess they might, eventually." Caleb put down his tea and held out his hand to Einstein. The old dog left his spot near Gracie to snuffle at Caleb's fingers. Then he flopped down on the porch with a blissed-out sigh while Caleb scratched behind his ears. Only then did Caleb look up at Gracie. "The thing is, do you really want to wait around, letting all this stuff bother you and mess up your life, while you hope that it will fade away? Even if it did fade, that might take years."

"I hadn't thought about it that way." Years of this? Suddenly medicine didn't sound so scary.

"I'd hate for you to lose out on a big chunk of your life just because you're too scared to tell your doctor what's up."

"I'm not scared!" She noted his smile. "You did that on purpose."

"It worked, didn't it? If you need a doctor, we've got someone good here in town. He helped me out a lot. If you'd rather talk to a woman, I'm sure he could help you find someone."

"I'll go see him." Though just the thought had anxiety slithering up her spine. But she couldn't let fear keep winning. This was her time to really face it.

"I'll write down his information for you tomorrow."

"You're a good man, Caleb. Thank you so much for talking to me." Gracie picked up her tea and stood. "I think I'm going to go to bed. It's been a really long day." Maybe it was heartbreak and the aftermath of way too many tears. Maybe it was relief that she was going to get help. Whatever the reason, she was suddenly wrung out. A popped balloon, losing air fast.

"Get some rest. I'll feed Rio in the morning so you can sleep in if you want."

"You don't have to do that."

"Soup," he said, lifting his mug toward her in a salute. "Potato leek soup."

"It's a deal." She gave Caleb a wave and headed inside, so grateful that she'd found the courage to talk with him. He'd given her a lot to think about, and a little bit of hope to hang on to.

CHAPTER TWENTY-ONE

THE DRIVEWAY AT the Bar D had never seemed this long before. Maybe any drive was long when there was so much potential happiness or heartbreak waiting at the end of it. Adam was hoping for a chance to talk with Gracie. He'd been awake most of the night trying to find the right words to apologize and win her back. But here it was, just before noon on Sunday, and he still didn't have them.

Adam took in the neat fences along the road, the cattle grazing on the bone-dry September hills in the distance. This place had come a long way in the past couple years. Adam was grateful for that. He'd spent way too many nights pulling Caleb out of bar fights, even tossing his friend in the drunk tank, hoping it would teach him a lesson. Maybe his tough love had played a small part in Caleb's present-day happiness and success. He liked to think so.

Today Adam was here to reach for his own happiness. As the big wooden barn came into sight, he remembered the last time he'd been here, for Maya and Caleb's barbecue. How he'd watched Gracie console Penny when she'd gotten hurt. He'd been so struck by her sweet, humorous way with his daughter. It was a memory he'd cherish.

He pulled his truck alongside the barn and Caleb came out to meet him. His friend put a big hand on the door frame, looking down at him through the open window with a slight smile. "I don't see you groveling."

"I don't need to grovel for you, do I?" Adam cut the engine and Caleb stepped back to let him get out of the cab.

"You just might. I'm pretty fond of Gracie. And stay away from Maya. She's got extra hormones, and you are currently on her bad side."

"I'll keep that in mind. Is Gracie in the barn?"

"Nope." Caleb paused as if he wanted to torture Adam just a little. "She took Rio into the round pen. She's doing some training with her."

Something in Caleb's eyes had Adam hesitating. "Is there something else you want to say?"

"Yes, there is." Caleb paused as if collecting his thoughts. "We all mess up sometimes. Or a lot, in my case. You saw me ruin my life over and over. And you were always there for me, encouraging me to shape up, buying me breakfast at the diner, even shoving me in the back of your patrol car. Now you've messed up with Gracie, and I want to have your back now."

"But…" Adam could read the conflict in Caleb's eyes.

"Gracie was pretty broken up when she came home last night. I don't want you to talk to her today if you're just going to make it worse. I don't think she's up for much more heartache."

"I hate that I hurt her. It won't happen again."

"Are you sure?" Caleb crossed his arms over his chest like a judge in a cowboy hat.

Adam's pride could take a few hits, but only so many. "Do I have to answer to you?"

"Think of me as one of her big brothers. Or her dad."

Adam took a deep breath to keep from just shoving his friend out of the way. He needed to see Gracie, not waste time here with her self-proclaimed dad. "I love her. You know I do. More than I've loved anyone, besides the kids. And that's a different kind of love anyway."

Caleb moved out of his way. "Then why don't you go tell her that?"

Adam clung to the last thread of his patience. "Because you're standing here like the troll at the bridge, not letting me cross."

"You passed the test. Go get her." Caleb walked a couple paces backward and pointed a finger at Adam. "Do not make her cry. Do not mess this up. For both your sakes."

"Yes, Dad."

Caleb grinned and turned away, disappearing into the shadows of the barn.

That was a hurdle Adam hadn't expected. But he could understand Caleb's loyalty. Gracie was special. He felt protective of her, too. Which made it even worse that he'd been the one to bring her so low.

The round pen was beyond the barn. Its high wooden fencing made it a good place to train a horse. Less for them to see, easier for them to focus. Quietly, Adam climbed up on the rails. Gracie was circling the edge of the pen with Rio. It took a moment for Adam to realize that she didn't have a lead rope on her mare. Rio was following her just because she wanted to.

Gracie turned toward the center of the pen and Rio was right behind her. They both saw Adam and stopped in their tracks. Rio's ears came forward like she recognized him. Gracie's mouth curved into a frown.

"You two look good together."

Gracie took a step back and put her hand on Rio's neck. "What are you doing here?"

"I was hoping we could talk." Adam pulled his hat off. It seemed like the right thing to do when he was begging. "I brought some lunch. Are you hungry?"

"No."

She looked pale and tired as she shoved her hair out of her face in a gesture so familiar it tugged at Adam's heart.

"I made a huge mistake yesterday at the party. I would love a chance to apologize. And to explain."

"I don't think I can handle your explaining today," she said quietly. "I don't need any more reasons anyway. You were pretty clear."

"No, I was pretty wrong. *Really* wrong. I love you, Gracie. I love you so much. Can we just talk? Not over this fence. Do you want to go for a walk? You can bring Rio."

Gracie hesitated for an infinite moment,

studying him with a solemn expression on her
face. He'd never seen her look so vulnerable,
and it was all he could do not to leap over the
fence and take her in his arms. But he'd lost
that right yesterday and it might just take a
miracle to get it back.

"Okay." She walked over to the opposite fence, with Rio plodding faithfully behind her. She'd hung the lead rope there, and
when she snapped it onto Rio's halter, Adam
opened the gate so she could bring the mare
out. He shut the gate behind them and when
he turned around, Gracie had already started
along the dirt lane that led across a small valley toward the hillside pastures. She and Rio
were ambling slowly; it didn't take more than
a few strides for Adam to catch up.

"Thanks for doing this." He glanced over at
her, but she was looking straight ahead, and
he could see how tense the muscles were at
the back of her jaw. This was his moment, and
he glanced at the sky, sending up a quick plea
that he'd somehow find the right words. "I
am in love with you. Totally in love with you.
That hasn't changed. It will never change."

The deep breath she took was audible, but
she still wouldn't look at him. "That's nice to

hear." He'd never heard her voice so hoarse, or so tentative.

"I don't want us to be apart. What I said yesterday about this being too complicated… that was me worrying, as a dad. The kids had been so upset because Tanya was going to skip the party. Then she showed up and all I could think was *here we go again*. More drama. More long talks trying to help the kids process her behavior. I lashed out at you when really, I was angry with her."

She glanced his way with a faint flicker of interest, then turned her gaze forward again.

Adam cleared the emotion from his throat. "Gracie, you've been there for the kids every time they've wanted you. Even when you barely knew them, or me. You are *not* the problem. It's the opposite. You've brought so much goodness into their lives. You've made them feel important and cared for. You make me feel the same way."

Gracie stopped and let Rio nibble on the grass at the side of the lane. When she looked at him, Adam was struck again by the glorious blue of her eyes, like windows into a summer sky. But he could see that her eyelids were puffy from crying. "I really hate that I hurt you."

She lifted her slim shoulders in a small shrug. "I hurt you, too, when I left."

"You did. It hurt like heck. But I understood, on some level, that you needed to go."

"I had something I needed to learn. As soon as I learned it, I came back."

He was intrigued. "What did you learn?"

"What you'd already tried to tell me. That I was so intent on proving that my attacker hadn't broken me, or changed me in any way, that he became the driving force in my life. I was determined to return to my work and triumph over my fears, and I made that goal more important than the people I love." She flashed him a wry smile. "I guess I should have just listened to you and saved us both a lot of heart ache."

Adam returned her smile, relishing the connection building between them. "It's nice of you to say it, but I think there are things we have to learn on our own. We can't really hear them from another person."

Gracie nodded. "I had to go back to the place where he attacked me. I had a hunch that I'd never feel free of him unless I faced what happened."

"That hunch took a whole lot of courage," Adam said.

She nodded. "I guess it did. It was scary, but I stood in the exact spot where he attacked me. I thought it would be this big emotional moment, but there was nothing. Just birds flying around and new growth on the pines, and all I could think was that life there had moved on. I was the only thing stuck back in that day, in that place. And once I realized that, I didn't feel stuck there anymore."

Man, she was tough. Would he have the courage to go back to a place like that, alone? "I'm really glad it helped you. It was a bold move to go there."

"It was worth it. Because then everything became clear and I knew that what I truly wanted was time with you and the kids, and to do some good work with wildlife. Shelter Creek offers me all of that, and so much more."

"I'm happy to hear you say that."

She was twisting the end of Rio's lead rope in her hands. "Will the kids be okay, though? I don't want to cause any problems in their lives."

"My kids are tougher than I realized. Do

you know what they did yesterday after you left?"

She shook her head.

"They sat down with their mom and told her how they feel. How much they missed her. How hard it was to never know when they'd see her, or if she'd keep her plans with them. I might have facilitated the talk a tiny bit, but it was Jack and Penny who did the talking."

Her smile was like sunshine emerging from the clouds. "That is incredible. What a brave thing for them to do."

Adam could see the pride in her eyes and hear it in her tone. The fact that Gracie was proud of his kids made him fall a little harder for her, if that was even possible.

"How did she take it?" Gracie put her hand up. "Wait, I'm sorry. I'm not trying to pry. But was Tanya kind to them?"

"She was. And it seems like she truly wants to do better. She told me, when I walked her out to her car, that she's thinking of moving to Santa Rosa, so she'll be closer to the kids. And she wants to go back to school and study accounting." Adam had to smile at the memory of that revelation. "I've known her most of my life. I had no idea she even liked numbers."

"It will be so good for the kids if she's close by. As long as she keeps her promises to them."

"That's the catch," Adam said. "We'll just have to wait and see."

"We?" Gracie's brows rose in their graceful questioning arc.

Adam realized his blunder. "If that's what you want. I don't want to assume anything. Not after the way I acted yesterday."

"We." She smiled at him. "I like the sound of it."

"Gracie…" If there were any other words to say this moment, they were lost in his sense of awe. At her faith in him. At her willingness to change her life, so they could be together. He stepped toward her in a wordless plea. She answered by folding herself against his chest.

Adam wrapped his arms around her and closed his eyes, reveling in the pressure of her body against his. Every piece of his world was perfectly in place, now that she was here. "I love you," he whispered into her thick silky hair. He kissed her softly, just above the ear. "I love you so much."

She answered by holding him closer, her strong arms on his back, pulling him in. "I love you back," she whispered. Adam inhaled her scent—fresh air, a little vanilla and a lot of…horse?

Adam opened his eyes just as Rio's pink-and-gray nose tipped his hat brim back. "Hey!" He stepped away from Gracie as the mare nuzzled his ear, bathing him in her grassy breath.

"Rio!" Gracie laughed as she looped fingers through her mare's halter and backed her up a couple paces. "Are you jealous?"

"Either that or she's just happy. Maybe she thinks we make a good team." Adam straightened his hat and held out his knuckles. Rio nibbled at them with her soft lips. "Don't worry, Rio. Gracie has enough love for both of us."

Gracie hugged Rio's neck. "I have so much love right now, I'm not even sure what to do."

"I have an idea." Adam said. "Excuse us for a moment, Rio." He took Gracie's hand and pulled her toward him. He tipped his head to kiss her once, long and slow. Afterward he kept his lips near hers, reluctant to have more than an inch or two between them. "I promise

I'll do everything in my power to help you be happy in Shelter Creek, Gracie. Anything and everything you need, I will find a way to make it happen."

"Thank you," she whispered and brought her lips to his in a perfect, soft caress that lingered until Adam stepped back, needing air and sunshine and a reminder that they had time now. A lot of time. They could take this slow.

"How about that picnic? The kids are with Tanya. She stayed at the inn in town last night and took them to the beach for today."

"I'd like that." She looked at him in wonder. "I'm actually really hungry."

Adam smiled. "Does that mean you're feeling better? That you can forgive me for yesterday?"

"We've each backed away once. I think we're even."

"I know I'm all done with backing away. That was way too painful."

Gracie reached up to trail her fingers lightly along his jaw. "*Way* too painful. You are it for me, Adam Sears. You're stuck with me. I'm not leaving again."

She'd always been so guarded, but now her

shields were down and Adam could see the warmth and love shining in her eyes. "I'm the luckiest man on this planet. Thank you for coming back to me."

"Thank you for coming here, for me." She kissed him one more time, then slipped her hand in his and gave a gentle tug. "Let's walk back." She clicked her tongue to get Rio walking with them and the mare followed obediently.

As they strolled along the lane, Adam tried to find a way to take it all in. To imprint this moment into his memory so he would be able to bring it out again to study and cherish. Not just because of Gracie's love but all of it—her hand holding his so firmly, Rio's hooves clopping softly in the dust behind them, a couple of crows arguing up on the roof of the barn, the sun so bright it seemed to bleach the color out of the landscape.

Gracie squeezed his hand. "It's perfect, isn't it?"

"Absolutely." Adam brought their clasped hands to his lips and brushed a kiss over her knuckles. "Absolutely perfect."

CHAPTER TWENTY-TWO

THE LOBBY OF the Shelter Creek Wildlife Center was crowded with visitors, talking and laughing and occasionally attempting to supervise over-excited children. Even though Gracie had been working here for less than a month, she felt pride as she looked around at the busy Fall Family Fling, a fundraiser to help pay for permanent animal habitats.

"The kids are loving this." Adam put his arm around Gracie's waist. "Am I allowed to do this if you're on the job?"

"For a moment. When no one is looking." They were standing at the side of the lobby while most kids and their parents clustered around tables set up all around the room. There were arts and crafts stations, animal identification games, touch tables where little fingers could handle samples of bones and fur. The buzz of excitement and the smiling faces were strong evidence that this event was a huge success.

Gracie leaned against Adam, relaxing into the tall strength of him for just a moment. She was still getting used to this. That they could touch each other, show their feelings—that they were a couple. Adam was her boyfriend, though that flimsy word didn't do justice to a man like him. Adam was a father, an experienced lawman, and the tall, dark and handsome love of her life. He wasn't a *boy*friend.

Penny came running toward them and instinctively Gracie pulled away from Adam. The kids knew they were a couple, but she didn't want to overwhelm them with it, or cause them to feel left out. "What do you have there?" She knelt down to see the drawing Penny displayed so proudly. "Is that a fox?"

Penny nodded. "Vivian took a bunch of us to the fox pen. We had to be really, really quiet. Then we could peek through the fence and observe them. We drew what we saw."

"Observe." Gracie looked up at Adam. "That's a mighty scientific word."

"Vivian says it means to look really carefully at what an animal looks like and what it's doing."

"Vivian is a good teacher." No wonder she was head of education here at the wildlife center. She was a natural with kids. Gracie had *observed* Vivian over the last couple weeks and was in awe of the way she could hold the attention of large groups of children and guide them through a complicated, hands-on lesson. Gracie had barely learned how to talk to Penny and Jack; she couldn't imagine being able to connect with a bunch of kids that way.

"Let me take a look at this fox." Adam knelt down, too, and took the drawing from Penny. "That bushy tail is something else." Penny had started the drawing with accuracy but seemed to have gotten a little carried away. Something like sparks seemed to be flying off the fox's tail. "Is that sunlight?"

"It's the fox's superpowers." Penny might as well have said "duh" to her dad, from the tone she'd used, and Gracie pressed her lips together to hide a smile. "Vivian said the fox has superpowers. Like big ears to hear a lot of stuff. And a big tail so it can climb and keep its balance."

Gracie's jaw dropped a little. "You learned a lot out there. And now that you mention it,

I can see the superpowers around the ears, too." She pointed to more little yellow sparks emanating from the fox's head and glanced over at Adam. He was watching his little girl with such a proud expression that Gracie's heart melted.

"I am not sure I've ever seen a picture of a fox that I enjoyed more than this one." He gave Penny's ponytail a tug and stood up. Gracie stood, too. "Do you want me to hold your drawing for you while you do something else? I see an opening over at the touch table. And isn't that a friend of yours from class, at the animal track stamps?"

"That's Emma. Can I go over there?"

"Of course. We'll be right here if you need us."

Penny ran off and Gracie leaned against Adam while they both studied the lovely little drawing. The fox's black nose was a little smeared and its body was rounder than any real fox could be. "It's beautiful, isn't it?" Gracie looked up at Adam. "I love her creativity."

He grinned. "Superpowers. Awesome."

She could stay here a long time, talking about Penny and Jack and anything under the sun. But she was supposed to be working. "I should probably walk around and see if I can be useful."

"I should probably go find Jack. He said he was going to see the hospital. I guess Emily is doing a demonstration?"

"She's giving tours of the wildlife hospital and trying to show people what it's like to be a wildlife veterinarian," Gracie said. "She put up a bunch of X-rays, and photos of wounded wildlife and things like that. I hope it doesn't gross any kids out."

Adam laughed. "I think I may need to check that out. Maybe I can sneak in there while Penny is busy."

"It's pretty fascinating. I got to watch her sew up a rabbit's ear the other day. She definitely knows what she's doing." Gracie tapped the fox picture lightly. "Keep an eye on Penny and I'll look around for Jack as I wander."

Outside, Gracie found Vivian kneeling by the raccoon habitat with a small group of kids and their parents, pointing out the raccoon's den, which looked like a hollow log. "Vivian, do you need anything?"

Vivian straightened and put a hand to her lower back. "I'm good. Just a little tired."

Wisps of Vivian's dark hair had slid out of her ponytail and wafted around her face. She was so sweet and always seemed just a bit delicate to Gracie. "Would you like to take a break? I can fill in here if you want. I'm not sure what to say, but I can make some stuff up. I have some good raccoon stories, too. Like the time they ate a huge hole in my backpack and stole most of my food when I was twenty miles in from the nearest trailhead."

Vivian laughed. "Remember, we're trying to get them to like raccoons and donate to improve their habitat. Maybe save that story for another time."

Though they'd only gotten to know each other in the past couple weeks, Vivian already felt like a good friend. It was so easy to laugh with her. "I'll save that story. But seriously, why don't you go get a drink or a bite of something?"

Just then a girl and boy ran up. They were older than Penny by a few years at least. "Aunty Vivian, can we go inside and do the stuff in there?"

"Of course. Where is your uncle?"

"Right here." Jace tipped his hat to Gracie. "Good to see you again. Congratulations on your new job. Not quite as exciting as trapping poachers in the forest in the middle of the night, though, is it?"

Vivian smiled up at her husband. "Jace talked about that night for a week straight."

"It was like being in the cavalry," Jace said. "It was awesome riding down that dark fire road in a big group of riders like that. Anytime you need help catching a poacher, sign me up. Oh, and the other great part of that night? Seeing those guys handcuffed and heading off to jail."

"That was satisfying," Gracie said.

Jace nodded. "How's the case against them unfolding?"

"We turned all of our evidence over," Gracie explained. "Including everything we found in the barn. The Department of Wildlife should have a pretty strong case against them."

"I hope you do." Jace scowled. "What a couple of lowlifes."

Just then, Maya and Adam joined them. "It's getting kind of stuffy in that lobby," Maya said, fanning herself with a flyer for the fundraiser. "Or maybe I'm just getting more pregnant."

Vivian laughed. "I am pretty sure it's both. Do you want to go take a break in the office, Maya? Gracie and I can handle anything that comes up."

Maya smiled at Gracie. "Speaking of which, something has come up. I know today was supposed to be a fun day hanging out here, but I might need you to go out to a ranch."

"Sure," Gracie said. "Though after watching you sweet-talk these ranchers all week, I'm wondering if I'm even qualified for this job. You know I'm not known for my diplomacy skills."

Adam laughed abruptly then stopped, putting his hands up in apology. "Sorry, don't know what came over me."

Gracie delivered a light punch to his upper arm. "Be nice."

"Always." He pulled her in close to his side, his arm around her shoulders.

Maya looked from one of them to the other and then at Jace and Vivian. "Can you believe these lovebirds? Were Caleb and I ever like that?"

"Don't get me involved in any relationship analysis," Jace protested. "You and Caleb were your own unique pile of trouble."

"That's one way to describe it," Maya said. "Anyway, Gracie. You won't have to talk to the rancher today, I don't think. But he is having a mountain lion problem. He lives south of Shelter Creek and his property borders Windy Ridge Open Space Preserve. A lion came onto his property and went after his sheep."

"Uh-oh. Did it get any?"

"His livestock dogs sounded the alarm, and since this guy was already nearby in his truck, he managed to get over there and take a shot at it as the dogs chased it off. He says he thinks he might have hit it, but he's not sure."

"I thought the whole point of those dogs was that you didn't have to shoot at wild animals. They'd just scare them away," Gracie said.

"That's the idea." Maya shrugged. "This is the kind of stuff we deal with. We can go out and talk to him about it later, but right now someone needs to try to track that lion and see if it's hurt." She glanced down at her belly. "That person can't be me."

"Rio and I will go." Gracie tried to sound professional, but she knew her excitement came through loud and clear. "I haven't had a work mission on horseback for too long."

Maya grinned. "I figured you'd be happy to get out on the trail." She looked at Adam. "I'd rather send two people out on this mission, since it's a wounded lion and all."

"Viv and I can take your kids back to our place, Adam," Jace said. "Amy and Alex would love to hang out with them. Maybe we can grill some burgers and they can all have a picnic dinner outside."

"Are you sure?" Adam looked at Gracie, a smile building in his eyes. "If it's not too much trouble, I'd like to go along. Seems like a long time since Gracie and I roamed the woods looking for wild animals."

"Mainly you'll be looking for tracks and traces of blood," Maya said. "I don't actually want you guys to get cozy with a possibly injured mountain lion."

"Fine, tracks and blood then," Gracie said. "We're on it."

"I'll go talk to the kids," Adam said.

"I'll go back to the Bar D and get Rio ready." Gracie wanted to run full tilt for her SUV. Her new job had been interesting so far, but tracking a mountain lion was the kind of work she loved most.

"Bodie and I will pick you up. I know the area Maya's talking about," Adam said.

"I don't know that I've ever seen two people more excited to go to work on a Saturday." Jace grinned. "Adam, I'll come with you to find your kids, so they know that they're my rug rats for the rest of the day."

Adam gave Gracie a quick kiss on the cheek. "I'll be at the Bar D as soon as possible."

He and Jace hurried off to find Penny and Jack.

Maya put a hand on Gracie's arm. "Be careful, okay? If you find it and it's wounded, you'll have to make the call."

A chill sent bumps over Gracie's arms. "You mean euthanize it?"

Maya nodded. "I'm sorry to have to even say it, but we shouldn't let it suffer if it can't be saved."

Gracie was used to stopping other people from killing animals. She'd never had to kill one herself. "What if the wound doesn't seem bad?"

"Use your GPS to note where it is. We can get out there and try to trap it early tomorrow morning."

"I hope this rancher is a really bad shot," Gracie said.

Maya nodded. "Me, too. Best-case scenario is that you find the lion, or at least its tracks, and there's no blood anywhere. But regardless, enjoy it out there and let me know what you find as soon as you can."

Gracie could see the twinge of regret in her friend's eyes. "Hey. You'll be back chasing lions in no time, okay? Maybe we can chase some together."

"You're right. It's just funny how life can change so quickly."

"Things are definitely changing." She took Maya's hand and gave it a quick squeeze. "We can handle it, though, right? We're the toughest women we know."

Maya laughed. "You got that right. Now go get Rio and hit the trail."

THE SUN WAS setting in a haze of orange and pink. Adam watched Gracie, sitting tall in the saddle as Rio picked her way along the narrow deer trail that led back to where he'd parked his truck. He stood up in his stirrups to stretch his back. It had been a couple weeks since he'd spent several hours in the saddle like this. They'd zigged and zagged along this ridge. They'd followed the fence line where the rancher had shot at the lion. Fortunately, there'd been no sign of blood anywhere. Finally, way on the other side of the ridge, they'd found the big cat, lounging gracefully on the branch of a huge old oak, as if it hadn't a care in the world.

Relief had washed over him from head to toe. He'd brought his gun along but had dreaded finding the lion so wounded that he'd have to use it.

He'd wanted to chase the lion off, once they spotted it. To get it running away from the ranch and the temptation of the livestock and the danger of the rancher and his shotgun. But Gracie had told him no. Maya would call in a research team from a local conservation group to come back out here and try to catch, study and put a radio collar on the lion tomorrow. She'd call the rancher back and try to convince him to put his gun away and trust his dogs to do their job.

They reached the dirt road where they'd left his truck and trailer and Gracie swung her leg easily over Rio's back and dropped to the ground. "That was amazing." She smiled up at him. "And tomorrow I might get to learn how to collar it. I think I like my new job."

He didn't want to dampen her enthusiasm, but he had to ask. "Does it bother you that, if you catch it, it will wear a big collar around its neck from now on?" He swung his leg over and landed on the ground next to Bodie, then turned to look at Gracie.

"It makes me sad. In my perfect world, every animal would be free to live how it was meant to. But we don't live in that world. This lion's terrain sits between two ranches, a small town and a local highway. If we put a radio collar on it, we can map where it goes."

"What do you learn from all that, though?"

"A lot." Gracie ticked ideas off on her fingers. "We can see if it's heading onto private property. We can see if it goes into town, which could be a bad sign that it's trying to scavenge or snack on people's pets. We can see if it crosses that highway to hunt. If it does, and we learn where it's crossing, we can try to prevent it getting hit by a car, which happens to mountain lions way too often."

Adam flipped up his stirrup and loosened the cinch on Bodie's saddle. "I had no idea you knew so much about lions."

She laughed and walked Rio a little closer to the trailer. "I've spent the last two weeks following Maya around at work. I can't help but learn about lions. But with bears migrating south into this area, pretty soon we'll be talking to folks about them as well."

She looked so happy as she slid Rio's bridle off that Adam laughed.

"What's so funny?"

"It's just really nice to see you so enthusiastic about work. I was worried this new job might not be exciting enough for you."

Her shoulders raised in a slight shrug. "It's not perfect, but I feel like I can help make a difference here. And if I get to spend some time like this, wandering out in wild places with you and our horses, I know I'll be just fine."

Adam walked Bodie close enough that he could reach for Gracie's hand. "I'll wander with you any time. Lions, bobcats, bears, we can chase them all, as long as you look as happy as you do now." He tipped his hat back so he could kiss her as she smiled. And kiss her again. And send out a silent thank-you to all the migrating bears out there. If they hadn't wandered down this way, he'd never have met the love of his life.

CHAPTER TWENTY-THREE

"GRACIE, COME UP here with me!" Penny swished her princess skirt as she sashayed around the gazebo in the park at the center of Shelter Creek.

"Yeah, Gracie, get on up there." Jack, dressed as a cowboy, was grinning so hard he looked like one of the thousands of jack-o-lanterns scattered around town tonight.

"Don't rub it in," Gracie muttered. She picked up the pink satin skirt of her princess dress and looked around the square, glad that most families were wandering the neighborhood streets, trick-or-treating. "Why couldn't *we* have dressed as twins?"

"Because it would be lame to twin with my dad's girlfriend. And Dad and I are kind of twins."

"Which means you're both just wearing what you wear every weekend." Gracie looked over at Adam, who was following their exchange with barely concealed mirth. She glared at the phone in his hand. "No photos, please."

"Excuse me? My adorable daughter and my gorgeous girlfriend dress up as twin princesses and I'm not supposed to take photos?"

"Well, no video, then. There's a good chance I won't make it up the gazebo steps without falling on my face." Gracie tottered across the grass in the silver high heels Penny had insisted she wear to look like a "real princess." Her enormous skirt, a swishing and swaying bell, made it hard to see where she was stepping. And who was the moron who invented heels? Now she knew why she'd never worn them before.

Adam hastened to her side and offered his arm. "I'm no Prince Charming but let me help you."

Gracie accepted his support gratefully, trying not to cling to his arm for dear life. She eyed the gazebo, trying to judge if her feet, lost somewhere beneath the giant skirt, were near the base of the steps yet.

"Come on, Gracie," Penny called. "You look so pretty. Just like Snow White. Except your crown is crooked."

With her free hand, Gracie managed to catch her tiara before it slid down her nose. "This isn't working. I don't have tiara hair."

Adam laughed. "I don't know what tiara hair is, but I know I owe you big-time for tonight." He took off his cowboy hat and kissed her cheek. "You've made Penny's Halloween so special. And she's right. You look beautiful. Though it's a little hard to get used to seeing you in a dress."

"Don't get used to it. Please." Gracie inched forward until the tip of her toe hit the riser of the first step. "You will probably never see me in a dress again. Especially after I fall and break my neck, which is looking pretty likely."

"I won't let you fall. I promise." He gave her a wink. "Unless you want to fall into my arms, that is."

Gracie made a face at him and navigated the first step.

"Only two more to go," Adam announced cheerfully. "Ready? And…step."

Gracie stepped, and stepped again, and realized with relief that she was on the deck of the gazebo. No more stairs, at least until it was time to leave. Maybe she *would* just fall into Adam's arms. It would be a lot safer than walking down stairs in this getup.

"Let's dance, Gracie!" Penny took her by the hand, gliding back and forth in her best impression of a singing Disney princess. Gracie swayed awkwardly next to her, cheeks blazing. How had she let herself get talked into this?

The truth was she hadn't been able to say no when Penny had asked her. No way could she crush the excitement in the sweet girl's eyes. She looked down at Penny's beaming smile and relaxed a little, lifting their joined hands so Penny could turn under them. "Adam Sears, put that camera away," she murmured as they danced by him.

"Not on your life. I want to remember this moment forever."

"Are you guys ready to go trick-or-treating?" Jack had joined them in the gazebo and was leaning against one of the columns.

"Not until you dance with us," Gracie crooned in her best princess voice.

"Seriously? No way." Jack crossed his arms and shook his head.

"Plus, you already went trick-or-treating in downtown Santa Rosa with your mom this afternoon," Adam reminded him. "You've got a whole lot of candy waiting for you at home."

"Yeah, but there is no such thing as too much candy," Jack said. "It's a known fact."

"Ah," Adam said, snapping a picture of Jack. "I guess I never learned that one."

"Come on, Jack." Penny went to her brother and tugged at his arm. "Be happy. This is a special night. *Remember?*"

Jack rolled his eyes, but after glancing around to make sure they were alone, he let his sister tug him to the middle of the gazebo. He picked her up and spun her around, making her shriek with laughter.

Adam held out his hand to Gracie and pulled her in to dance close, or as close as her skirt would allow. "I didn't know Halloween could be so romantic." He smiled down at her. "Yet here I am, in a fancy gazebo, dancing with my very own princess."

"With a crooked crown." Gracie took her hand off Adam's shoulder to push the tiara away from her face again.

"I wish I had a better crown to offer you." Adam took a step back from her and knelt down. He reached into his pocket and pulled out a ring. A ring that sparkled in the lamp-light. "Will this do?"

Everything around her froze, her breath caught, even her heart seemed to take a pause. They'd talked about marriage a couple times. They both knew, so clearly, that they'd be to-gether forever. But she'd never thought he'd actually get down on his knee and propose like this. She put her fingers to her cheeks and found tears there.

"Gracie, I love you more every day, if that's even possible. I want to spend my whole life making you happy. Please marry me."

Gracie looked over at Jack and Penny. They were standing side by side a few feet away. Penny nodded solemnly. Jack gave her a thumbs-up. Gracie sniffed and tried to wipe her tears away with the side of her hand. "I can't believe you got me a pretty ring." Her voice was shaking so hard her words were like gasps. "You didn't have to do that. You know I want to marry you. Yikes, why am I crying so much?"

Adam looked up at her with tender humor. "You feel things more deeply than most of us. It's one of the things I love about you." He stood and pulled her close to his chest. "It's okay," he whispered into her hair as she held tight to his warmth and strength and tried to pull herself together. He stroked her back over and over. "We found each other. We're going to be together."

"It's just so unexpected. I didn't know you were going to ask, and I just—" oh no, the tears were starting again "—I love you so much and I didn't think I was the kind of person who could feel like this. It's just...a lot."

"It is a lot," Adam said quietly. "And I like it that way. I went a lot of years without feeling much. I'm so grateful that you help me feel it all."

"Gracie!" Penny threw her arms around Gracie's waist, her small tiara askew, her smile wide and trusting. "Will you marry my daddy?"

"Oh gosh." Gracie put her hand on Penny's shoulder. "You're going to give me even more happy tears. Yes, I would love to marry your daddy." Embraced by Adam and Penny, Gracie looked over at Jack. "Is there any way you'll come join us?"

To her surprise, Jack nodded and came to them, putting a hand on his dad's shoulder.

"You have to put the ring on," he said. "We helped pick it out."

"You did?" She looked from Jack to Penny in wonder. "Thank you!"

Penny stepped back, looking so proud. "I wanted one of the big diamonds that stick up from the band, but Daddy said you'd hate that kind because it would get caught on things."

Gracie laughed. "Your daddy knows me very well." She took the ring that Adam held out to her. The band split into two thinner bands of diamonds that twined around each other. "It's just gorgeous."

Adam took it back from her. "It reminds me of the winding paths we took to get to this moment."

"I love it. I love you. You know I'll marry you any time you want."

Jack held up a hand. "Hang on. This is too much mushy stuff for me. Come on, Penny, let's get out of here. When you guys are done, we'll be at the nearest bench."

Adam's laugh boomed out into the twilit night. "I appreciate that, son."

Penny followed her brother down the steps and Adam slid the band of diamonds onto Gracie's finger. It fit perfectly, and Gracie put her hand out to admire it. "I can't believe you planned this, and that the kids helped."

"I wanted to make sure they felt included. And ring shopping was hilarious. It turns out Penny has some pretty outrageous taste in jewelry."

Gracie put her arms around Adam's neck and kissed him softly. "Thank you for trusting me with them. I know I might not be the best stepmother material, but I will try my hardest to be good to them."

"You are perfect for them. They love you. How could they not? You ride with them and play with them and help them when they're hurt. You even wore this poofy dress, which is perhaps the biggest, most selfless act of devotion I've ever seen."

His laughing smile was infectious. Gracie stepped back and tried her best to curtsy without falling. "What do they say? No good deed goes unpunished?"

"Something like that." Adam pulled her in close again and kissed her lips, taking his time, settling her emotions, centering her world. "I'll tell you what," he murmured as he pulled away. "After this we'll swing by your house and you can put some jeans and boots on under your dress. Would that help?"

"Yes. Most definitely."

"Can we go trick-or-treating now?" Jack appeared at the top of the gazebo steps, Princess Penny right behind him.

"Absolutely," Gracie said, going on tiptoes to give Adam one last kiss. "Thank you," she whispered.

He settled her tilted tiara carefully in place. The love and wonder in his gaze stole her breath. "You shook my whole world up, Gracie. You made it so much better."

She wanted to stay here. To spend more time wrapped in his arms, pressed to his chest, listening to the beat of his heart. But the kids had waited so patiently, for long enough. She stepped back and playfully tipped down the brim of Adam's hat. "Enough romance. Let's go get some candy. But someone has to help me down these stairs."

Adam scooped her up in his arms. "That would be my job."

She held tight to his neck and pressed her cheek to his chest while he carried her easily down the steps and across the grass.

"I'm not putting you down, now that I've got you," he teased.

"That's fine with me. Then I don't have to walk in these heels."

"Kids, we're stopping by Gracie's house first," Adam called. "This gal needs her boots."

Gracie was content to stay in his arms for a few moments longer, with Penny running alongside in her pretty dress and Jack jogging ahead so he could pretend he didn't know them. They were her family, and they were her future. They were so much more than she'd dreamed possible. Yet somehow here she was, surrounded by love, in this little town of Shelter Creek.

This was her new life, and she didn't miss her old one at all.

* * * * *

Get 4 FREE REWARDS!

We'll send you 2 FREE Books plus 2 FREE Mystery Gifts.

Love Inspired books feature uplifting stories where faith helps guide you through life's challenges and discover the promise of a new beginning.

FREE
Value Over
$20

YES! Please send me 2 FREE Love Inspired Romance novels and my 2 FREE mystery gifts (gifts are worth about $10 retail). After receiving them, if I don't wish to receive any more books, I can return the shipping statement marked "cancel." If I don't cancel, I will receive 6 brand-new novels every month and be billed just $5.24 each for the regular-print edition or $5.99 each for the larger-print edition in the U.S., or $5.74 each for the regular-print edition or $6.24 each for the larger-print edition in Canada. That's a savings of at least 13% off the cover price. It's quite a bargain! Shipping and handling is just 50¢ per book in the U.S. and $1.25 per book in Canada.* I understand that accepting the 2 free books and gifts places me under no obligation to buy anything. I can always return a shipment and cancel at any time. The free books and gifts are mine to keep no matter what I decide.

Choose one: ☐ **Love Inspired Romance Regular-Print**
(105/305 IDN GNWC)

☐ **Love Inspired Romance Larger-Print**
(122/322 IDN GNWC)

Name (please print)

Address   Apt. #

City   State/Province   Zip/Postal Code

Email: Please check this box ☐ if you would like to receive newsletters and promotional emails from Harlequin Enterprises ULC and its affiliates. You can unsubscribe anytime.

Mail to the Harlequin Reader Service:
IN U.S.A.: P.O. Box 1341, Buffalo, NY 14240-8531
IN CANADA: P.O. Box 603, Fort Erie, Ontario L2A 5X3

Want to try 2 free books from another series? Call 1-800-873-8635 or visit www.ReaderService.com.

---

*Terms and prices subject to change without notice. Prices do not include sales taxes, which will be charged (if applicable) based on your state or country of residence. Canadian residents will be charged applicable taxes. Offer not valid in Quebec. This offer is limited to one order per household. Books received may not be as shown. Not valid for current subscribers to Love Inspired Romance books. All orders subject to approval. Credit or debit balances in a customer's account(s) may be offset by any other outstanding balance owed by or to the customer. Please allow 4 to 6 weeks for delivery. Offer available while quantities last.

Your Privacy—Your information is being collected by Harlequin Enterprises ULC, operating as Harlequin Reader Service. For a complete summary of the information we collect, how we use this information and to whom it is disclosed, please visit our privacy notice located at corporate.harlequin.com/privacy-notice. From time to time we may also exchange your personal information with reputable third parties. If you wish to opt out of this sharing of your personal information, please visit readerservice.com/consumerschoice or call 1-800-873-8635. **Notice to California Residents**—Under California law, you have specific rights to control and access your data. For more information on these rights and how to exercise them, visit corporate.harlequin.com/california-privacy.   LIR21R2

⟨H⟩HARLEQUIN

HEARTWARMING

#391 A COWGIRL'S SECRET
The Mountain Monroes • by Melinda Curtis
Horse trainer Cassie Diaz is at a crossroads. Ranch life is her
first love...until Bentley Monroe passes through her Idaho town
and helps with the family business. Will this cowgirl turn in her
boots for him?

#392 THE SINGLE DAD'S HOLIDAY MATCH
Smoky Mountain First Responders
by Tanya Agler
Can a widowed cop and single father find love again? When
a case leads Jonathan Maxwell to single mom Brooke Novak,
sparks fly. But with their focus on kids and work, romance isn't
so easy...is it?

#393 A COWBOY'S HOPE
Eclipse Ridge Ranch • by Mary Anne Wilson
When lawyer Anna Watters agreed to help a local ranch, she
wasn't supposed to fall for handsome Ben Arias! He's only in
town temporarily—but soon she wants Ben and the peace she
finds at his ranch permanently.

#394 I'LL BE HOME FOR CHRISTMAS
Return to Christmas Island • by Amie Denman
Rebecca Browne will do anything for her finance career. Even
spend the summer on Christmas Island. But she didn't expect
to have to keep secrets...especially from the local ferryboat
captain she's starting to fall for.

Visit ReaderService.com Today!

As a valued member of the Harlequin Reader Service, you'll find these benefits and more at ReaderService.com:

- Try 2 free books from any series
- Access risk-free special offers
- View your account history & manage payments
- Browse the latest Bonus Bucks catalog

Don't miss out!

If you want to stay up-to-date on the latest at the Harlequin Reader Service and enjoy more content, make sure you've signed up for our monthly News & Notes email newsletter. Sign up online at ReaderService.com or by calling Customer Service at 1-800-873-8635.

RS20